Praise for *In Bad Faith*

A novel worth your time puts you in interesting company, takes you to interesting places,and makes you care about what happens—Geoffrey Carter's latest "In Bad Faith" does all of that and more.

Writing with a crisp, sparse style that puts the reader in the midst of the action, Carter creates multidimensional characters that become traveling companions on a fascinating quest to right wrongs in a world of outrageous schemes and loud-talking big money.

From the tough streets of Chicago to even tougher remote Mexican towns with their religious/gang entanglements, Carter invites the reader along to listen in as Nelson, Mia and Lionel sort through one complexity after another as things go from bad to worse to where is the missing five million dollars and were the Mexican miners actually murdered for money?

In the midst of all of this is the mental health issue that started it all and the sensitive way treatment is approached.

Carter has done a lot of good work here, and "In Bad Faith" measures up in all the ways a good novel should.

—Bill Stokes, author of *Margaret's War* and *Treeson*

"

In "In Bad Faith," Geoff Carter's private eye Nelson West joins a long line of detectives whose talk, brains, scrapes, and adventures keep readers enthralled for hours on end. Like Sara Paretsky with V. I. Warshawski, Carter has created a rough-edged Chicagoan with a troubled past, a nose for lies, and a habit of getting in (and out of) jams. Ex-cop West's prickly, complicated, relationship with super-rich Lionel Bing—at once a client, boss, patient, sidekick, teacher, and student—adds emotional intensity and comic relief to a well-crafted story. Geoff Carter's skill in shaping characters with many layers, creating a plot that twists as it sprints, and writing dialog that crackles with tension make "In Bad Faith" a delightful story. West's inner monologs heighten the tale's intensity. At times they made me laugh out loud. Once you start this book, you'll find it gripping. After you finish, you'll be more than pleased you read it.

—David Riemer, author of
Putting Government in its Place: The New Deal 3.0

In Bad Faith is a masterfully plotted mystery/suspense novel that will keep you guessing right up to the climax. The narrative moves along at a crisp pace as the clues lead Nelson closer to the answer, but also closer to peril. Readers will delight in this twisty ride that results in a well-earned surprise ending.

—Gregory Lee Renz, Award-winning author of
Beneath the Flames and *Beyond the Flames*

IN BAD FAITH

(A NOVEL)

Other books by Geoffrey Carter

The PS Wars

Thicker than Water

IN BAD FAITH

(A NOVEL)

GEOFFREY CARTER

Three Towers Press
An imprint of HenschelHAUSbooks.com

MILWAUKEE, WISCONSIN

Published by Three Towers Press
An imprint of HenschelHAUS Publishing, Inc.
www.henschelHAUSbooks.com
Milwaukee, Wisconsin

ISBN: 9798992107050
LCCN: 2025932425

Cover art by Michael deMilo

For Frankie

Chapter 1

IT FELT AS IF A FIRE ALARM WAS going off inside his head. Nelson cracked open one eye, glanced at the clock, and wrapped the pillow around his head. *Christ,* he thought. *Who would be calling at 6:30 in the morning?* The ringing finally quit, but it seemed to echo on, caroming off the sides of his skull. He rolled over and shut his eyes, trying to will away the dull ache in his head, and fell into an uneasy sleep.

Again. Nelson opened his eyes. Seven o'clock. The sun was streaming through the slightly opened curtains. He sat up, took a deep breath, and lay back down. Not yet. *That cheap bourbon,* he thought. *You'd think I'd know better.* The ringing stopped. Nelson sighed. No way he'd get back to sleep now. He got up, dragged himself into the kitchen, and put on some coffee. He thought about eating but quickly rejected the idea. He sat at the chipped Formica table, cradling the coffee mug in his hands, and waited.

Sure as hell, as soon as the clock struck 7:30, it started ringing. Nelson paused a moment before picking up the phone—composing himself on the off-chance it might be a client.

"Hello?"

"Mr. West?" It was a deep voice, but it was a woman's voice. There was no mistaking that.

"Yes, this is Nelson West."

"Of the West Detective Agency?" *Client,* he thought, and took a deep breath.

"Yes, ma'am."

"My employer might have a job for you. He'd like to talk to you about it. How soon could you be here?"

"Well, that depends on where you are," he said. He paused. *Nothing.*

"Well, where are you?" he finally asked.

"On LaSalle between Illinois and Ohio." She gave him the number of the building.

River North, he thought. *Nice neighborhood. The address was in those big new apartment towers. That could mean money.*

"I could be there in an hour. What kind of job is it?"

"I'll let Mr. Bing explain that to you," she said and hung up.

Bing. Bing—that name is familiar. He rattled it around in his head for a minute but came up empty. *Well, I'll know soon enough.*

All right, thought Nelson, headed for the shower. *A job. Things are looking up.* He showered, shaved, dressed in his only suit, put on the nicest tie he had, and left. He took the train to the LaSalle station and walked to the building. It was a little chilly for the middle of September, but the sun was out. He felt better than he had earlier. The trip had cleared his head.

He found the building, walked in, and told the doorman he was there to see Mr. Bing. It was a nice lobby—a lot of dark wood, brass fittings, and high windows. The doorman was ancient. He looked about ninety but was probably older. He gave Nelson the once-over, frowned, and went behind his desk to make a call.

I guess I don't make a good first impression.

The doorman hung up the phone and motioned him towards the elevators.

"Mr. Bing is in the penthouse," he said. "Press 'P.'"

"P? You're sure?"

The guy made a face. Nelson smiled, stepped into the car, and pressed the button.

The elevator stopped at the top floor and opened. Nelson stepped out into a small room—a sort of foyer. There was no hallway, only a massive set of double doors directly across from him. He walked over, looking for a doorbell. Nothing. He raised his fist to knock when one of the doors opened suddenly. A young woman stood there, examining him through a pair of black, thick-rimmed glasses. She was tall and her hair was cut into a shoulder length bob. It was dyed sort of a maroon color.

"Hello," she said, sticking out a hand suddenly. "Mr. West, I presume."

Nelson nodded as he took her hand. She was the woman who'd called. He recognized that voice—husky, sort of a cross between Scarlett Johansson and Kathleen Turner.

"Please come in," she said, going back inside. He followed.

Nelson had been expecting a high-class, even opulent space, but this was something else. The interior foyer opened up into a cavernous living room. The exterior wall was glass from the floor to the ceiling, which was at least fifteen feet high. The hardwood floors were covered with luxuriant area carpets. Nelson spotted a leopard skin rug near the stone fireplace, and if he wasn't mistaken, that was a genuine Monet on the wall. *Holy shit*, he thought. *I've hit the jackpot.*

He followed the woman through the living room and into a small dining space just off the kitchen. A man was sitting at the table, reading the newspaper, his bare feet up on a chair. He didn't look up as they walked in. Nelson judged he was in his early to mid-30s. His long, dark, shoulder-length hair hung loose, and he was wearing a black bathrobe that looked like very expensive—probably mulberry, maybe even Muga—silk. A half-consumed plate of toast and eggs sat off to the side.

"Lionel?" said the woman softly.

The man looked up suddenly, and Nelson felt rather than saw his eyes clamping onto him. They were dark brown, so dark they seemed black. Nelson held back the man's gaze with his own.

"Lionel, this is Mr. West. Mr. West, Lionel Bing."

"Yes," said Bing, putting down the paper and standing up. "I've been expecting you."

He was a shade taller than Nelson—six-foot-two or so—and slender. His dark eyes were framed by a set of high cheekbones and a sharp, thin nose. As he tilted his head back, Nelson couldn't help thinking he was looking down that nose at him. The guy had that vibe. He was pale and dark bags hung beneath his eyes. Bing extended his hand. It was large and delicate-looking with tapering fingers. Nelson took it and was surprised at the strength of the man's grip—delicate-looking was all it was.

"Please, Mr. West. Have a seat. Would you like a cup of coffee?"

"Thank you. That'd be great," said Nelson, sitting down. The coffee smelled good, a lot better than the swill he had at home. Bing sat down slowly, never taking his eyes off Nelson, who looked back and smiled. Bing simply kept staring at him. It was a little creepy, but Nelson kept his mouth shut and kept smiling. This was a job interview. Bing finally broke eye contact.

"Mia," he said to the woman with the burgundy hair, "would you mind getting Mr. West a cup of coffee?"

"Not at all."

Nelson watched her saunter off into the kitchen. He hadn't noticed her legs before. Bing waited until after Mia wandered off into the kitchen. He leaned over toward Nelson.

"Mia Wentworth is my full-time assistant," said Bing, with kind of a proprietary air. "She assists me with my—projects—and helps around here during the day." He crossed his legs and leaned back.

"But don't let appearances fool you," he said. "She's not just another pretty face. Mia has a master's in chemistry from Stanford and a PhD in physics from the University of Chicago."

"Wow."

"Yes. I sought out a candidate with those specific qualifications and hand-picked her. She's indispensable."

Nelson nodded. He wasn't sure exactly how advanced science skills were useful for a secretary, but he didn't say so.

"I see," said Nelson, looking up as Mia came in with his coffee. He thanked her and took a sip. Nice. Much better than what he was used to. "This is great," he said.

"Yes," said his host. "I have it specially imported from a private grove in Jalisco."

Nelson smiled and took another sip.

"So, Mr. West. I'm sure you're wondering what this is all about, and we'll get to that shortly. But first things first. My name is Lionel Bing. My father is Reginald Bing."

Reginald Bing as in Bing Contracting, thought Nelson. *The company that handles outdoor lighting contracts for the city. That company that's responsible for nearly every streetlight in Chicago. Sure. That's why the name seems familiar.* The Bings were rich—filthy rich. The son, Lionel, the guy sitting in front of him, was heir apparent to the one of the biggest family fortunes in Chicago.

Nelson nodded to himself. *Yep. I know all about this guy.*

Lionel Bing. The black sheep. And he'd earned that bad-boy reputation. Partying, drugs, slumming, and accumulating a slew of drunk driving, resisting, and drunk and disorderly arrests along the way. He'd also gotten involved in a few altercations, a couple of them nasty. Nelson remembered one that made the rounds in the daily news cycle a few years back. Lionel had beaten a man so severely he'd been hospitalized for a week. There'd been rumors he was chemically dependent, mentally unstable, and then—finally—in treatment. Of course, young Bing had gotten away with it—all of it—until he crashed his Porsche on Lake Shore Drive and nearly killed somebody. After that, his father had reined him in and got him into rehab. That was maybe a year or so ago. Nelson looked at his host. Bing was staring at him intently, as if reading his thoughts.

"Yes, of course I've heard the name, Mr. Bing," said Nelson. "Bing Contracting."

"Yes," he said slowly, "my father's company. His baby. He's a great man, Mr. West. An institution. A visionary. Shrewd. Ambitious. He built that business up from nothing."

Nelson noticed an odd vibe in Bing's voice. Dry. Cold. It didn't exactly sound like an admiring son. More like a schoolboy reciting the pledge.

"You must be proud of the old man."

Lionel frowned, nodded slightly, and stared into his cup for a moment. He cleared his throat.

"Yes," he said, without looking up. "Of course, I'm proud."

Nelson nodded and waited.

"Anyway," Bing continued, looking up suddenly, "for the past year or so, I've been working for my father, helping some friends of his solve problems that they would rather keep quiet. Under the radar."

"Problems?"

"Yes, Mr. West. Problems. All sorts of dilemmas. For example, a few months ago one of my father's old fraternity brothers asked me to help track down a granddaughter who had been spirited away to New Orleans."

"Spirited away?" asked Nelson, trying not to smile.

"Yes," said Lionel brusquely. "The girl fell under the spell of a rather glib charmer who swept her off her feet. She followed him all the way down to the Tremé."

"And you went down there and got her back?"

"Yes," said Bing. "Once I found her, all it took to get her to come home was a little bit of leverage."

"Money?"

"That and a little persuasion," said Bing.

"Persuasion?"

"Yes, the man who convinced her to accompany him wasn't very happy about her leaving so suddenly."

"And the leverage didn't quite bring him around to your way of thinking?"

"It did at first," said Bing, "but then he changed his mind and said he wanted the girl to stay with him."

"I see. So, what sort of alternate persuasion did that call for?"

Bing stood up and stretched.

"The man was quite confrontational and needed to be persuaded physically," said Bing. He smiled slightly.

"I'm on probation, Mr. West. I also have a family reputation to protect. I can't afford to get into trouble with the law anymore, so I enlisted the help of a local private investigator. He helped me persuade the young man in question."

"I see—", started Nelson.

"I have to be careful," said Lionel, sitting down. "I can defend myself, of course, but I have to consider the consequences. I can't embarrass my family by having any further run-ins with the law." He opened his mouth as if to add something, but then paused.

"Which," he added, "is why I called you."

"Because I'm a violent man?"

15

"Not exactly," said Bing. "You are when you need to be. I know that. But the real reason you're here is because of your experience as a police detective. Apparently, you were very good at it. You did your work quickly, cleanly, and quietly. You still have a good reputation in the department."

"Thank you," said Nelson, wondering who might have said something nice about him.

"Yes," continued Bing. "According to Chicago Police Department records, your cases had a ninety-four percent clearance rate. Which is excellent." He leaned back in his chair and folded his hands in his lap.

"My father insisted I hire someone with experience in the field. That's why you're here. If it were up to me, I would go it alone, but this is his show."

"Okay," said Nelson. *I'll take what I can get.*

"He told me to interview you specifically. He said he got your name from a very reliable source."

"However, Mr. West," he said—a bit stridently, "I have misgivings. The records also show you also had some conflicts with your superiors and that you sometimes carried out your assignments a little too zealously. That you have, on occasion, used excessive force. Is that true?"

"I did my job the best I could," said Nelson. "If that meant using force, that's what I did. It's part of the job sometimes."

Bing leaned back and scratched an eyebrow.

"Part of the job," he repeated. "Then what about Oswald Press? What happened with him?"

Nelson nodded. It figured this would come up again. He sighed. *Screw it. Here goes.*

"Well," he said, and cleared his throat. "That happened just after I'd left the force and started working freelance. I'd been hired to track down an old lady's niece, her only living relative. The girl's name was Janie. She was seventeen and had run away from home. The aunt—the great-aunt—had just been diagnosed with cancer and wanted to speak to the girl about her inheritance, so she hired me to track her down. The parents weren't really in the picture at that point."

Nelson paused and took a sip of coffee.

"It didn't take me long to find her. She was being held against her will by a man named Oswald Press, a known felon. A pimp. He was keeping her in his stable. He'd confined six girls he'd picked up on the street. He had them living in dog cages. Janie was the oldest. The youngest was eleven. Press was pimping them out. I told him I was taking Janie back to her family and he didn't like that. He wanted to get rough, so I had to take care of the situation. I guess I got a little carried away."

"If I remember correctly," said Bing. "Mr. Press suffered a fractured skull, a broken arm, and a fractured orbit."

Nelson shrugged. *Yep. The son of a bitch got what he deserved.*

"The city nearly pulled your private investigator license, but the board ultimately determined it was a case of self-defense."

Nelson nodded. "That's right. I'm kind of on probation myself."

"And because of you, the police were able to restore all of those girls back to their families. And prosecute Mr. Oswald Press."

"A couple of the girls went to foster care," said Nelson. "That's no picnic."

"Well, I'm sure it was better than the alternative. Personally," said Lionel. "I thought Mr. Press had it coming. I understand there's still a civil suit pending?"

Nelson nodded.

"Press' family is suing me for damages. I don't know why. I don't have anything. I think their lawyer is trying to get at the old lady who hired me. She's loaded."

"All right," said Lionel. He leaned forward in his chair. "So, Mr. West, are you still willing and able to ply your trade?"

"Yep." *They hadn't taken that away. Not yet.*

"Good." Bing stood up. "Let me tell you a little about the position," he said. "The person I hire will be helping me fix problems for my private clientele who typically want their issues solved quickly and quietly with as little police involvement as possible."

"So, this is kind of a private detective agency?"

"Not exactly," said Lionel. "I'm more of a troubleshooter. A fixer. Although some investigation will usually be involved, which happens to be something I excel at."

He paused a moment, scratching an eyebrow. Thinking.

"It's not easy to explain how this works," he continued. "I occupy a niche that's difficult to describe. Perhaps a little background information might help."

Nelson nodded and crossed his arms. Lionel cleared his throat and began.

"I earned a bachelor's degree in psychology with a minor in abnormal psychology at the University of Chicago when I was nineteen. I have a master's degree in sociology and a PhD in criminology."

"And," he continued, "I have what has been called an uncanny knack for solving real-life problems. I recently helped an associate of my father's analyze some irregularities inside his company. There were a few discrepancies in the accounts. It took me all of two hours to find the aberration and track down the perpetrator. A straightforward case of embezzlement."

Nelson nodded politely. *Real-life problems. Sure.*

"After that," he said, "and with my father's encouragement, I decided to pursue this line of work. And so, I studied forensics, psychological profiling—anything that I felt could help me."

"You went back to school?"

"Not exactly. It wasn't necessary. I did most of the work myself, although I did commission a few experts to tutor me on the finer points. You might know of some of them. I studied with Eric Diedrich, John Maxwell, and Dr. Frances Wilhelm. And others."

Nelson nodded. He knew about Diedrich, a forensics guy, but that was it. "You hired them to teach you?"

"My father did," said Bing, smiling. "And after working with them, I feel prepared—with Miss Wentworth's help—to tackle any sort of problem my clients might encounter."

"That's great," said Nelson. "Quite an accomplishment."

Bing nodded and looked down at his hands.

"Why focus on crime?" asked Nelson. "If you don't mind me asking. I mean you can do anything you want. Why do you want to be an investigator?"

"Why?" answered Lionel. His voice quavered a little. He swallowed and his mouth tightened. "It's not necessarily something I would have chosen to do, Mr. West, but after my last—incident— my father told me I needed to straighten up and start being a productive member of society. He—we—decided this would be the best course for me to take." He shrugged. "Which is fine. It's all right. I like it. And doing this is the easiest way to keep him happy."

And to keep yourself in the will, thought Nelson.

"So, he wants you to hunt down the bad guys? Those hardened criminals from the boardroom? Your father wants you to make them pay?"

Bing stared at him a moment, opened his mouth, shut it, and then leaned forward, squeezing his hands together so tightly his knuckles began to turn white. His whole body tensed up. His shoulders raised up and a muscle in his throat had begun to twitch.

"I want to—," he said, his voice tight. "I want to stop—, I need to help—."

He took a deep breath and opened his hands. Nelson noticed red crescents where his fingernails had bit into his palms.

"But it's more than that," he said, "—it's—it's something I need to do. For me. It's complicated. I—," Nelson noticed Lionel's hands shaking. A sheen of sweat appeared on his forehead. He swallowed again and clenched his hands together.

A dark expression passed over the man's face—a cloud of pain and anger—and something else, something Nelson couldn't read. Bing's breathing quickened into raspy gasps and the cords stood out from his neck, tense as wires.

Seizure? thought Nelson.

He moved closer, ready to catch the man if he passed out. Bing suddenly exhaled, leaned on the table, and took some deep breaths. His face slowly began unclenching, and he swallowed. His color began to come back, and his breathing returned to normal.

"My apologies, Mr. West," he whispered, glancing up at Nelson. "I get these panic attacks sometimes. It's nothing. It'll pass."

Lionel's face was covered in sweat. He sat down heavily.

That's not like any panic attack I ever saw, thought Nelson.

Bing took out a handkerchief and mopped his forehead. He took a few deep breaths and then squared his shoulders.

"To answer your question," said Lionel, taking another deep breath. "Yes. This is more than something I need to do for myself and for my father. It's a responsibility—an obligation. I don't have a choice, Mr. West."

No choice? Why would he say that?

"Hey," said Nelson. "You don't have to explain anything. I think I know what you mean. I tell myself I got into this line of work to help people, but that's not really it. I wanted to put away the scum. That's why I became a cop."

"The scum," said Lionel, in a low tone, almost a whisper, nodding. The same darkness flitted across his face. His eyes became distant, focused on a point beyond the walls of the room. He grimaced and clenched the arms of his chair.

Nelson wondered if he should call in Mia. Bing didn't look so good. He leaned over and placed his head in his hands. Nelson glanced toward the kitchen and then back to Bing.

"Are you okay, Mr. Bing?" Nelson asked in a low voice. *It'd be just my luck to get a job and have my boss keel over on my first day.*

Bing raised his head and looked at him as if he'd just awakened. He closed his eyes and nodded.

"Yes," he said, sitting up slowly. "I'm sorry, Mr. West. This happens from time to time. It's nothing serious. I've had these attacks since I was a child. They're mostly under control now with medication."

Nelson nodded. *Mostly under control.*

"Back in prep school," continued Bing, "my classmates assumed I was handicapped or mentally deranged. Brain damaged, they said. I had to put up a with a lot of crap."

"Sure."

"It helps," said Lionel, "that I'm rich. People tend to be a little more understanding."

Nelson allowed himself a smile.

"I believe that, Mr. Bing."

Bing smiled. "Call me Lionel, Mr. West."

"Sure. I'm Nelson."

"So, this is how we're going to do things," said Lionel slowly, sitting up straight. "We have a very exclusive clientele that does not like publicity. I fix problems that come up for them."

Nelson nodded. *Sure. Private eye to the rich.*

"So, our investigations have to be kept quiet," Lionel continued. "We need to be discreet. We might run into some violent situations during the course of our work. And, because of my legal situation, I won't be able to handle those myself. That's where you come in."

"I'd be the muscle?" asked Nelson.

"Partly. And, of course, you'll assist with our investigations. We're also hoping you can talk to the right people at CPD should any of our cases get their attention. Is that something you can help us with, Mr. West?"

"Yeah, I think I could handle that."

"My father is not very comfortable with me being out there on my own," said Lionel. "He's worried that I lack experience, especially dealing with the police and other authorities. Even if I'm on the right side of the law. He's worried I may do something rash."

He glanced up at Nelson, who nodded.

"He told me," continued Lionel, "I need to have someone with experience assisting me. Someone like you. He said it isn't every day I can work with a twelve-year veteran of the police force. A homicide detective, no less."

No less, thought Nelson.

"So that's about it," said Lionel. "I have a case pending that I wanted to get started on this afternoon. I would like to have you work with me on it."

"So," said Nelson, "about the job. Is this a one-time deal for this particular case or is it more permanent? And how exactly how does it shake out in terms of a job?"

"If you would find it acceptable, you will be hired as a full-time consultant. We will work on my cases as a team."

"And you would be the lead investigator?" asked Nelson.

"Of course. I think you'll find the salary quite competitive. Per year, $95,000. You will also enjoy full health coverage under our insurance plan."

Health insurance. Damn!

"Mia is also part of the investigative team. She is my analytics and forensics expert. My science officer, as it were."

Spock, thought Nelson, smiling to himself.

"So, what do you think, Nelson?"

Well, thought Nelson, *I've got a rich guy here who wants me to babysit him while he plays cop with his nerdy girlfriend. And I'll be making more than I ever did for the city. Plus health insurance. That's a big yes.*

Nelson stood up.

"This sounds great, Lionel," he said. "You've got a deal."

They shook hands. Lionel smiled and said something about how pleased he was to have Nelson on the team, but it seemed flat and a little forced. Nelson smiled and kept his mouth shut. Lionel excused himself and went to get dressed.

Nelson sat down and finished his coffee. He stood as Mia came into the room.

"Don't," she said. "I hate it when people do that."

"Do what?"

"Stand up when I walk into a room."

"I'm just trying to be polite," he said, sitting back down.

"I know, but please don't do it." She started clearing the table.

"Mia?"

"Yeah?"

"Do you mind me asking you something?"

"What?"

"Why would a PhD be working as a maid?"

"I'm not a maid."

"You're serving coffee. You're clearing the table," Nelson said. "I'm pretty sure that's what maids do."

"I'm employed as Mr. Bing's consultant," she said. "I do forensics and scientific analysis. That's my job." She shrugged. "I help out here between cases because I like to keep busy. At any rate, I know a fair number of PhDs who are also waiting tables and mopping floors. There's no shame in it."

"Do you live here?"

"No, but Mr. Bing expects me to be here during working hours, whether there's a case or not."

"Why?"

She paused a moment, then looked Nelson straight in the eye.

"He enjoys the company."

Nelson nodded and grinned.

"It's not like that, Mr. West. I have my own apartment and my own life. Lionel enjoys having people around. He doesn't like being alone." She paused a moment, as if to say something else, then continued. "That's all it is."

"All right," he said. "All right. I didn't mean anything."

Mia grunted and walked the dishes back into the kitchen. Nelson watched her. *If she's not attached to Lionel, I wonder who she goes home to at night. A cat?*

Nelson heard someone coming and turned. Lionel walked in, wearing a plain cotton button-down shirt and a pair of black jeans. He was carrying some manila folders. He seemed fully recovered from his—attack.

"Are we ready, Nelson? Have you eaten breakfast? I'm sure Mia wouldn't mind whipping something up for you."

She might mind, thought Nelson. *I'd mind.*

"No, thanks. I could use another cup of coffee, though."

"That's a good idea," said Lionel. "Mia," he called. "Could you bring in a fresh pot of coffee, please?"

"Sure thing," she said from the kitchen. *A PhD*, thought Nelson. *Man, I'm glad I never finished college.*

"So," said Lionel, sitting down across from Nelson and opening one of the folders. "I mentioned that we were going to be getting started on a new project this afternoon. I thought we could start by going over some of the basic facts of the case."

Nelson glanced over at Lionel. There was a different sort of tone in his new boss' voice. A gravity that hadn't been there before.

"Sounds good."

"All right," said Lionel, handing a sheaf of papers to Nelson. "I'll go fast, so please try to keep up."

Nelson nodded. *All right, boss.*

"You're looking at a file on a Mr. Bradley Baker," said Lionel, speaking rapidly. "He has been employed at the Consolidated Union Bank for the past twenty-seven years. He's presently an executive vice president and doing quite well. Mr. Baker is—or was—very likely next in line to become CEO."

Mia came in, put a pot of coffee on the table, and sat down. Lionel slid her a copy of the file.

Nelson started reading Baker's file. BS in Economics from the University of Illinois, an MBA from Booth School of Business, and a two-year apprenticeship at a major Wall Street brokerage firm. He'd been hired by Con Union after that and stayed at the bank since. He'd been working mostly in real estate loans. Sterling record. A wife and two kids, one grown, one in college. Big house in the suburbs. *Well*, thought Nelson. *It's a wonderful life. They probably have a little purebred dog, too—one his wife keeps in her purse.*

Nelson turned the page to a financial report that looked to be a compilation of Con Union real estate transactions. It was a summary of acquisitions, liquidations, everything. Everything listed took place in Mr. Baker's department.

"Where'd you get these records?" asked Nelson.

Lionel glanced up at him and frowned. "I compiled the information in that report from tax records, sales reports, and bank records, which Con Union was exceedingly reluctant to let go of. If you notice," said Lionel, leaning over and pointing at a column, "there seems to be a deficit in Mr. Baker's area."

"Five million dollars' worth," said Mia.

Well, thought Nelson. *Things are getting interesting.*

He leaned over, puzzling over the spreadsheets. Nelson was no expert, but it looked to him as if a loan for the Hindman Group had been approved by Con Union. Baker and several other loan officers had signed off on the transaction. It all looked pretty straightforward until Hindman abruptly defaulted on the loan—a five-million-dollar loss. Nelson leaned back in his chair and looked up. Lionel was watching him and smiling. He started tapping a pen against the table.

Oh, boy, thought Nelson. *I guess I'm under the gun.* He kept reading.

"Well?" asked Lionel after a moment.

"Fraud and embezzlement are not my areas, but I'd have to say if looks as if there's something pretty funky going on with this Hindman Corporation."

"Uh-huh," said Lionel, nodding.

"Out of curiosity, Lionel, how did you find these numbers?" asked Nelson.

"Well," said Lionel. "I followed the money. Hindman applied for and received a five-million-dollar loan to support a business venture—a mine in Mexico. They defaulted shortly after the loan was granted. Con Union was ready to write off the losses until they were alerted to a number of irregularities by Reynolds Hanson, the CEO. Irregularities that he maintains point to Baker. Reynolds thinks Baker created the shell company, diverted the loan, and pocketed the proceeds."

Okay, boss. Not bad.

"How'd you get this case?" asked Mia. Nelson glanced over at her. He'd almost forgotten she was there.

"My father referred it to me earlier this week," said Lionel. "I assume Reynolds asked him to help. They want to keep it quiet so the shareholders don't panic. Reynolds knew a sum that large couldn't have been embezzled by just anybody, so he figured that the culprit was upper management. That narrowed the field of suspects down quite a bit. After looking at their financial records, I—"

"How'd you get hold of those?" asked Nelson. "That's quite a trick. You usually need subpoenas to get that stuff."

Lionel shrugged one shoulder and frowned. *He doesn't like being called out*, thought Nelson. *Too bad.*

"The bank wants this fixed. Besides, money talks, Nelson. As does reputation. I don't usually have much trouble getting the information I need."

Nelson nodded. *That kind of clout would make life a hell of a lot easier.*

"What tipped you off to Baker? Why not the other loan officers?" asked Mia. "Was he gambling? Spending it on young girls? Buying little red sports cars?"

Lionel held up his hand.

"Whoa, Mia," he said. "No. There was no evidence that Mr. Baker had been up to anything wrong, let alone criminal. No unexplained money flow, no new business ventures acting as fronts for money laundering, and no unusual expenditures."

"What tipped you off that it was him?" asked Nelson. "Did he crack during questioning?"

"No," said Lionel, leaning back and clasping his hands together. "I haven't spoken to Mr. Baker yet. This has all been very civilized. So far. No, I knew he was our man when I discovered that he had been taking long walks at night."

He stopped and smiled at the two of them, waiting. Nelson glanced over at Mia, who didn't even twitch.

Fucking games, thought Nelson. *This is all I need.*

"I give up," he said.

Lionel leaned forward, grinning. *Like the goddamned Cheshire Cat.*

"First, I narrowed my list of suspects down to three executives who were the only ones with the opportunity to get at that much money. I had each of them trailed. Only Mr. Baker strayed outside his normal routine. He started taking long walks every night that took him into the downtown of his little suburb. He'd stop at the local bar, Harvey's, have a drink, go to the payphone outside—yes, they still have a working payphone—and make a short call. An international call. Every night at nine-thirty. On the dot."

Nelson nodded.

"Did he ever meet anyone?"

Lionel shook his head. Nelson went back to the report and scanned it again.

"No affairs, no gambling, no drug habits, nothing untoward?"

Lionel shook his head.

"Where does his son go to college?"

"Rice," said Lionel. He nodded at Nelson. "I thought of that, too."

"Did you try to reach the boy?" asked Nelson, the hairs on his neck rising. *It was the cop in him. It never went away.*

Lionel shook his head. "No, we didn't want to put anyone on guard."

"What is it?" asked Mia. "Do you think he's been kidnapped or something?"

"Maybe," said Nelson, "or it could be blackmail if the son is involved in something he shouldn't be."

"I don't think so," mused Lionel. "He's not that type of kid. No, the motivation is somewhere else. Something we're not seeing."

"The first thing we have to do is find out whether the kid's okay," said Nelson. "Where is Rice exactly?"

"Texas," said Lionel, "but I'm not sure of the city."

"Houston," said Mia. Lionel and Nelson looked at her.

"I interviewed there for a tenure-track position," she said. "It wasn't a good fit."

"Mia," said Lionel, "could you call the university under some pretext and find out if this kid is a student in good standing?"

"Sure," she said, "no problem," and stood up.

"Wait a minute," said Nelson. "Wait a minute. What are you going to say exactly? We don't want to get this kid hurt."

Mia shrugged.

"I'll think of something," she said.

What the fuck? thought Nelson. *Really?*

"This is not some sort of game," said Nelson, rising. He realized he had raised his voice. *Control, Nelson, control.* He took a deep breath.

"No," said Mia, tilting her head back, "it's not. And you're not dealing with amateurs, Mr. West. We do know what we're doing."

She turned on her heel and left. Nelson sat back down. Lionel leaned toward him.

"Nelson," he said, his voice icy. "Never, ever presume that I don't know what I'm doing. Not if you want to continue to work here. I'm running things. You're not here to supervise me. I know what I'm doing. Don't embarrass me again."

He leaned back in his chair. "I know I hired you to provide support and advice, but understand I am not a dilettante. I am a professional. I take care of my clients and I am very careful that no one involved in my investigations will ever be harmed. The boy will be safe. Mia knows what she's doing. She is more than qualified to handle this. All right?"

"All right," said Nelson. He hoped he sounded convinced. And contrite. He had always hated getting this sort of shit from his supervisors. *The more things change... Meet the new boss.*

"The boy," continued Lionel, "is named Mark. He doesn't present with anything out of the ordinary. Decent grades, member of a fraternity, parties on the weekends. No known criminal activity."

"What about the wife?"

"Nothing," said Lionel, shaking his head. "Younger—but not too young. Apparently she plays around, but there's nothing there to indicate any sort of suspicious activity."

"Where's the money?"

"We don't know yet. Probably offshore somewhere."

"And Baker's still in town?"

Lionel nodded.

"Could he be getting ready to bolt?"

"Possibly," said Lionel, "but I don't think so. I don't think he knows we're onto him, or even that the bank knows about his little escapade yet. I think he might be working with someone right here in the city."

"To launder the cash?"

"Or to act as a straw man."

"A girlfriend, maybe," mused Nelson. "He could be using her as a mule."

"Well, if he has one, he never goes to visit her," said Lionel. "Not since we've been tailing him."

Nelson nodded. *All right. So this guy Baker embezzles a ton of money, gets out of the house every night, and makes a midnight phone call. No gambling, no payoffs, and no money laundering. It added up to blackmail. Or just plain greed.*

"Lionel," asked Nelson, "did you get the phone records on that payphone?"

"We tried that. The calls were all to disposable cells. The receiver could be anywhere."

31

Mia came back in.

"I just spoke to student services," she said. "Mark is fine. He's cutting a 3.7 grade point average, attending his classes, and has not gotten into any sort of trouble on campus. He was in class this morning." She sat down.

"Good work, Mia," said Lionel, reaching over and patting her on the arm.

"Nice," said Nelson. "How'd you do it?"

"I said I was Mark's mom and I told them how concerned we were given our darling son's predisposition to bouts of depression. The assistant was more than glad to help."

"Just like that?"

"Just like that, Mr. West. They wanted some personal information, but we have all that, so it was no big deal."

"And," she added, "no one got hurt."

Nelson nodded. *Okay. I deserved that.*

"So, Lionel," said Nelson, leaning back in his chair. *Boss,* he thought. "We've come against a series of dead ends. Where do we go from here?"

"Well," said Lionel, leaning forward on the table, "what would you do, Nelson? Dazzle me with your vast expertise."

"I would say it's time we pay Mr. Baker a visit," said Nelson. "I'd like to ask him a few questions. Discreetly, of course."

"Good," said Lionel, getting up from the table. "Very good. Exactly what I was thinking."

Lionel glanced at his watch.

"I have a few errands to run this morning," he said. "Could we meet back here at one?"

Nelson nodded.

"Good," said Lionel. "Mia can show you out."

He disappeared into the rear of the apartment.

"Come on," said Mia. "Welcome aboard, by the way."

"Thanks."

"I'll walk you out."

They got into the elevator together. Nelson glanced at her on the way down. She was looking sideways at him through her thick-rimmed glasses.

"What?" he asked.

"What yourself?" she answered.

He shrugged.

The elevator door opened, and Mia led the way through the lobby and onto the sidewalk.

Jesus. Does she think I don't know where the street is?

She stopped near a long, black limousine standing at the curb and beckoned him over. Nelson glanced at the logo.

A Rolls Royce. Are you kidding me?

Mia opened the rear door. "There's someone here who needs to speak to you, Mr. West."

Nelson hesitated, then walked over and peeked into the back. An older man sat in the far seat, glaring at him. Reginald Bing.

Now what the hell is this? thought Nelson.

"Get in," whispered Mia. "Mr. Bing doesn't have all day."

Nelson glanced back at her, took a deep breath, and got into the car.

Chapter 2

NELSON SLID INTO THE REAR SEAT of the Rolls and was struck immediately by the rich smell of oiled leather. A television hung on the panel facing them, hardwood trim lined the seats and door interiors, and a fully stocked bar, complete with what looked like Waterford crystal, stood on the console between himself and Reginald Bing.

Well, thought Nelson. *What a morning. The hits keep coming.*

"Mr. West."

Nelson glanced over at the man sitting next to him. He'd recognized Reginald Bing immediately, and no wonder. The man's face was everywhere. Bing was a philanthropist, a bit of a celebrity, and richer than God. He had a reputation as a tough, sometimes ruthless businessman, but he also donated generously to local museums and colleges as well as several charities. Lately, he'd been focusing primarily on mental health advocacy groups.

Reginald Bing looked smaller and slightly less imposing in person than he did on TV. His immaculately groomed white hair was parted on the side, and his gray eyes were partly hidden behind horn-rimmed glasses. He was dressed in a blue pinstripe suit and held a cane with a snarling wolf's head carved onto the handle. His face was etched with deep lines. The papers said he was seventy-three, but he looked older.

He looks tired, thought Nelson. *Worn out.*

Bing nodded toward the front, and the car pulled out into traffic.

"Mr. Bing," said Nelson. "This is a surprise. I wasn't expecting you."

"I imagine it is," said the old man, smiling a little. "I see that you have a sense of humor, Mr. West. That's a good thing. You're going to need it."

Nelson nodded. "Thank you. It's a pleasure meeting you."

The old man nodded and coughed slightly.

"You're probably wondering why you've been kidnapped by one of the wealthiest men in Chicago."

"Now I'm wondering about your sense of humor."

Bing chuckled. "It's not as sharp as yours, I'm afraid. But unfortunately, this is no joking matter. And," he added, glancing at his watch, "I'm a little pressed for time."

"I am curious what a man like you would want with a lowly private detective like me."

Bing straightened up in his seat. *Time to get serious*, thought Nelson.

"I understand you had an interview with my son Lionel this morning. A job interview."

"That's right."

"And that he spoke to you about working with him on some — difficulties that associates of mine could be facing."

"Something along those lines, yes," said Nelson, glancing out the window. He wasn't going to say more until he knew what this was all about. He glanced over at Bing, who was staring at him.

"Did you accept the job?" asked Bing, a note of concern in his voice.

"Yes. I did accept it. I think it's a good opportunity."

"I believe you're right about that," said Bing.

"Listen," he continued, "before you start work with my son, I want to make a few things clear. The first is that I am the one who suggested he hire you. I gave him your name after speaking to Deputy Chief Larson, who recommended you highly."

Nelson nodded. Larson was a good guy. He'd told Nelson he owed him after the Hightower thing.

"I, along with some others, have been encouraging Lionel to get into this sort of work for some time. I've done this for a variety of reasons. First and foremost is a lack of direction in his life. He's spent the lion's share of his time since college spending money and getting into trouble."

The old man grimaced and leaned back into his seat.

"In fact, about a year ago, after he'd had a rather serious car accident, I insisted on it."

Nelson nodded.

"He was lucky," Bing continued, "that no one was killed. As it was, it cost a pretty penny to clear things up."

"I heard about that."

Bing snorted. "Of course you did. I think every paper and television station in the country covered it."

Nelson nodded.

"So, I gave my son a rather—shall we say gentle but stern—ultimatum. Either he straightens out and finds some meaningful work, or he would be cut out of the estate. Entirely."

Okay, thought Nelson. *That's not what I would call gentle, but what do I know?*

"I suggested something along the lines of being an investigator—that was for a couple of reasons. First is that Lionel is quite intelligent—he tested out with an IQ of 155. That's Einstein territory. He also has good instincts for getting to the heart of a matter. He always has."

The old man coughed.

"Secondly, this was a course recommended by Lionel's analyst, and it is one that I heartily agree with."

Nelson looked at the old man, who was gazing at him steadily through his thick-lensed glasses. It was impossible to get a read on him.

"His analyst?"

"Yes," said Bing. He gazed out the window. They were passing Millennium Park. He turned back to Nelson, the lines in his face highlighted by the sun.

"Yes," he continued. "There's something about Lionel's condition that you need to know—provided you still want to work for him."

Nelson nodded.

"When he was about twelve—about twenty years ago now, while Lionel and his mother were shopping on Michigan Avenue, they were kidnapped in broad daylight by a gang of thugs. They killed the chauffeur and carjacked them."

"I remember that," said Nelson. "Sure. I was still in uniform. Everybody was following it."

I should have known that was him, thought Nelson. *Why didn't I put two and two together?*

"Yes, thanks to our friends in the media, it was quite difficult to negotiate with the kidnappers. And of course, the public was enthralled by the spectacle."

"Yeah," said Nelson. "They were."

"The kidnappers demanded ten million dollars for the release of my family. Of course, we told them we'd comply. My attorneys got the cash together and we prepared the exchange. But," he said, sighing, "something went wrong."

The old man stared out the window.

"Yeah," said Nelson. "I remember. The press got wind of it and some reporter tried to crash the party."

"Yes," said Bing. "The person doing the pick-up was scared off. The payoff was never made." He cleared his throat. "The next morning, a package was found outside the front door of my home. It contained a human finger with my wife's wedding ring on it."

Nelson took a breath. He hadn't heard this before.

"It also contained a note demanding fifteen million dollars. Interest, you see. Well, we got the extra cash together and made the drop. Things went exactly as they should have this time. The money was picked up and there were no complications. We waited but heard nothing. No word of my wife and son, just silence. The police started a massive manhunt."

Nelson nodded. He remembered.

"Two days later, some deer hunters found Lionel wandering in a cornfield on the Wisconsin border. He was in shock and so deeply traumatized he couldn't speak. He'd been beaten and was dehydrated but had no other serious injuries."

Nelson nodded. He remembered now. Somehow he hadn't equated the kidnapping with the man he'd been talking to just an hour ago.

Reginald Bing cleared his throat.

"They found my wife's body floating off Promontory Point two days after that. She'd been beaten, tortured, and sexually assaulted. Mutilated. The ring finger on her left hand was missing. The police estimated she'd been dead at least a week. She'd been shot in the back of the head. Execution style."

"Lionel was hospitalized. It took a few weeks for him to start speaking again, but he still couldn't function properly. After they released him from the hospital, he refused to leave the house. He'd become hysterical at the prospect. The police interviewed him several times, but he couldn't remember anything about what happened, which probably was a blessing. After examining him again, the doctors decided he was suffering from PTSD and as a result, couldn't remember anything. He'd blocked everything out, you see."

Nelson watched the old man. He was staring down at the floor, lost in thought. Nelson let him stay lost.

"Lionel suffers from that trauma to this day. His temper and aggressiveness, his inability to maintain a healthy relationship, the nightmares, and his self-destructiveness are all textbook examples of PTSD." He glanced up at Nelson. "Or so I'm told."

"Does he have flashbacks? Or seizures?"

The old man looked at him sharply.

"Not seizures," he said, "but he does have episodes of dissociation. Emotional flashbacks where he relives the experience even though he can't consciously remember it. The doctors don't know what triggers them. Honestly, I sometimes wonder if they know what the hell they're talking about. Why do you ask?"

"He had a sort of an episode this morning," said Nelson. "He called it a panic attack, but it didn't look like that to me."

Mr. Bing leaned back in his seat and looked him straight in the eye. Nelson felt a little like an insect pinned on a board.

"Part of what you'll be doing, Mr. West, when you work with Lionel, is helping him with his therapy. His doctors believe that reliving aspects of his trauma might help him overcome some effects of the PTSD. It's called narrative therapy. It usually involves reliving the trauma, but since Lionel can't remember exactly what happened to him, his doctors think having experiences mirroring his particular trauma may help. They also believe he suffers from a massive guilt complex for not being able save his mother. He can't forgive himself for it."

"He was twelve years old."

Bing nodded. "Yes. Even so, his doctors feel that he believes he abandoned her. And God knows what he witnessed during that time."

The old man fell silent again and slumped back into his seat. He looked even smaller now.

"What do I have to do?"

"Just your usual work. Lionel has to work through his own demons, but I want you there to keep an eye on him. And to keep him from doing anything too extreme or reckless. He's been known to snap at times—to become violent."

"I can do that."

"Good. That's as expected. Mr. West," he said, his voice booming in the small space. "Now, I brought you here to make both a demand and a request."

"All right."

"First, I want you to promise me you'll do your utmost to keep Lionel out of harm's way. The boy is not only inexperienced, but he is reckless, over-confident, and suffers from poor judgement. Keep an eye on him. That's the most important part of your job."

Nelson nodded. *That's some request. I can't wait to hear the demand.*

"And," said Mr. Bing, leaning forward, "Lionel does not know we're having this conversation. He knows I recommended you for the job, but that's it. Do not tell him we spoke. Ever. If Lionel finds out that this, this, um—situation—has been engineered, his analyst, Dr. Ribot, is afraid that all the progress they've made could be ruined. It's very possible that Lionel could bottom out. He cannot know this is for his own good."

Weird on weird, thought Nelson. He nodded.

Mr. Bing nodded toward the front. The car immediately pulled over to the curb.

"It's been a pleasure, Mr. West." He held out his hand. Nelson shook it.

It was time to go.

"It's mutual, sir," he said, and opened the car door.

"Remember," said the old man. "We've never met. And this conversation must remain our little secret."

Chapter 3

NELSON LOOKED THROUGH THE open office door at Lionel Bing and Reynolds Hanson, the CEO of Con Union. Mr. Hanson was sitting behind his desk and listening as Lionel talked. Somehow, he looked as if he wasn't taking Lionel very seriously.

He's not going to like that, thought Nelson wryly. *Lionel has a thin skin.*

Lionel certainly didn't look like a private eye. He had long hair, he was skinny, he slouched, and he didn't—despite his bravado—always seem very sure of himself, which was hardly surprising considering what he had gone through. The guy looked like an overgrown kid. On the ride over, he had been quiet, mostly staring out the window.

Even though Lionel had done his homework on the case—and done it well—Nelson wasn't totally convinced that he wasn't just a flake or a snotty rich kid playing cop. If nothing else, he was a well-paying flake.

It's not like I have a choice, thought Nelson. *I can't turn down the money. And who knows—this could turn out to be something interesting.*

Nelson caught a motion out of the corner of his eye and looked up. Lionel was gesturing for him to come in. He got up and went. The office was about what Nelson had expected—huge and expensive. There were some windows with a big view, a lot of expensive wood, and a ton of leather. The place smelled like money. Reynolds Hanson stood with Lionel at the head of the teak conference table that sat in front of his desk. He was a short, stout man who probably couldn't stand any straighter if he tried. And he was trying. His stance reminded Nelson of an undersized rooster—all noise and no meat.

"Mr. West," said Lionel. "I'd like you to meet Mr. Hanson, the CEO of this establishment."

"My pleasure," said Nelson, stepping forward and extending a hand.

Reynolds didn't take it. His eyes never left Nelson's face.

Little prick, thought Nelson. *He's trying to intimidate us. I used to love busting these guys.* Not that he had many chances. Men like Reynolds were always surrounded by lawyers.

"Mr. Bing tells me that you're some sort of hotshot investigator," said Reynolds.

"I'm a private investigator. I don't know if I'm a hotshot."

"You used to be with city homicide?" asked Reynolds.

"That's right."

"I heard you worked the Hightower case. Is that true?"

Nelson felt Lionel glance over at him. He kept his eyes on Reynolds.

"That's right. I was the lead investigator."

"You got the wrong man, you know," said Reynolds, crossing his arms.

"Is that so?"

"Yeah. That spick never did it," said Reynolds, trying to stand even straighter.

That still doesn't make you any taller, thought Nelson. "Is that right?"

Reynolds nodded, smirked, and then went back behind his big desk. He sat down and picked a cigar out of a large humidor. He took his time trimming it before he lit up.

"Tell me about the Hightower case," said Reynolds.

"That's not why we're here, Reynolds," said Lionel, sitting down. "Mr. West is helping me look into the Baker case."

He said the word case as if it were something very valuable. *Well, maybe it will be,* Nelson thought. *Let's see.*

"I don't mind, Mr. Bing," said Nelson. "I don't mind at all."

Nelson rocked back and forth on his heels a couple of times. Felicity Hightower, he recalled. *The case of a lifetime.*

"You probably know the particulars," said Nelson. "A fifteen-year-old girl, Felicity Hightower, was found raped and strangled in Millennium Park. Her body had been placed under The Bean—"

"The Cloud Gate," said Lionel. Both men looked at him. "That's its real name. The Cloud Gate."

Nelson turned back to Reynolds.

"We traced the physical evidence back to Aurelio Montego, a transient. He'd been seen in the park that day, he had a history of sexual assault, and we discovered traces of his DNA at the scene."

"I happen to know," said Reynolds, putting his feet up on the desk, "that the crime was committed by the son of a very well-known political figure. A United States senator, in fact."

"Is that so?"

"It's common knowledge," added Reynolds. "Right, Lionel?"

"I heard something like that," said Lionel. "But I assumed it was just talk."

Nelson didn't take his eyes off Reynolds.

"If you have information about the murder, you should have reported it to the police," said Nelson.

"Right," said Reynolds, chuckling. "You're not serious."

"I'm dead serious," continued Nelson. "If you're right"—*and the little asshole was right*—"then an innocent man is rotting in jail and a psychopath is still out there on the streets." Nelson leaned forward, putting his palms on Reynolds' desk. "Concealing that information could make you an accessory after the fact."

Reynolds started laughing. Nelson straightened up. He felt his hands twitching. Lionel cleared his throat.

"Maybe we should focus on the matter at hand," said Lionel. Nelson glanced at him. He didn't look like a kid anymore—there was iron in his voice.

Reynolds noticed, too. He frowned and slid his feet off his desk, banging them on the hardwood floor.

"Have a seat, West. Lionel here is right. We should get down to business. So," he continued, smiling at Nelson, "wow me with your prowess. Show me how you go about arresting the wrong man."

Nelson sat. Lionel cleared his throat.

"Let's make one thing clear, Mr. Hanson. I'm here because my father is doing you a favor. I don't know why that is and I don't care, but I will have your complete and utter cooperation, or Mr. West and I will walk out of this office and this will become a matter between you, your stockholders, and the district attorney."

"Are you threatening me, you little twerp?"

Lionel stood up.

"Let's go, Nelson. We can let Mr. Hanson stew in his own bullshit."

"Okay, boss," said Nelson. He stood.

"Whoa, take it easy," said Reynolds. "Take it easy. I was just kidding around, Lionel. I was just messing with you. My God."

Lionel remained standing, staring down at Reynolds.

"You need to apologize to Mr. West."

"What for?"

"Because Mr. Bing told you to, you little prick," said Nelson. "He's right. One of your executives managed to walk away with five million dollars of your money. Right under your fucking nose. Lionel's made it his problem, and now I've made it my problem. The last thing we need is for you to be part of our problem." Nelson reached over the desk and helped himself to a cigar. "So, lose the fucking attitude. Or I'll run you in as a material witness on the Hightower case."

Reynolds sneered and then took a deep breath.

"All right," he said. "All right. I'm sorry, Mr. West. I apologize. Okay? Please, have a seat, Lionel. Mr. West."

They sat. Lionel cleared his throat and turned to Nelson.

"Mr. Hanson was telling me that until the auditors called, he had no idea that Mr. Baker had been up to anything."

"That's right," said Reynolds, puffing on his cigar. "It seemed like a straight-up default before they took a close look at Hindman. We didn't suspect anything. Of course, I was being advised by Baker at the time."

Nelson took out his notebook.

"Are all loans usually audited?"

"Not always," said Reynolds, "but defaults are always checked out."

"Tell me about Bradley Baker," said Nelson.

Reynolds took a puff from his cigar. "Brad has been with us for over thirty years. He was an exemplary employee. Family man, very active in his church, and by all accounts, a good father. Excellent at his job, too. Meticulous, very detail-oriented. He was the kind of guy who worked twelve-hour days without blinking."

"Why do you think he was the one who did it?" asked Nelson.

"The amount of a transaction like that demands that upper management signs off on it. That was either Baker, Quinn, Ravelli, Majors, or me."

"Why Baker?" asked Nelson. "Why not you or one of the others? You had the opportunity, too, Mr. Hanson, and five million bucks is a pretty good motive."

Lionel opened his mouth and then shut it. He smiled slightly.

"Because I didn't do it," said Reynolds, sneering. "You're after the wrong man again, Mr. West."

Nelson turned to Lionel. "Did we take a look at Mr. Hanson's financial records along with everyone else's?"

"No, we didn't," said Lionel.

"You'd better check them out. Just to be on the safe side. It's standard procedure. You checked everybody else in upper management, right?"

Lionel nodded. *How come he never takes notes?* wondered Nelson. *He can't be remembering all this.*

"This is outrageous," said Reynolds. "This is harassment."

"You can take it up with the DA if you want," said Nelson. "Now, who was this loan issued to?"

"It's all in the transactions record."

Nelson stared at him.

"The Hindman Corporation," Reynolds finally muttered.

"Who were the loan officers under Baker? Their names weren't on the records."

Reynolds frowned. "I wouldn't know. Baker would know all that. Listen, you don't need to be investigating anyone else. It's unnecessary. A waste of time. Baker did it."

Nelson leaned back in his chair. Reynolds wasn't being very forthcoming with details. Victims weren't usually this resistant.

"If Baker is such an exemplary employee, why do you point the finger at him?" asked Nelson. "Why not the other executives? Why not"—he glanced at his notes—"Ravelli or Majors or Quinn?"

"Real estate wasn't their area," said Reynolds. "If they tried to pull off something like this, it would have sent up red flags all over the place."

"I'm glad something alerts you to wrongdoing in your company, Mr. Hanson," said Nelson, "because I'm a little surprised you've been so blissfully unaware of this little bit of embezzlement."

Lionel stood and looked at Reynolds a moment. Nelson couldn't tell what he was thinking.

"Maybe we should go and talk to Mr. Baker now," he said. "I think we have everything we need from our friend Mr. Hanson."

Reynolds rose. "That would probably be a great idea," he said. *I bet you think it's a good idea, you little prick.* "Except for the fact Mr. Baker isn't in today."

"What?"

"He hasn't been in since Tuesday."

Two days. Long enough for him to get anywhere. Nelson looked over at Lionel, who was glaring at Reynolds.

"Do you have any idea where he is?" asked Lionel. He sounded angry.

No wonder. It's pretty tough when your own client fucks with you.

"You could try his home number," said Reynolds. "Or his cell." He smiled slightly as he puffed his cigar. Lionel nodded slightly.

Yep, kid, thought Nelson. *You've been punked.*

"I'll be in touch, Mr. Hanson," said Lionel. He left quickly. Nelson followed, leaving Reynolds grinning in a cloud of cigar smoke.

Man, I'd love to take that asshole on a perp walk, thought Nelson. He caught up to Lionel at the elevator. Lionel turned to Nelson.

"He's in—" started Lionel. Nelson put his finger to his lips. Lionel stopped and glanced around him. You won't see them, kid.

The elevator door opened. They rode it down to the parking ramp. Lionel made a call. The driver was there in two minutes.

I could get used to this, thought Nelson as they climbed into the back seat. *Beats standing in the rain.*

"Nice guy," said Nelson. "Friend of the family?"

"No," said Lionel, shaking his head. "He's worked on financing with my father in the past. I never met him before. His dad and my dad are old friends."

"Nice people your father knows."

"Reynolds is par for the course. You know, Nelson, these guys generally have two things in common. They never admit when they're wrong and they never apologize. Ever."

"You made him apologize," said Nelson. "Thanks, by the way."

"Sure."

"You don't like them much. Your father's friends, I mean." He glanced over at Lionel, who shrugged.

"I don't really know them all that well. Nor do I wish to," he added, smiling. "I've met enough of their sons and daughters to know better." He turned and looked out the window.

Well, at least he's not one of them, thought Nelson. *So far. That's one in his favor.*

"So," said Lionel, still gazing out the window. "What's our strategy with Baker? How do we go about questioning him?"

"It's probably best to go out there. Surprise him. Don't let him get his guard up. If he's there, we'll sit him down and get some answers."

"If he's not?"

"If he's not," said Nelson, "then we talk to his wife." He paused a moment.

"So, Lionel?"

"Yes?"

"What's the deal when we resolve this thing? I know the bank doesn't want any publicity, so we won't be giving Baker to the cops. What's the plan?"

"That's a good question," said Lionel. "Getting the money back is our primary objective. I think anything after that is up to Con Union. Maybe the SEC."

Nelson sat back. It figures. The rich have their own set of rules. It was true with Hightower, and it was true here. *Except*, thought Nelson, smiling, *when I made sure Senator Dance's kid got a little bit of payback.*

"What's so funny?" asked Lionel.

"What?"

"You were smiling."

"Was I? I don't know. I was just thinking."

Lionel nodded.

"Lincoln," he said to the driver, "take us to Arlington Heights, please. I'll look up the exact address for you."

Nelson leaned back in this seat. *We won't find Baker. He'll be long gone. But if we can talk to his wife and maybe his kid, we might get lucky. Maybe.*

Chapter 4

THE WOMAN WHO ANSWERED THE door was not exactly a spring chicken, but she still looked too young to be the wife of a senior vice president of a bank. Clear skin, firm, not many wrinkles, and no tell-tale neck sags. A lot of eye make-up. She might have been in her early forties. Maybe. There was a hardness in her face that no amount of plastic surgery could hide. Her hair was jet black, although it looked dyed. Brittle. She wore it tied back in a ponytail.

"Yes?" she asked, crossing her arms and leaning on the door jamb.

She was wearing black yoga pants and a workout pullover with a Rice University logo emblazoned on it. Her body—what he could see of it—looked trim. It was obvious she worked at it. She had that look of someone who was very aware of her appearance. One of those people who always know when their picture is being taken.

"Are you Marilyn Baker?" asked Lionel. The woman nodded.

"Is your husband at home?"

"Why?' she asked, tilting her head and frowning. "Who are you?"

"I'm Lionel Bing, and this is my associate, Nelson West. We're here on behalf of Consolidated Union and wanted to talk to your husband about some problems they've been having at the bank."

"What sort of problems?" she asked, barely moving a muscle.

Lionel opened his mouth and then shut it. He took a deep breath.

Take it easy, Lionel, thought Nelson. *Relax.*

"Is he here, ma'am?" asked Nelson. Mrs. Baker shifted her eyes over to him. They were green with little brown specks.

"No. He had to go out of town on family business."

"Really?" asked Lionel curtly. "Where?"

"Wisconsin."

"Do you have an address or a phone number?" asked Lionel. "He's not answering his cell."

"I don't know where he's staying," she said.

"I don't think I should be talking to you," she continued. "If the bank had a problem, they'd be talking to Brad directly. How do I know you're who you say you are?"

Lionel cleared his throat and took another deep breath. He looked uncomfortable and more than a little frustrated. Nelson couldn't tell if he might be getting ready to snap. Mrs. Baker smiled and chuckled.

"You all right?" she asked Lionel. "You look a little nervous."

Lionel frowned and the color rose in his face. Nelson took a step toward her. She didn't seem too impressed.

Time to play hardball, he thought.

"You know exactly why we're here, Mrs. Baker," he said. "And you know exactly what we want. If your husband plays ball with us, this all goes away quietly. If not, he gets dragged into court, goes to prison, you lose this beautiful house, and watch your name get dragged through the mud. Is that what you want?"

She smiled at him and shrugged. *Cool as a cucumber*, thought Nelson. *Tough. If this were a movie, she'd be sneering at me like Barbara Stanwyck.*

"I don't know what you're talking about. Has something happened to Brad?"

"We believe he has a mistress," Lionel blurted. Nelson looked at him.

"What?" said Mrs. Baker, almost laughing. "Brad? You've got to be kidding me."

"Yes," said Lionel. "We're sure of it. He's paying for her apartment in the River North neighborhood."

"Is that a fact? Is that supposed to make me upset?"

"Well, it has more to do with the bank. Our clients are wondering how Mr. Baker is able to afford a $7,000 a month apartment," answered Lionel, "as well as purchase a brand-new Mercedes for his girlfriend."

Mrs. Baker shrugged, still trying to look nonchalant. *She's thinking about it,* thought Nelson. *She's doing the math, thinking that's her money.*

"Who is this supposed woman?"

"That's not the focus of our investigation," answered Lionel. "Our clients don't really care. But we thought you might."

"What's this all about? What happened?"

She's thinking, thought Nelson. *Hard. She either can't figure it out or she's trying to think of a story.*

"Money," said Nelson. "We're looking for a lot of money."

"Do you think Brad stole it?" She laughed. "You can't be serious. He never stole anything in his life. He's never even gotten a speeding ticket."

"Men your husband's age can do odd things," said Nelson. "They might wake up one morning, realize that they suddenly got old, and then something snaps. I've seen it a hundred times."

"What are you, a psychiatrist?"

"He used to be a cop," said Lionel. "City homicide."

She nodded and made an "O" with her mouth.

"Your husband took the money," said Nelson. "We know that. If we don't get him, the cops will. If the cops do, they won't care about keeping it quiet. They might keep Reynolds Hanson out of it, but they'll crucify your husband. And you'll be right up there on that cross with him. Your friends won't be your friends anymore. You'll lose the house, the car, your kid's college education, everything. It'd be a shame if Mark couldn't finish college."

She stared at him a moment, then dropped her eyes.

"Rice, isn't it?" asked Lionel. "That's where Mark goes to school, right?"

"Yeah," she answered, after a moment. "He goes to Rice." She looked up.

"Listen," she said. "If you really think that Brad did this—I don't know. I'd be surprised. We don't share much. He has his own little world, and I have mine. He takes the train to the city, works, and then he comes home and reads or looks at his maps. He goes to church. A lot. That's what he does. That's what he's done for the past twenty years. I find it hard to believe that he has a mistress—and that he would be spending that kind of money on her. That's definitely not like him. And unless he's skipping work, he wouldn't have the time. That wouldn't be like him, either."

The fact he might have something on the side—something expensive— is bugging the hell out of her, thought Nelson.

"I'm sorry you had to find out this way," said Lionel. "Did he tell you anything?"

"No. We don't talk much. As far as I'm concerned, he can do whatever he wants. I don't care. All I know is that the other morning he mentioned that he had to go away for a couple of weeks. He said it was a business trip."

"Any idea where?" asked Nelson.

"No. He packed light, though. One suitcase."

"Does he have a passport?" asked Lionel.

"Of course."

"Could we see it, please?"

She shrugged and went back into the house. Nelson waited until she'd disappeared up the stars and whispered to Lionel.

"Why'd you make that up about the mistress?"

Lionel smiled—almost a smirk. "I had a hunch she might be upset when she found out he was spending money on another woman. Especially that kind of money."

Nelson nodded.

"Good call. It rattled her cage."

"Do you think she knows anything?" asked Lionel. Nelson glanced over at him.

"What do you think? This is your field experience, right? What does your gut tell you?"

"She doesn't know," said Lionel. "She never thought about it before, but now that it's in her head, she's worried the other woman will get her money. She wants her cut."

"You know your women. That kind of woman."

"Yeah," said Lionel. "I've met a thousand just like her." He smiled. "It's not easy being rich, Nelson."

"You poor bastard."

Lionel almost chuckled and then stopped suddenly.

He raised his head. "She's coming," he whispered.

Marilyn Baker came to the door, breathless. Her face was pinched, and her neck was a blotchy red. She was pissed.

"The passport is gone," she blurted. "So is our cash reserve."

"Cash reserve?" asked Lionel.

"Yeah," she said. "Twenty thousand dollars. We had cash on hand in case of an emergency."

Like what? thought Nelson. *The zombie apocalypse? Jesus.*

"Anything else missing?" asked Lionel.

"No," she said. "I can't believe that son of a bitch left me. He left me."

"Well, Mrs. Baker," said Nelson, "it might help us find him if you let us look through his things, his papers. Anything that might shed light on where he went. You know, if we could look at his study or home office or anything like that."

Marilyn Baker looked at him, glaring. *Although,* thought Nelson, *she's not pissed at me. She's just pissed.*

"Yeah, come back tomorrow and I'll let you look through his stuff. After lunch."

Nelson nodded. *Not ideal. If she's in on it, she'll have time to hide anything she wanted.* But his gut told him she didn't know.

"Good. Thank you."

"Listen," she said, taking a step closer to Lionel, "I want you to tell me the name of that woman and I want you to do it now. She's not getting away with this."

"I'm sorry," said Nelson, stepping between the two of them, "but that's against company policy. We can't have you getting in the way of our investigation, now, can we?"

"You get him," she said, her voice rising, "and you bring him back here to me." She turned on her heel, stomped into the foyer and slammed the front door behind her.

Nelson and Lionel turned to leave.

"You might have hit a nerve there, Lionel," said Nelson, as they walked toward the street.

"Yes. I think so, too. What do you think she'll do next?"

"Call her lawyer, I imagine," said Nelson. "Start counting up her stack in case it comes down to a divorce. She'll probably freeze as much of the mutual money as she can."

The driver got out and opened the door for them.

I wonder what she thinks of Lionel Bing, thought Nelson, turning toward the house as he got into the car. *Sure enough, there she was— watching them from the living room window as they drove away.*

Chapter 5

"So your name is Lincoln?" asked Nelson.

The driver turned in his seat, took a short look at Lionel, and glanced back at Nelson. He turned back toward the road.

"Yeah," he said. "Lincoln DuPree."

"Great name for a driver."

"Well, I guess you could say I stumbled into both my name and my profession."

Nelson felt himself smiling. He glanced over at Lionel, who was staring out the window.

"Where to, Mr. Bing?" asked Lincoln. They were already on the Edens Expressway, headed back toward the city.

Lionel looked up at the sound of his name and then glanced absently at Lincoln and then over at Nelson. He frowned.

"Head back to the Consolidated Union Bank, Lincoln. Mr. West gave me an idea."

Lincoln turned his head so that Nelson could see it in profile.

"Don't do that, Mr. West," he said.

"Do what?"

"Don't give Mr. Bing any ideas. That's the last thing we need."

Nelson chuckled and glanced over. Lionel was staring out the window again, lost in thought.

* * *

It didn't take long to get the key to Baker's office. They called Reynolds Hanson and his secretary was out in two minutes, key in hand. She was nice-looking, young. Probably fresh out of college. Squeaky clean. She'd hadn't quite lost that flush of first job excitement.

"Thank you," said Lionel, taking the key.

"You're Lionel Bing, aren't you?"

"Yes," he said curtly, not making eye contact.

"I thought so," she said, smiling. "I recognized you."

"Oh," said Lionel, finally glancing at her. "That's nice." He sounded as if he was telling a dog to sit.

"Yes," she said, oblivious. "I actually read an article about you in *People*, but it was mostly about your dad. Wow. He's amazing. He's so wealthy. It's got to be crazy being that rich."

Lionel looked at her a moment and quickly looked away.

"Thank you," he said. "Thank you so much for sharing. Tell me—"

"Heather."

"Heather. Where exactly is Mr. Baker's office?"

She smiled and pointed down the corridor. Lionel nodded and left. Nelson caught up. They walked for a while in silence.

Man, thought Nelson. *I thought he was going to go off on her for a minute.* He hesitated a moment.

"Gee, boss, I didn't know you had groupies."

Lionel grimaced. "My God. Look at her," he said, gesturing back toward Miss Squeaky Clean, who was still standing in the corridor watching them. "She's like a rat terrier. She can smell money."

"Maybe a cross between a terrier and a poodle," said Nelson.

Lionel shook his head. "Stupid girl doesn't know what she's talking about. My dad. Huh."

"Maybe she likes you for your personality, Lionel."

Lionel scoffed and glanced sideways at him, his mouth twitching.

Well, well. The boss almost smiled.

They reached Baker's office and went inside. Nelson thought it was a smallish room for a vice president. Maybe eight by ten. A desk tucked against the far wall. One window with not much of a view. A couple dozen pictures adorned the walls. Most were photographs of what looked like a South American village. Jungle, mountains, a plaza, and a church. A lot of pictures of the church. People. Mostly kids. Most of the buildings had the same small blue and white sign on them. Nelson couldn't quite make out the writing on the signs. Lionel started poking around on Baker's desk. He leaned over and started typing on the computer.

"May I help you?"

It was a tough voice, gravelly, the voice of a smoker. Nelson turned. A tall, middle-aged woman stood in the doorway, her arms folded over her chest. *Well,* thought Nelson, *I don't think it's a question of diddling the secretary.*

"Yes," said Lionel. "I think you can."

"Who are you? What are you doing in Mr. Baker's office?"

"I'm Lionel Bing, and this is my associate, Nelson West. I'm sorry, but I don't think we were properly introduced."

"My name is Charlotte Schmitz. I'm Mr. Baker's secretary."

"Mr. Hanson hired us," said Lionel, "to look into a matter that involves Mr. Baker in a kind of peripheral way. When was the last time you saw him?"

"Why?"

"You'll have to ask Mr. Hanson that," answered Lionel. "I'm not at liberty to say. You can call him if you want. We'll wait."

Charlotte looked from one man to the other, frowned, and then sighed. *I guess she doesn't like talking to Reynolds Hanson,* thought Nelson. *I can't say I blame her.*

"All right," she said. "If you really want to know, I haven't seen Mr. Baker for a few days now."

"Any idea where he might be? Any messages, voicemails, anything like that?" asked Nelson.

She shook her head. "I still don't understand this. Why are you here? What are you looking for? Don't you need a warrant or something?"

"Nope," said Nelson, opening a drawer in the bureau. "We were hired by Mr. Hanson, so we have every right to look around." *Books. Bibles. Four of them.* He picked one up and turned it over. *Leatherbound, old. It looked valuable.*

"We are here to look through Mr. Baker's office as part of—an investigation," said Lionel. "We want to ask him a few questions."

"Isn't he home? I thought he was out sick."

"Do you know," asked Lionel, "where he keeps his schedule? There doesn't seem to be anything online."

"Mr. Baker doesn't believe in computers," she said. "He only uses them when he has to. He doesn't trust them. He wrote down all his appointments in his book that he always keeps in the top drawer there." She pointed.

Lionel walked over to the desk, opened the drawer, and took out one, two, and three appointment books, opened the top one, and riffled through it.

"These are from last year and the years before that," he said. "Where's his current date book?"

Charlotte shrugged. "It's usually in there."

"Why would he keep appointment books from a year ago?" asked Nelson, walking over to the desk. He took one from the pile and flipped through it. *Nothing unusual. Business meetings. Lunches. Nothing much on the weekends or after hours except for* meetings with a Father Mike. Church stuff, apparently. It all looked straight.

"He's odd that way. He always keeps his old datebooks."

"Does he have a safe?" asked Nelson. She shook her head. Lionel put his hands in his pockets and stared at Charlotte a moment.

"Why don't you sit down?" he finally said, motioning to one of office chairs. She sat. Lionel sat down in the chair opposite.

"Could you tell us about the last time you saw Mr. Baker?" asked Lionel.

"Well," she said, leaning back and placing her hands on the arms of the chair, "let me see. That was on Monday. He came in, poured his coffee, and then closed the door."

"Any calls?"

Charlotte shook her head.

"No, wait," she said. "There was one call that morning. A man with an accent."

"Accent? What sort of accent?"

"Spanish."

"That sounds a little mysterious," said Lionel, smiling a little.

He's trying to be charming, thought Nelson, *but it's coming off as a little forced. Charlotte didn't seem to mind, though.*

"Did Mr. Baker often get calls from foreign gentlemen?"

"Once in a while," said Charlotte, after a moment's thought. "The same one, I think. He never leaves a message. It's just, 'Is Mr. Baker there?' and if I say no, he'll hang up."

"When was the last time he got one of those calls?" asked Nelson. "Before the one on Monday, I mean. Do you remember?"

"About a week ago or so, I think," she said. Nelson glanced at Lionel, who nodded. *That should show up on the phone records—unless they used one of those disposable cells.*

"I have a question," said Nelson. Charlotte leaned forward in her chair. "Why did Mr. Baker have all those Bibles?"

"Oh, he's a very religious man," she said, "and very involved with church charities. His church, St. Alphonso's, does a lot of work overseas."

Lionel got up, walked over to the bureau, and picked up the leather-bound Bible. He flipped it open and started paging through it.

"Did he ever conduct any of his church business while he was here in the office?" asked Nelson. "Did he ever talk about what they did or where they did it?"

"Well, yes," she said, turning in her seat and gesturing behind her. "Of course. You can see for yourself. It's everywhere."

"What's that?" asked Nelson, looking around. "Where?"

"The photos," said Charlotte. "These photographs from San Pablo. That's where he did his church work."

Nelson walked over and started reexamining the photos. Lionel joined him. Pretty standard stuff. Adobe houses, a big plaza, a church, marketplace. The photos could have come from anybody's Mexican vacation.

"St. Alphonso's did a lot to help the people in that village," said Charlotte, "after that terrible accident."

"An accident?" asked Lionel, gazing at one of the photos.

"There was an explosion in the mine right outside of the town. Over eighty people were killed." She shook her head. "I guess it was just awful."

"An explosion?" asked Nelson.

"I don't know too much about it, but there was a gold mine there," she said. "Nearly all the men and a lot of the boys from San Pablo worked there. It had a name. I think they called it La Fuente or something. I forget the name of the company that owned it, too."

"What happened?" asked Lionel, his voice low, almost a whisper.

"Some sort of explosion," said Charlotte, "and then a cave-in. I'm not sure exactly what happened. I do know that most of the workers were killed. They left behind wives, children, families. They had nothing after they were gone. The company didn't do anything to help them."

"How did St. Alphonso's become involved?" asked Lionel.

"I'm not sure about that," said Charlotte. "Through Mr. Baker, I imagine."

"Do you know the name of the priest there?"

She furrowed her brow. "Oh, I must know it," she said. "He's said it a hundred times. Mike. That's it. Father Mike."

"Do you know the name of the San Pablo church?" asked Nelson.

Charlotte pursed her lips, thinking.

"Was it Santa Barbara?" asked Lionel softly.

"Why, yes, it is," exclaimed Charlotte. "How did you know?"

Lionel held up the leatherbound bible and smiled.

"This bible is signed by Father Ignacio from the Santa Barbara Church in San Pablo. It was a thank-you gift to Mr. Baker. It's dated three months ago. Did your boss travel to Mexico recently? More recently that that?"

"Not that I know of."

"All right," said Lionel, walking over and offering Charlotte his hand. "Thank you so much, Charlotte. You've been a big help."

She smiled and took the proffered hand.

"Do you mind if we borrow this Bible?" asked Lionel. "I'd like to show it to Mrs. Baker to see if she recognizes it."

A look of distaste crossed Charlotte's face.

"That one," she said.

"What do you mean?" asked Nelson.

"He's too good for her. The way she carries on."

Nelson crossed his arms and waited. She was ready to start rolling. He could feel it. He glanced over at Lionel, who was standing with his hands in his pockets.

That's right. Don't rush her.

Charlotte put her hands in her lap and squared her shoulders.

"You know, she's been having an affair for at least three years. At least one."

"Really?" asked Nelson.

She nodded. "A much younger man. I understand he's some sort of trainer. I believe he works for the Racine Cougars."

"Really?" asked Nelson. The Cougars were a minor-league ballclub up in Racine, Wisconsin, about an hour away.

"Yes," she said. "The two of them carry on everywhere, right out in the open. Mr. Baker lives out in Arlington Heights and a few friends of mine live out there, too, so I know. Believe me, I know."

"Carrying on?"

"Oh, yes, you know, they usually meet two or three times a week for lunch and then… well."

She paused. Nelson waited. Charlotte leaned forward and whispered, "They've been seen going into hotels together."

"What's his name?" asked Nelson. "The trainer."

"Lance Malkowitz," she replied instantly. "One of my friends knows his sister."

Nelson wrote it down, glancing over at Lionel.

"Did Mr. Baker know about this?" asked Lionel.

"I don't think so," said Charlotte. "That poor man. She barely gives him the time of day."

Nelson nodded. They'd have to check out Malkowitz. A philandering wife with a rich, older husband who just happened to be missing. It was possible—just possible—that Bradley Baker was the victim of foul play. Nelson half-smiled to himself. Marilyn Baker and a young stud. *Who says people aren't predictable?*

"Did Mr. Baker ever talk about his wife?" asked Lionel.

"Not to me," said Charlotte. "No, he only talked about those poor Mexicans and that terrible accident." She glanced up at Lionel. "That's all he ever talked about, Mr. Bing. They were his life."

"The last time you saw him," asked Nelson, "did he happen to have a bag or a suitcase with him?"

"No," she said. "No, just his briefcase."

Nelson glanced over at Lionel, who nodded. They thanked Charlotte and left, Lionel clutching the Bible under his arm. He stood silent as they waited for the elevator. Nelson wanted to ask him about going after Malkowitz, but he waited. No rush. He'd talk when he was ready.

The elevator door opened. Lionel turned and looked at Nelson and smiled and then got onto the car.

He thinks he knows something, thought Nelson. *I have no idea what, but he knows something.*

Chapter 6

Lincoln was there waiting for them at the curb. Lionel climbed into the backseat and Nelson followed. Lincoln pulled out into traffic.

"You know," said Lionel, "I think we're making progress. This was a productive day. I had misgivings about you, Nelson, but I think this is going to work."

"Good," said Nelson. "Thanks." *Sort of a left-handed compliment, but I'll take it.*

"I like the way you complement me—the way we play off each other," said Lionel. He smiled. "You know, I hate to admit when my father's right, but I think you'll be a good addition to the team."

"Yeah, I think so, too," said Nelson. *Well,* he thought. *The boss likes me. There's a change.*

"So tomorrow," continued Lionel, "I'm thinking we need to go back to see Mrs. Baker. We should also touch base with the priest at his church. That Father Mike. Okay," he said. "That's our agenda."

"Sounds good."

"What time is it?" asked Lionel.

"About five," said Nelson, glancing at his watch.

"You should join us for dinner tonight, Nelson. We should brainstorm some more."

It wasn't exactly a question. Nelson paused before answering.

"I don't know," he said. "Thanks for the invitation, though."

"You should come. Mia will be there, and we'll be having our study hall a little later."

"Study hall?"

Nelson heard something coming from the front seat. Laughing? He glanced at the rear-view and caught a sidelong glance from Lincoln. He might have had a smile on his face. It was hard to tell.

"Yes," said Lionel, "that's what we call it. Some of my friends and I have a little get-together about once a week. They come over and we discuss wine. Everyone brings a bottle and we taste and compare." He shrugged and smiled. "Sort of a study group."

"I don't know much about wine," said Nelson. *Nothing, in fact.*

"Well, this might be a good opportunity for you to learn. You like wine, don't you?"

"Sure," said Nelson. *I like bourbon better*, he thought, but didn't say so.

"We'll be tasting white burgundies tonight," said Lionel. "We're going to have a 2010 Louis Latour Corton-Charlemagne and some other producers from the Côte de Beaune. You should come. You'll enjoy it."

"I'm not going to know anyone," said Nelson. *Or anything*, he thought. *What the hell is Côte de Beaune?*

"You might," said Lionel. "Let me think. Do you know John Sellers?"

"The news guy from Channel 3?"

Lionel nodded.

"I know who he is," said Nelson. *I should. The son of a bitch roasted me over the Hightower case.*

"He'll be there—he always is—and so will Derrick Nickleby, the author."

"The mystery writer? Wow. I didn't know he lived in Chicago."

"He doesn't," said Lionel. "He has a house in Asheville but flies in to visit every month. We're pretty close. We went to school together."

"Wow," said Nelson, feeling smaller by the minute.

"There are others, too," said Lionel. "People you'd recognize."

Nelson nodded.

"So," said Lionel, after a moment. "Are you coming?"

Nelson glanced over at him. Lionel was smiling at him now, brimming with enthusiasm. *Quite a switch from this morning,* thought Nelson. *He's excited, like a big kid planning a sleepover. Well, what the hell?*

"Sure," he said. "Why not?"

"Excellent."

Nelson leaned forward.

"Hey, Lincoln? Could you drop me off at home first?" he asked. "I should change and take care of a few things."

"Nonsense," said Lionel. "You can change at my place. I'm certain we have clothes that'll fit you."

"Thanks, but I really do need to stop in at the apartment for a minute. What time does the fun start?"

Lionel frowned. He seemed a little irritated by Nelson's detour but shrugged and nodded.

"Eight or so. Dinner will be at seven."

"Sounds good," said Nelson. He shared his address with Lincoln, who soon pulled up to his building. Nelson got out and nodded to Lionel, who waved as the car pulled away. Nelson went in. The elevator was broken again. He trudged up the three flights of stairs, opened the door, and walked into the apartment. It looked even smaller and shoddier than usual. The dirty dishes were still soaking in the sink and a sour smell hung over the bed. He needed to change the sheets. And do the laundry. And take out the garbage. And everything else. The place badly needed cleaning.

But even so, he thought, loosening his tie and sitting down in the lone kitchen chair, *it's all mine.* He could sit here without listening, without thinking, without reacting. He didn't have to do anything he didn't want to do. Lionel was all right. He seemed like he was going to be a good boss, even with all the TLC he needed, but he tended to wear on a person after a while. *And I'm not getting paid to be his friend. Or his therapist.* He didn't want to be on call for the guy 24/7.

Nelson put his feet up on the table, closed his eyes, and listened to the silence for a moment—the near-silence, the silence of a second-rate building. He could hear a television blaring next door, an argument somewhere above him, and kids playing in the hall. It wasn't the Ritz or the Bing house, but it was home.

What a life, thought Nelson. *I'm going to be a combination babysitter, bodyguard, and detective. To help this guy get over a childhood trauma by what? Stopping crime? Good luck with that. It's impossible to make a difference out there. When you do try to do the right thing, they shoot you down.*

Nelson opened his eyes. *Felicity Hightower.* Reynolds Hanson had stirred up a lot of old memories. That morning in the park, finding that poor little girl curled up under The Bean—he remembered it like yesterday. The anger that welled up in him hadn't faded, either. It never would, not until Simon Dance was doing hard time at Joliet—and that wasn't going to happen. That son of a bitch Reynolds was right. They had gotten the wrong man. The worst thing about it was that he knew it. Everyone knew it.

Nelson stood up, walked to the kitchen cabinet, and reached for the bottle of bourbon. *Nah,* he thought, pulling his hand back. *I'd better be good tonight. I'm still making an impression.* He went into the bedroom and opened his closet. There had to be at least one clean shirt in there. Nope. Bare. He looked in his shirt drawer and rooted around until saw the black turtleneck he'd gotten from Mary, his ex-wife, for Christmas. *Boy*, he thought, *was that four years ago? Five?*

Nelson hadn't worn it in years, but desperate times called for desperate measures. Besides, it was probably just old enough to be fashionable again. Now that he had steady work, he'd have to head down to Macy's or one of the other department stores to go clothes shopping this weekend. *I'd better keep that to myself*, he thought. *I don't want Lionel tagging along.* He had a feeling that his new boss—despite his initial brusqueness—was going to be more than a little needy. They were buddies now. The fact that Mia said Lionel liked to have people around and the way he had invited Nelson to come up before dinner seemed to indicate Lionel expected him to be a paid companion as well as an associate.

Well, thought Nelson. *We'll see how long that lasts.* It was a good job—*health insurance, for Christ's sake*—but Nelson wasn't sure if he'd be able to take Lionel Bing 24/7. He liked the guy, sure, but he didn't want to be his big brother. Or his dad, his therapist, or whoever the hell it was he needed.

Nelson glanced at his watch. He needed to get going. This time of day, it would take a good forty-five minutes on the train. *Maybe,* he thought, as he clattered down the stairs, *I should get a car. I can afford it now. Unless he could talk his boss into getting him one for the job.* Nelson smiled to himself. *Maybe,* he thought. *Maybe.*

* * *

He knocked. Mia opened the door almost immediately. She was wearing a green pullover and blue jeans. She looked good.

"Hello, Mr. West," she said, stepping into the foyer and shutting the door behind her.

"Hello, Mia."

"Tell me, how did it go this morning?"

"How did what go?"

"The meeting."

"What meeting? Oh," he said, snapping his fingers, "the meeting with Mr. Bing? The original Mr. Bing?"

"Quiet. He'll hear."

"It went well. We mostly talked about women we've known."

"Stop it. This is serious."

"Why do you want to know?" asked Nelson, crossing his arms.

"Why do you think?" she whispered, glancing at the door. "I'm part of this, too, Nelson. I helped Lionel's dad pick you out."

"So, what—"

"Mia," called someone from inside. Lionel.

"Just play dumb for now," she said. "That shouldn't be too hard for you. We'll talk later."

She opened the door, and they went in.

"Coming," she called.

"Remember," she whispered to Nelson, "don't say anything about this to Lionel."

"Okay. By the way, you look nice."

"Shut up. Give me your coat."

He shrugged out of his jacket and handed it her, wishing it was clean. Mia took it and went into the apartment. He followed and watched her disappear into one of the side rooms. Nelson put his hands in his pockets and glanced around. Apparently, he was the first one there. He wasn't early, though, he knew that. Maybe dinner was just for the three of them, and the wine thing—the study hall, as Lionel had called it—would be later.

There was a large, mirrored cart sitting in the middle of the living room—or great room, or whatever it was, with a large assortment of booze arrayed across the top shelf. Nelson strolled over and took a look. There were at least a dozen bottles. He didn't know many of the scotches. There was Johnnie Walker Blue, Lagavulin, and a Laphroaig, whatever that was. The bourbons he knew, and they were prime. Expensive. Old Weller Antique, Buffalo Trace Hancock, and even a Pappy Van Winkle. He'd only heard of the legendary Pappy—it was supposed to be phenomenal.

"Do you like what you see, Nelson?"

Nelson turned around. Lionel stood in the doorway to the kitchen, smiling. He seemed cheerful, almost ebullient. Quite a change from earlier in the day. *Were mood swings part of the PTSD?* He'd have to check. Lionel hadn't changed his clothes, which surprised Nelson a little. He'd figured Lionel would have dressed for dinner, since that was what the wealthy did. He was holding a glass of red wine.

"Yeah," said Nelson, glancing down at the cart. "I've tried the Johnny Walker Blue, but I don't know many of the other ones. I have heard of Pappy Van Winkle," he said, picking up the bottle, "but I've never had the pleasure."

"It's as good as advertised," said Lionel. "Everything here is the best. Would you like to try some?"

Nelson shrugged and then nodded. *Sure. Why not? Who knew when he might have another chance to try the best of the best?* From what he'd heard, the cost of Pappy could be astronomical, sometimes going for ten times the listed price. He watched as Lionel poured out a glass.

"I assume you take it neat?" he asked, handing Nelson the glass.

"Of course. I'm not an animal."

Lionel chuckled and raised his wine glass. They toasted and Nelson took a sip. *Damn, that's good.* It was smooth, buttery—with a surprising caramel taste.

"Jesus," he said, taking another sip. "Jesus, that's good."

"This is a fifteen year. The best. Much better than the twenty. You know, considering its quality, it's remarkable how affordable Pappy is," said Lionel. "If you know the right people," he added.

"Affordable for you, maybe," said Nelson, smiling.

They both glanced over as Mia entered from the side room. She came over to the table and glanced at the bottle Lionel was still holding.

"You go right for the cream, don't you, Mr. West?" she said. She took a wine glass from the bottom shelf of the cart and went into the kitchen. Lionel stood there holding his wine glass and the Pappy, staring at the empty doorway.

"She's really something," said Lionel, taking another sip.

Nelson grunted.

"We're lucky to have her," continued Lionel. "She could be working for Dow, Monsanto, the government. She had all sorts of offers right out of school."

"Did you meet in college? Is that how you know her?"

"College?" asked Lionel. "No, no, no. An acquaintance of my father's at the university told me about her. I'd asked him to keep an eye out for someone with her qualifications."

"Qualifications?"

"Yes," answered Lionel, nodding. "Her intellectual qualifications and her analytic talents. Not only is Mia a great scientist, but she also has a fine, intuitive feel for problem solving. She has excellent instincts for getting to the heart of a problem."

Mia walked back in, holding a full wine glass in one hand and a bottle in the other.

"So," she said, "what's going on, boys?"

Lionel smiled. Nelson nodded to himself. Despite her abrasiveness, he was starting to like Mia. She was funny. And she had a funky exuberance underneath that tough exterior. *And*, he thought, gazing at her hair, *not always that far under the surface, either.*

"Mr. Bing," called a voice from the kitchen. "Dinner is ready to be served."

"Thank you, David," called out Lionel. "Shall we?"

Mia led the way. Nelson followed them past the little room they'd met in that morning into a large dining room, also with floor-to-ceiling windows. They were facing southeast, toward downtown. The lights of the city spread out before them.

"Nice view," Nelson murmured.

"Yes, especially in the summer," said Lionel. *He certainly is talkative now*, thought Nelson. *On his meds or off?*

"The entire lakeshore comes alive," he continued. "We see runners, swimmers, sunbathers, families—the whole city comes out." A wistful, almost sad, expression crossed his face.

Lionel guided Nelson to the table. The table was big but not huge. It could easily have seated ten people but was still small enough to be cozy. It was simply set, just the basic silverware. *Thank God*, thought Nelson. Fine dining was not his forte. They sat.

"Nelson," said Mia. He looked up. She was passing a bottle of white wine. He took it and glanced at the label.

"This is an Albarino," said Lionel. "A Spanish white. It pairs quite well with chicken, also with fish. We're going to be having seafood risotto tonight, and it's absolutely stellar with that."

Nelson nodded and said, "Ah."

"You'll see," said Lionel.

Nelson poured himself a glass and took a sip. It was nice, crisp, and had a little bit of a bite.

"Nice," he said. "I don't know much about wine, but this is really good." He smiled. "I guess I know that I like it."

"That's the only criteria that matters," said Mia. "Cheers," she said, raising her glass. They toasted.

"So, how did it go today?"

Lionel gave her the rundown. Nelson listened closely, interjecting a comment only every now and then. He wanted to see how his boss had digested the day's information and what he thought was important. A good detective had to be able to strip away the bullshit and get to the heart of a case—to see through the lies and smokescreens and inconsequential evidence. Some cops were born with that knack. Others learned it. Some never really got it. Lionel was doing all right.

He's pretty good, thought Nelson. He had given most of Charlotte Schmitz's information the attention it deserved, concentrating mostly on the church angle. *And that's a big part of it with Baker. The church.*

Mia was nodding her head and listening closely, too. The questions she asked were pertinent and to the point. *She's sharp, too. Really sharp.* Nelson hoped he wasn't going to be outclassed.

"So, what we have," Lionel was saying, "is a banker who disappeared with about five million dollars. There's no evidence of debt, drug use, recent spending, or a mistress—none of the usual motives for fraud. The wife is unhappy but seems to be unaware of any illicit activities." He glanced at Nelson, who nodded.

"Yeah," he said. "She was surprised he might have stolen that much money." Nelson turned to Mia. "I think she felt a little left out. She wanted her cut."

"She sounds like a real piece of work," said Mia.

"And apparently," continued Lionel, speaking rapidly, "according to Charlotte, she's been playing around with a trainer for a local baseball team. A much younger man."

"The Racine Cougars," said Nelson. "The minor-league team."

"Apt name," murmured Mia. Nelson smiled and had some more risotto.

"This is really good," he said. *I have to quit saying that,* he thought.

"Doesn't it pair well with the wine?" asked Lionel.

I guess, thought Nelson. He nodded.

"Why is Cougars an apt name?" Lionel asked suddenly, turning to Mia.

Really? thought Nelson.

Mia smiled. "Well, Nelson said he is a much younger man. So, she would fit the description of a cougar. On the prowl."

"Oh," said Lionel. "Of course."

Nelson cleared his throat.

"Oh," said Mia. "Did you say something, Mr. West?"

He shook his head.

"An older woman," she said. "Did you find her attractive, Mr. West?"

Nope, he thought. *She looks too much like my ex-wife.*

"No," he said. "She's not really my type. Plus, she's a little mercenary for my taste."

"But is she attractive?"

Nelson glanced over at her. Mia had her head cocked and was smiling at him.

Flirting? he thought. *No. No way. She's just giving me shit.*

"She's attractive," he said, "but you can tell she works pretty hard at it. There's nothing natural about her—nothing genuine. If that makes sense."

Lionel nodded in agreement.

"Definitely," he said. "You're right on the mark with that one, Nelson. She's had at least one face lift, probably more."

Nelson looked at him. *Where the hell did that come from?*

Lionel glanced at his watch.

"Ah," he said. "The study hall will be starting in about fifteen minutes." He turned. "David," he called.

David, a rangy man, probably in his middle forties, appeared in the doorway from the kitchen, and nodded.

"Thank you for a wonderful dinner." David nodded and moved to clear the table.

"Let me help," said Mia.

Nelson rose, grabbed his plate, and started stacking silver on it.

"No, please, Nelson," said Lionel. "You're a guest."

"He works here now," said Mia. "Let him help."

Lionel frowned and glared at Mia. He opened his mouth but then snapped it shut and turned away.

"Sir," said a voice at Nelson's elbow. He turned. David stood there.

"Let me help you with that, sir."

He glanced over at Lionel, who still looked upset. Nelson realized he was making his host—his boss—uncomfortable. *No*, he thought. *Don't push his buttons, Nelson.*

"Thank you," he said, handing his plate to David. He turned to Lionel.

"So, Lionel, what is this study hall thing?"

Lionel took a breath. He looked relieved.

"Oh, it's just an informal get-together," said Lionel. "We're almost like a book club, except we sample and discuss wine. We're all fanciers, I guess some of us might even be called experts. Mr. Angelis would definitely fall into that category."

"Angelis. Why is that name familiar?"

"Preston Angelis?" said Lionel. "The restaurant owner? Does that ring a bell?"

Sure, thought Nelson. *The guy who owns Miranda's, the most elite restaurant in Chicago.* He'd heard dinner there cost over a thousand bucks a plate.

"Sure," he said.

"Yes," said Lionel. "Preston is quite the wine connoisseur. His sommelier is a good friend of mine. Preston could have been a sommelier himself."

Nelson nodded, not quite sure exactly what a sommelier was—but he sure wasn't going to say so.

"And, as I was saying earlier, John Sellers will probably be here. We're expecting Mason Pillsbury, too."

"The fashion designer?" asked Nelson.

"Right."

"Man," he said.

"There will be quite a few others here, too. Don't worry, Nelson. We'll have a great time. And you, my friend, will be introduced to the world of fine wine."

* * *

Sellers arrived early—for a party. Mia let him in a little after eight. He looked shorter than Nelson expected—not nearly as imposing as he did anchoring the 10 o'clock news. He had a well-groomed, maybe over-groomed, look to him. He looked soft, pink, and puffy, like a big Beanie Baby.

Well, thought Nelson. *I guess it goes with the territory.* He wasn't sure if Sellers would remember him. They'd never met, but he had led the coverage on the Hightower case. He'd been extremely critical of the investigation, calling it—among other things—a sham and a disgrace. Sellers had mentioned Nelson by name more than a few times.

Nelson smiled and shook Sellers' hand as Mia introduced them. He watched Sellers' face for a glimmer of recognition. Nothing. *He doesn't remember me. Well, that's a good thing.*

"So, Lionel mentioned you're going to be working with him?" he asked.

"That's right," said Nelson.

"I think it's great that he's found a calling. He should be very good at it, don't you think?"

Nelson nodded.

"Definitely," he said. "He has very good instincts."

"Well, it'd be a great story. You know, rich kid giving back to his community, that sort of thing. I'd love to do a feature on it."

Nelson nodded. He wasn't really sure how Lionel was giving back to the community. It seemed to him he was simply helping out other rich people—for free.

"What did you bring tonight?" asked Sellers.

"Bring?" asked Nelson.

"Yeah," said Sellers. "Typically, we all bring a wine we'd like to share."

"Sorry. This is my first time. Lionel just invited me this afternoon."

"Ah," said Sellers. "Do you know wine?"

Nelson shrugged. "Not as well as I'd like."

"Come with me," said Sellers.

He followed Sellers into the kitchen, where Lionel was taking several bottles out of a wine refrigerator. He looked up as they walked in.

"Hello, John," he said enthusiastically, standing up. "I see you've met Nelson West, my newest associate."

"I have indeed."

"You better be careful," said Lionel. "You know he's a retired cop."

Sellers turned and looked at Nelson, a glimmer of recognition flickering.

"Nelson West. Sure. Detective West. I thought the name seemed familiar."

"I was wondering if you'd remember," said Nelson. "What was it you said? 'The Hightower investigation is a shining example of everything that is wrong, filthy, and corrupt with the CPD.' Did I get that right?"

Sellers shrugged.

"Something like that. I call them as I see them, Detective."

The two men stared at each other.

"Mr. West is working for me now," said Lionel, handing Sellers a bottle. "As far as I'm concerned, he's the best in the business."

Sellers nodded at Lionel and glanced down at the bottle.

"Oh," he said. "Perclos?"

"That's right," said Lionel. "We have to have it on white burgundy night. You know that. What did you bring?"

"I brought," said Sellers, producing the bottle, "Domaine Leroy Corton-Charlemagne." He smiled. "The 2004."

"Beautiful," said Lionel. "When did you open it?"

81

"Noon or so."

"Perfect," said Lionel, gazing at the bottle as if it were made of gold.

Who knows, thought Nelson. *In this world, maybe it is.*

Sellers turned to Nelson.

"I hope there's no hard feelings about our coverage of the Hightower case, Mr. West. I was only doing my job."

Nelson shrugged. "We were all trying to do our jobs."

"It was a tough case," said Sellers. "There were a lot of extenuating circumstances. I know you did the best job you possibly could." He paused as Lionel handed him a glass. "We found out a lot more than we could report. Without all the—" he paused, "—outside political pressures, I think we might have ended up with a better result for everyone."

Nelson nodded. *Keep your mouth shut*, he said to himself. He felt a nudge and turned. Lionel was handing him a glass of wine.

"Try this," said Lionel. "It's Domaine d'Eugénie, Les Perclos, Chassagne-Montrachet, 2018. Great stuff. This is a recent vintage but very nice."

"Okay," said Nelson. He took a sip.

"Try smelling it first," said Lionel. "Get your nose right in there."

Nelson took a whiff. He smelled some sort of fruit and a kind of buttery aroma.

"Try a slow sip."

It was good.

"This is good," said Nelson. He paused as the sensation sunk in. *No,* he thought. *This is fucking great.*

"It's really good," he added.

"Well," said Lionel, "we'll make a gourmand out of you yet. Excuse me."

Someone was at the door. Mia opened it and a short, rotund man bustled in, clutching a brown paper bag to his chest. He peered around the room intently until he finally caught sight of Lionel.

"Ah, there you are," he said, trotting over to him. Lionel gave him a hug.

"Here." He handed Lionel the bag, shrugged out of his coat, and handed it to Mia, who had come up beside him. "Thank you, Mia."

"Sure thing, Derrick. How are you?"

"I am all right. Things are going quite well. And whom," he asked, peering up at Nelson, "do we have here?"

"This is Nelson West, who is going to be working with Lionel and me," said Mia. "He's an ex-homicide detective."

"Really?" asked Derrick. "Excellent. We'll have to talk. I need to pick your brains—all of them—but first I have to get my bottle opened. It needs to breathe." He trotted off toward the kitchen, where Lionel had disappeared. Mia went toward the closet to hang up Derrick's coat. Nelson followed.

"Who was that?"

"Derrick Nickleby," she said. "The writer."

"Huh," said Nelson. "He's quite the character."

"He is that," she said, putting the coat on the hanger.

"So, Mia, what do you know about all this wine stuff? I don't know what people are talking about half the time."

"I don't know much yet either," she said, smiling, "but I'm learning. Here. Follow me."

David was at the door. At least four or five other guests had arrived. Nelson glanced around the room. Beside Sellers and Nickleby, there was an extremely well-dressed middle-aged woman—late forties, maybe a well-preserved fifty—who was conversing with a youngish man dressed in a button-down shirt and sport coat. He was tall, lanky, and leaning against the wall, swirling his wine glass with one hand as he listened to the woman.

A cool boy. Nelson knew the type. One of those guys able to glide through life without breaking a sweat. Women and money were never problems for them. The only problems cool boys had were the ones they made themselves. Nelson smiled to himself. *They always think they can get away with murder.* Nelson had busted dozens of them—genuine cool boys, wannabes, and has-beens. It was part of the job he never minded. He turned and followed Mia into the dining room, where she was setting up some glasses.

"Hey," he said, as she was getting a bottle, "what was up with the limo and Mr. Bing this morning? I'm not used to that cloak-and-dagger stuff."

Mia glanced over her shoulder. Lionel was busy talking to a new group of guests.

"Do you understand it?" she whispered.

"I guess, but I'd like to know how it's supposed to work."

"Let's talk later," she said. "We really do need to be discreet. It is pretty straightforward, Nelson. Believe me. All right?"

He shrugged. She'd set up three wine glasses in a row and was pouring wine into the first.

"This was the way Lionel first taught me how to taste wine. He said, 'The best way to appreciate a wine is to taste it relative to another wine.'"

"Have a seat," she said. "I'll give you a crash course on white burgundies."

"What is burgundy, anyway?" he asked, glancing over his shoulder. No one was there. *Good. This was embarrassing enough with just Mia.*

"Chardonnay," she said, leaning over him and pouring.

"Why don't they call it that?"

"Because they're French, stupid," she said. "They do everything differently."

"They," she continued, picking up a second bottle and pouring the next glass, "name the wines after the towns where they're produced, not after which grape they're made of."

"So burgundy is from Burgundy?"

"Yep," she said, pouring the last glass. "That's the region." She handed him the bottle. "Check that out."

He took the bottle and glanced at the label.

"Is that Pouilly-Fuisse?" he asked.

"That's pretty close. It's pronounced 'pwee'."

"Okay. What is it?"

"Well," said Mia, "it's the name—the appellation—of four small towns in the Maconnais region of Burgundy. Fuisse is one, Solutre-Puilly is another, and I'm not sure of the other two. The name is to let you know where the wine is made."

"Okay. And it's chardonnay?"

"That's all they make there. Try it."

He sniffed it. It didn't smell like any chardonnay he'd ever tried. He tasted it.

"Wow," he said. "That's different. It tastes really—I don't know—sort of like mineral water."

"Good," she said. "The Pouilly doesn't have that big buttery feel that American chards have. Try this one."

They went through the other two wines. *She's right*, thought Nelson. *Tasting them side by side gave it all a frame of reference.* All three all had a full-bodied kind of earthy taste that Mia said was because of the Burgundy region, but the differences were easier to spot.

"Shit," she said. "I forgot to tell you to spit."

"What?"

She reached across the table for an aluminum bucket. "You're supposed to taste and then spit it out into the bucket."

"Why?"

"So you don't get too buzzed," she said. She took a sip of wine, held it a second, then leaned over the bucket and spit it out. "Like that."

"Seems like kind of a waste," he muttered.

"Yeah," she agreed. "It's hard to spit out a $200 sip of wine."

"Man," he said. "This is a whole different world."

"Yep," she said. "It is that. One year ago, I was sharing a studio with a colony of cockroaches and three mice. Now I have a place in Hyde Park."

"Nice."

She looked at him.

"He's a good boss, Nelson. Definitely a challenge sometimes, but you know the reasons for that. That's why we're here."

He glanced at her. She was staring through the doorway at Lionel. Her face was flushed. She seemed a little buzzed. *Well, so am I.* She glanced over at him and shook her head.

"I should've told you to spit sooner. Come on."

He followed her into the main room. Lionel was engaged in a lively conversation with Derrick Nickelby and Sellers. The middle-aged woman was perched on the sofa holding court with the cool boy standing next to her, surveying the room.

I wonder who that is, he thought. *I know her from somewhere.* He took a sip of wine and leaned against the archway.

It wasn't a big party. Maybe a total of ten people, including him and Mia. He wondered how much money was in the apartment right now.

Nickleby's written at least two or three bestsellers. That puts him into seven-figure territory. Though you wouldn't know it when you look at him.

He glanced over at the cool boy—Angelis? It had to be. *There's another one. Income probably in the high six figure range. And who was that woman hanging on him?*

Mia was over by the kitchen doorway, talking to an older man and a youngish woman, maybe in her late twenties or early thirties. She wore her hair in a blonde bob. Nelson hadn't seen her before. The guy wore clear-rimmed glasses and a corduroy sport coat. He had college written all over him. Nelson walked over.

"Hello," he said. The blonde woman smiled. The guy merely nodded.

"Hello again, Nelson," said Mia. "This is Nelson West, the newest member of Lionel's staff. Nelson, this is Professor Thomas Enderby, and this is Violet Birdsong."

"Hello," he said. "Unusual name, Violet."

"Well," she said, sipping her wine, "it wasn't my idea."

Nelson laughed. Mia raised her eyebrows, and the professor continued to look bored. It obviously wasn't the first time they'd heard that joke. Violet giggled.

"Violet and I went to grad school together," said Mia. "She's still at UChicago."

Nelson nodded.

"Professor Enderby is from Northwestern. He's the psychology professor who tutored Lionel."

"Okay," said Nelson, holding out his hand. "It's a pleasure."

Enderby put his empty glass into Nelson's hand.

"Excuse me?"

"Oh," said Enderby. "I thought Mia said you were a member of Lionel's staff."

"I'm an investigative consultant," said Nelson, handing back the glass, "not the butler."

"My apologies," said Enderby, taking the glass. He put it on the counter and took a long appraising look at Nelson.

That was no accident, thought Nelson. Prick. He turned back to Mia and her friend.

"So, Violet," he asked, "what are you studying?"

"I'm working on my PhD in astrophysics."

"Oh. Rocket science?"

"No," she giggled. "Not really. Mostly trying to figure out what makes the universe tick."

"She's good at it, too," said Mia. "She's researching dark matter."

"That sounds mysterious," said Nelson, leaning against the wall.

"Not really," said Violet, swirling her glass. "It's mostly a matter of analyzing the chemical make-up of stars and cosmic matter. It actually gets pretty monotonous."

"Oh," said Nelson. "That's too bad."

"What I really find fascinating," said Violet, leaning on the wall and facing Nelson, "is astrobiology."

"Astrobiology? Do you mean alien life, like E.T.?"

"Maybe. We don't know what's up there. Our work might help us find out if E.T. is real."

"Are you really going to be doing research on that?" asked Mia.

"I don't know," said Violet. "Maybe. It'd be a lot of work. I'd have to write up a grant proposal and everything. I don't know."

"Well," said Enderby, "maybe you'd better get your dissertation done first, Violet. It's been five years."

She nodded. Mia gave Enderby a look. *Not much love lost there,* thought Nelson. *I don't think Mia cares much for our Mr. Enderby. I can't blame her.*

"I'm still on track," said Violet. "I'm just having a little trouble with the summaries of the data." She looked at Nelson. "My data is a little skewed. We're not sure why." She glanced down into her wine glass.

"So," said Nelson, turning to Enderby, "what's your specialty, Doctor?"

"Oh," he said, obviously warming up to the subject—himself. "I teach at Northwestern, but I mostly focus on my research, which is exploring factors in the developmental psychology of criminals."

"Really?" asked Nelson. "We might have a few acquaintances in common."

"Oh?" asked Enderby, frowning. "Why would that be?"

"I used to work homicide for the Chicago Police Department."

"Really?" asked Enderby. "Whereabouts?"

"Oh, I was pretty much all over the place," said Nelson. "There are only about one hundred homicide detectives in the city, so they sent us everywhere and anywhere."

"Why did you leave?"

Nelson shrugged.

"A lot of reasons," said Nelson. Enderby just looked at him. *I'd better think of one,* he thought.

"Mostly," he continued, "it was because I wanted to go private. I was getting fed up with the bureaucracy in the department."

"Excuse me, but your name seems very familiar to me," said Enderby, frowning. "And you look familiar, too," he said, peering at Nelson closely.

Nelson said nothing and waited. *Maybe he wouldn't remember.*

"My God," said Enderby. "You're Nelson West. You were the detective in charge of the Hightower investigation, weren't you?"

"I was," said Nelson. Enderby nodded vigorously and turned to Violet. He was excited.

Wonderful, thought Nelson. *Just wonderful.*

"Detective West—excuse me, Mr. West," said Enderby, "—investigated the Hightower murder. Remember? The young girl in Millennium Park a couple of years ago?"

He turned back to Nelson.

"I understand it was quite a difficult case. I heard there was some significant interference with the investigation by—shall we say—interested parties?"

Nelson said nothing. *Be cool. Stay cool.*

He wasn't sure what Enderby was after—whether he was trying to show off for the girl, was just that clueless, or was drunk.

"That's ancient history, Thomas," said Mia.

"And besides," chimed in Violet, "didn't they catch the guy?'

Nelson felt her looking up at him but kept his eyes locked on Enderby.

"They arrested a suspect who was tried and convicted, but there was some lingering doubt as to whether he was really the murderer," Enderby said.

"Really?" asked Violet. "I hadn't heard that."

"Yes," said Enderby. "There were some loose ends that just didn't fit."

"Like what?"

"Like the locket that was found in another suspect's posses-sion." Enderby nodded. "The victim's locket."

Enderby turned to Nelson and smiled. Nelson kept his eyes locked on him. All he had to do was to say that he couldn't comment on police business and that investigative files were classified. But all he could see was Enderby grinning at him like the smug bastard he was.

All right, you little prick. Do you really want to do this?

He opened his mouth but felt a hand on his elbow and turned. Lionel was standing there, holding a bottle. *How long had he been watching?*

"Hello, Nelson," he said. "Let me refresh your glass." He seemed calmer, less hyper now than at the beginning of the party.

Coming down off the meds? thought Nelson. *Or is it the excitement wearing off?*

Nelson nodded and turned back to Enderby. He felt Lionel pouring some wine into his glass.

"You know, Professor," said Lionel deliberately, "You are a professor, right?"

Enderby nodded, looking slightly offended.

"Mr. West is my colleague as well as my guest tonight. As are you. Violet is good friends with Mia. I understand the two of them go pretty far back. As such, and out of respect for her, I feel comfort-able asking you to treat everyone in my home with the respect they deserve. You're at a party, sir. My party. Not an inquisition."

There was an unusual firmness in Lionel's voice. Nelson glanced over at him. He was staring at Enderby, who had his lips pressed firmly together.

"So," continued Lionel, "I expect everyone here to act in a civilized manner. No more grillings, no interrogations, and definitely no rubber hoses."

Violet laughed. Mia smiled.

"Sorry," said Enderby to Lionel. He turned to Nelson.

"I'm sorry, Nelson. I didn't mean to offend you."

Nelson nodded. Violet smiled at him, took a sip from her glass, and left. Enderby followed her.

"Thanks, boss," said Nelson. "Your guest was about to get treated a little rudely himself."

"I am sick and tired of hearing about that case," said Lionel. He took a sip from his glass. "You know," he said. "When we get done with the current project, we'll have to go back and get it fixed."

Mia stepped in closer.

"Fixed?" asked Nelson. Lionel nodded.

"You're not happy with the way it turned out. That's obvious, Nelson. No one else seems happy with it, either. So, let's fix it."

Nelson shook his head.

"No, Lionel. You don't understand."

"What don't I understand?"

"There are issues involved," said Nelson. He glanced around. People were keeping their distance, but he still dropped his voice to a whisper. "City Hall, the police department, and other parties are involved, Lionel. Parties that the city of Chicago couldn't move."

"Well," said Lionel, "we'll see what we can do." He held his glass up to the light. "My God," he said, "look at that color. Liquid gold." He took a sip. "Beautiful. Try yours, Nelson."

Nelson raised his glass and sipped. He couldn't taste anything but nodded anyway.

"Great, Lionel." He glanced over at Mia. "Crisp. Almost like licking a pebble."

"Excellent," said Lionel, winking at Mia. "Very well done, Nelson. Excuse me." He trotted over to talk to Angelis, who looked like he was getting ready to leave.

"Jesus," said Nelson. "Who does he think he is?"

Mia laughed, sort of a snort. Nelson glanced over at her.

"He thinks he's rich and that he can do anything," she said. "And you know what?" she said, sipping her wine. "Most of the time, he's right."

"Excuse me."

Nelson turned. Derrick Nickleby was standing at his elbow, smiling.

"Hello," said Nelson.

"Hello. I am Derrick Nickleby. I write mystery novels."

"Hi, Derrick," said Mia. "This is Nelson West, Lionel's new associate."

"Hello, my dear. How are you?" He stood on his tiptoes and planted a kiss on Mia's cheek.

"I am glad to meet you, Mr. West."

"Me too," said Nelson, leaning over to shake his hand. "I've heard of you. I love your books." *Maybe I'll read one someday*, he thought.

"Excuse me," said Mia. She walked to Violet and Enderby, who had just opened another bottle of wine.

"I think it's a very good thing that Lionel hired someone like you," said Nickleby.

"Why is that?" asked Nelson. "I'm just another detective. A dick. That's what you call us in those mystery novels, right?"

"Oh, not me," said Nickleby, chuckling. "No." He cleared his throat. "No, what I meant was that Lionel could use a steady hand nearby, if you know what I mean."

Nelson raised an eyebrow. *Remember to keep it under your hat.*

"Oh, I see you don't know what I mean. Well, of course, when you consider everything Lionel has gone through, it's remarkable he's as well-adjusted as he is. But he still occasionally gets a little, well, shall we say overagitated?"

"What do you mean?"

"You are aware of the incident, aren't you? The kidnapping."

Nelson nodded.

"I've known Lionel for years," said Nickleby. "We went to school together. I knew him before it happened. It almost killed him. He never quite got over it. Not completely. Things are better now, but he went through some rough patches for a while."

"Rough patches?"

"Yes," said Nickleby, "he had trouble socially and dealing with anger management issues. Depression. There were days when the slightest thing would set him off."

Nelson nodded, watching Lionel talking and laughing with Violet. He took a sip of his wine.

"Some sort of PTSD," said Nickleby. "That's what the doctors called it. You know, being traumatized from the kidnapping and his mother's death. And from who knows what else he saw."

Nelson nodded. *That pretty much jibes with what Mr. Bing said.*

"Is he okay now?"

"Most of the time. He will get a little erratic on occasion. He still has mood swings. Sometimes he gets panic attacks, but his medications usually control that. He hasn't killed anyone for a few years now."

Nelson stared at the little man, who burst into laughter.

"You should see your face, Mr. West."

Yeah, thought Nelson. *Ha fucking ha. Jesus.*

He took a deep breath as Lionel walked up to them with bottle in hand.

"What have you been telling him, Derrick?" asked Lionel, grinning from ear to ear. "All the deep, dark family secrets?"

"You know it," said Derrick.

Lionel chuckled as he filled his friend's glass and then offered the wine to Nelson, glancing up at him as he poured, his dark eyes dancing.

Chapter 7

NELSON STEPPED OUTSIDE. IT was a pretty nice day. He took a deep breath and let it out. By all rights, he should be hung over—and badly—but he felt pretty good. *I guess that's what happens when you drink the good stuff.* He looked around. No sign of them yet. Lionel had called at 6:30, an absolutely ungodly hour, to say he'd be coming by to pick him up about eight.

"So, Nelson," said Lionel as soon as Nelson had picked up the phone. "Is it time to exact payment?"

That's an odd thing to say, he thought. Nelson rubbed his eyes and stifled a yawn.

"Yeah," he said. "Sure."

"I think we need to go to see Marilyn Baker this morning," said Lionel. "We should go through Baker's papers with a fine-toothed comb to see if we can figure out where he is."

"Or where the money is," he added.

I doubt if that's going to happen, thought Nelson, but didn't say it. In his experience, if they hadn't seen the money by now, they were not going to. It was buried—and buried deep.

"Okay," he said. "Sounds good."

"I think we should bring Mia," said Lionel.

Nelson thought a minute. *That probably wasn't a bad idea.* Ordinarily, he didn't like working with a team—too many cooks—but she might be helpful in handling Lionel if things went sour. And besides, she was smart.

"I guess," he said. "Sure."

"She is a first-class forensics specialist," said Lionel.

He's talkative today, thought Nelson, *just like last night.*

"Fiber and chemical analysis, DNA, spectrographic readings, and forensic engineering," continued Lionel. "She can handle it all. We'll farm out other forensics as we need them. You know, documents, accounting, that sort of thing."

"What about pathology?"

"Well," said Lionel, "we haven't run across any dead bodies yet."

You never know, thought Nelson. *With this much money floating around, I wouldn't be surprised if somebody winds up dead.*

"And the truth is," said Lionel, "we've been able to figure out as much as we need to on our own. Look how far we got with Baker's financials yesterday. I have a feeling we won't need specialists that often. You know, it's not as if we're preparing a case for prosecution. We're here to solve problems."

He sounds like he's trying to convince himself, thought Nelson.

"Yeah," said Nelson. "Bring Mia. She might see something we don't."

After Lionel hung up, Nelson got up, showered, dressed, and ate some old yogurt from the back of the fridge. *It seemed fine, but who knows?* he thought. Yogurt starts out spoiled.

* * *

Nelson didn't have long to wait. The car pulled up after about five minutes. He got in the back, plopping down next to Mia. She was wearing big, white plastic-rimmed sunglasses, a denim jacket over a t-shirt, and jeans. Lionel was dressed in a blue button-down shirt and black jeans. He was staring out the car window. *Seems to be his habit*, thought Nelson.

"Hello, Mia."

"Hello, Nelson. How are you?"

"I'm good. Got home and went straight to bed. Slept like a baby."

"Burgundy will do that for you," she said.

"How about you?" he asked.

"I'm good," she said. "Lionel and I were up early. We went over some details of the case this morning."

She glanced over at Lionel, but he was staring out the window, wound in his thoughts. Mia glanced back at Nelson and raised her eyebrows. Nelson started to say something but stopped. *Why bother the guy? Let him think.*

"I hope Thomas didn't offend you last night," said Mia. "He's basically clueless in social situations. And I should apologize for John Sellers, too. He gets a little pushy sometimes."

"Well," said Nelson, "the Hightower case pushes people's buttons."

"Yes, it does," said Mia.

"John is a good journalist," said Lionel curtly. Nelson glanced over. His boss was still looking out the window. His good mood from earlier seemed to have evaporated. He turned toward Nelson suddenly.

"You need to be aggressive to dig up the truth. Sometimes it's necessary to hurt people." His voice was stern, even a little harsh.

"Sellers wasn't looking for a story last night," said Nelson. "He was going after me."

"Don't take it personally," said Lionel. "It's not about you. That case still gets under his skin. He's still angry and frustrated. It's too bad you got in the middle of it, Nelson, but you're not the reason he's angry. He doesn't blame you."

Are we talking about the same guy? thought Nelson. *Sellers was pushing me a little, but I didn't think he was angry. Maybe a little aggressive.*

"I'm sure he didn't mean anything," said Mia.

"Yeah," said Lionel, "Other people, like Reynolds, might want to rub your nose in the case results. Now *he* is an asshole. But John's a good guy."

Mia smiled. Nelson frowned to himself and sighed. *That case was never going to go away, and I'll always be the goat.* He wished it would all disappear.

Lionel leaned over Mia.

"What I said last night stands, Nelson. You and I are going to fix that case." He held up his hand as Nelson started to protest. "I know it's going to be difficult, and I know who we'll be dealing with. But that case is a glaring example of everything that is wrong with us today. Our courts were bought. The city was bought. The police department—with one huge exception—was bought."

Lionel leaned back in his seat.

"I told you yesterday why I got into this, Nelson. To fix things. This work we're doing now for my dad and his friends is…" he shrugged. "It's good practice, but the Hightower case is an opportunity to fix things."

"Like what? What do you think reopening that case will accomplish?"

"Justice," said Lionel, staring straight at Nelson. "Punishing the guilty. Exacting payment." His face had become flushed, and his eyes were darting. He seemed upset.

"And how will you accomplish that," asked Nelson, "when nobody else could?"

Lionel smiled.

"We will fight fire with fire, my friend," he said, reaching over and patting Nelson on the knee. Nelson looked away.

Goddam it. Goddam it to hell. The last thing Nelson needed was for anyone—especially a rookie—to go sticking his nose into that case. He knew why Lionel was doing it, and he appreciated it, but he didn't want to go back there to revisit the worst time of his life, or back to that day he realized he couldn't be a cop anymore. He stared down at his hands. Mia cleared her throat.

"So," she said. "What's the strategy for when we go to the Baker house?"

Nelson took a deep breath.

"Well, she told us yesterday we could go through Bradley's papers. Maybe we'll get a clue to as to where he went, and maybe, if we're lucky—really lucky—get an idea of where the money is."

"What if she changes her mind?" asked Mia.

Nelson shrugged and glanced over to Lionel. He knew what he'd do, but Lionel was the lead on this one. His boss had returned to staring out the window.

"I don't think she will," said Nelson. "Lionel got her going yesterday. He insinuated Baker had a mistress and that got Mrs. Baker pretty pissed off. She's out for blood now."

Mia raised her eyebrows.

"Well," she said. "That's all we need. An angry cougar on the loose."

They pulled up to the Baker house and got out. Lionel led the way to the door and knocked. Nelson glanced around. Two cars were in the driveway—her Mercedes and a red Ford Focus. Everything else seemed the same—not a blade of grass out of place. *Good. Nobody had made any sudden moves.*

Lionel knocked again. The door opened suddenly. A youngish man stood in the doorway, glaring at them. He was short, maybe five six or so, but he was built like a fireplug. The kid was dressed in a polo shirt, some kind of nylon workout pants, and sneakers— expensive ones. *Those are the new Jordans,* thought Nelson, recognizing them right away. *I guess I haven't lost my street smarts—not yet.* The kid's brown hair was cut short, and he'd shaved that morning— though he probably hadn't needed to.

This has got to be Mrs. Baker's trainer friend. Lance Malkowitz.

"What do you want?" asked the kid, his voice surly. He seemed pretty wound up. Nelson edged in front of Mia and stood next to Lionel.

"We're here to see Mrs. Baker," said Lionel. "She's expecting us."

"What about?" asked the guy.

"I don't know if that's any of your business, Lance," said Nelson. He smiled. The kid looked at him, scowled, and stepped out onto the porch.

"How do you know my name, asshole?"

"We know all about you, Lance," replied Nelson. "We know you work for the Cougars, and we know all about the special training sessions you have going on with Mrs. Baker. We know all about your afternoon field trips to the local hotels."

Malkowitz balled his hands into fists, bent his knees slightly, and leaned forward. He looked muscular, like your garden variety gym rat, but he didn't seem dangerous. *No real meanness in him,* thought Nelson. *All bluster. He's no street fighter.*

"We do need to see Mrs. Baker," said Lionel. "Would you mind getting her, please?"

Malkowitz turned and took a step toward Lionel, who didn't move an inch.

"Why don't you get the fuck out of here?"

"I'm sorry," said Lionel, his tone even. "We have an appointment."

Malkowitz put his face right next to Lionel's.

"Fuck you," he whispered and grabbed Lionel's wrist.

Nelson took a quick step forward, but Lionel grabbed Malkowitz's wrist with his free hand before he could get there. He pulled away the kid's hand, twisted, and suddenly Lance was on his knees, gasping in pain. He struggled to get up, but went back down yelping as Lionel turned his wrist slightly.

"You need to relax, Lance," whispered Lionel through his teeth. "The more you struggle, the more pain you'll experience."

"Let him go."

Nelson looked up. Marilyn Baker was standing in the doorway. Lionel—to his credit—hung on.

"I said let him go," she repeated.

"You can let him go, Lionel," said Nelson, stepping up to them. "I've got him."

Lionel glanced at Nelson. His jaw was set, and his dark eyes danced with anger. He turned his wrist slightly and the kid yelped again.

He looks ready to blow, thought Nelson.

He grabbed Lionel's elbow.

His boss looked at him, took a deep breath, let the kid go, and stepped back. Nelson immediately moved between them.

"You motherfucker," muttered the kid, massaging his hand. He was still on the ground.

"You're lucky he didn't break it," said Nelson. "I would've."

"Hello, Mrs. Baker," said Lionel, trying to smile. Nelson noticed his hands were shaking.

"We met your friend," said Mia. Mrs. Baker looked at her and frowned.

"We're back," continued Lionel, "—as promised. Do you think we could examine your husband's papers now?"

"Who's she?" asked Marilyn, nodding towards Mia.

Lionel took a deep breath and let it out slowly.

"Miss Wentworth is one of my associates," said Lionel, starting to regain his composure. "Mia, this is Marilyn Baker. Mrs. Baker, this is Mia Wentworth."

Marilyn looked her up and down and raised her eyebrows.

"Associate," she said, raising her eyebrows. "All right."

To her credit, Mia didn't bat an eyelash.

Lionel frowned. *Easy, boss*, thought Nelson. *Take it easy.*

"Ms. Wentworth has doctorates in chemistry and physics," said Lionel, an edge still in his voice, "as well as experience in forensic accounting. That's why she's here."

"Really?" asked Mrs. Baker.

"Really," answered Mia.

"How impressive."

"So," asked Lionel, "can we take a look at your husband's papers?"

Mrs. Baker glanced at Lance, Nelson, back at Lionel, and finally nodded.

"Yeah," she said. "I looked through his stuff last night. I think I have an idea of where he could be." She turned to go into the house and motioned for Lionel to follow.

"Excellent," said Lionel, following her. Lance, still sitting on the ground and holding his wrist, watched Lionel go in.

"Well, now, Lance," asked Nelson, looking down at him. "Was your little temper tantrum really worth it?"

The kid started to stand up.

"Easy. Don't do anything stupid."

He stood up slowly and glared at the two of them.

"Hey," said Mia. Lance looked at her. "I'm just curious. Why," she continued, "would you want to do a stupid thing like that?"

"Fuck you," he muttered.

"Careful," said Nelson. "That's no way to talk to a lady. You don't want to end up on the ground again."

Malkowitz glared at him, glanced at Mia, and stalked away, rubbing his wrist. He got into the Focus and took off, squealing the tires.

Nelson motioned to Mia, and they stepped inside. Voices were coming from the back of the house, and they followed them into a study with a lot of windows looking out on a well-manicured backyard. Lionel was seated at the desk, going through some papers. Mrs. Baker stood behind the chair, looking over his shoulder.

"There," she said, pointing at a paper. "I've never seen that one before."

"El Banco Centro de Guadalajara," mused Lionel.

"We've never used any foreign banks," she said. "And that's a statement for over $100,000. That's all it says."

"Good," said Lionel, looking at the statement. "This is good."

She glanced over at Mia and Lionel.

"Where's Lance?" she asked.

"He left," said Mia. "He said to say goodbye."

Mrs. Baker turned to Lionel.

"I'm sorry about that," she said. "Lance is a little impetuous. He's young and not very bright."

Mia made a sound halfway between a snort and a cough.

"Excuse me?" asked Mrs. Baker. "Did you say something?"

"I was just agreeing with you," said Mia.

Mrs. Baker stared at her. Nelson looked down at his shoes, trying to hide a smile.

"He's not the best at self-defense either," said Mia. "He might want to work on that."

"Who the hell do you think you are?" asked Mrs. Baker.

"Mrs. Baker," said Lionel, "do you have your credit card receipts?"

"I think so. Why?"

"Well, obviously, we'd like to know if your husband bought any airline tickets, hotel reservations, or anything else that might indicate he had travel plans."

"I doubt if he'd be stupid enough to put any of that on our credit card," said Mrs. Baker, "but let me go and print the last couple months of charges on our Visa." She turned and left.

"Really?" asked Nelson, looking at Mia. "Were you *trying* to piss her off?"

Mia shrugged.

"Of course not," she said. "I was agreeing with her."

"Please, Mia," said Lionel. "This is serious."

"Sorry."

"Do you notice anything, Nelson?" asked Lionel. "About Mr. Baker's den?"

Nelson glanced at him, looked around the room, and shook his head.

"No pictures of San Pablo," said Lionel. "That little Mexican town. Bradley Baker's pet project."

Nelson nodded. *Good call, kid. We'll make a detective out of you yet.*

"Yeah," said Nelson. "It's a little strange he'd keep them exclusively at the office."

Nelson leaned over the desk and looked at the deposit slip. El Banco Centro del Guadalajara. *Just a straight deposit.* He put his finger on the numbers.

"Dollars, not pesos, right?"

"Yes," said Lionel. "Into this account. No name, but we do have the number. That will help when we make inquiries."

He glanced around the room.

"Do you see a map or an atlas?"

Mia took out her smartphone. "What do you want?" she asked.

"Find San Pablo, Mexico. There's probably more than one. Get the closest one to Guadalajara you can find."

Nelson looked down at Lionel and nodded. *That might be it,* he thought. *Baker might have chosen this Mexican village as his little getaway. Five million would go a long way down there.*

"Here it is," said Mia, coming over and sitting on the desk. She showed them her smartphone screen.

"Where is it?" asked Nelson. He could see Guadalajara but not much else.

"Here," she said, pointing at a little dot. "About twenty-five miles outside the city."

"Good," murmured Lionel. "Excellent. Mia," he added, "will you please take a photo of this bank statement and then email it to me?"

"Sure," she said, and did so. They all turned as Mrs. Baker came into the room.

"Did you find my money yet?" she asked.

Nelson smiled and shook his head. She smiled back.

"Sorry," he said. "Not quite yet."

"Well, here are the credit card statements," she said, handing them to him. "I didn't see anything unusual on them except for this." She pointed to an entry half-down. "Harper CE," she said. "What is that?"

Lionel shook his head. "We'll have to check it out."

"Mrs. Baker," said Nelson, pointing at a framed picture of a gray-haired man on the desk. "Is that your husband?"

She nodded—her lips tightly pressed together.

"Could we have that picture?"

"Sure," she said, grabbing it and handing it to him. "Take it. I don't want to see it anymore."

"Thanks."

"Well," said Lionel, glancing over at Nelson. "I think we've found everything we need here."

He stood and shook her hand. "Thank you so much, Mrs. Baker. We'll let you know when we find anything."

"Just make sure you get all my money from that two-timing bastard," she said. "I deserve it."

We'll get you what you deserve, thought Nelson as they made their way out. "Indeed, we will," he whispered.

Chapter 8

St. Alphonso's Church was in the Englewood neighborhood, forty minutes from Baker's house. It was an older church that had watched the neighborhood go from bad to worse. This was a rough area of town. When he was in homicide, they typically handled three or more murders a week down here. Mostly gang stuff. It seemed odd to Nelson that Baker would come all the way down here—to this neighborhood—to go to church. *Unless he had grown up around here.*

The building itself seemed to be in good shape. It was old and big, but not ostentatious, constructed mostly out of red brick and stone. Gargoyles and other stone creatures lurked near the roof that was topped with a copper-plated steeple. The grounds were a little ratty from wear and tear of the neighborhood. Lots of trash and litter. The grass needed cutting, but it was nothing that couldn't be fixed. *With a little work*, thought Nelson, *this could be a nice parish.*

Lincoln pulled up in front of the rectory.

"Should we go into the church?" asked Lionel. "I mean it's working hours, right? He should be in there."

"Depends," said Nelson. "At St. Boniface, Father John used to sneak into the rectory at 1 o'clock every afternoon for his nap. And a drink," he added.

"Did you go to Catholic school?" asked Mia.

"Yeah. Until eighth grade. Then my parents sent me over to public school."

"Why?" asked Lionel.

"It was too expensive," said Nelson. "And I had three sisters. My mom had to get them through St. Boniface, too. She wanted to make sure we all had a Catholic education early on." He shrugged. "I didn't mind. I liked public school better, anyway."

"Not as strict?" asked Mia.

"Yeah. No nuns. And the girls weren't as stuck-up."

"Really," said Mia. "You know, I went to Catholic school."

"That figures," said Nelson.

Lionel cleared his throat. "Lincoln," he said, "let's try the church first."

Lincoln nodded and backed up to the church doors. They got out of the car and stood a moment, staring up at the facade, and then Lionel went in. Mia followed, and Nelson—after a moment—walked through the massive wooden doors. Mia crossed herself at the holy water font and then walked into the church proper.

St. Alphonso was more spacious than it had looked from the outside. A vaulted ceiling arched over the beautiful stained-glass windows. Nelson took a deep breath; the room had that smell all churches had, a combination of old paper and incense. It brought back memories. It had been a long time. There'd been his dad's funeral. Ten years ago, now. Then there was the service for Officer Kovack three years ago. Shot and killed in the line of duty. Nelson walked slowly up the aisle between the pews. Most of them had spots where the stain had worn down. Graffiti was scribbled on some of them.

"Hello." The voice boomed in the cavernous space.

Nelson glanced toward the altar. A priest was straightening up, looking at Lionel. It looked as if he'd been arranging some flowers next to the lectern.

"Hello," answered Lionel.

"Greetings," said the priest. "May I help you?"

"Yes," said Lionel, his voice hushed. He was almost whispering now. "We're looking for Father Mike."

"He'll be back in about half an hour," said the priest, stepping down from the altar. "Could I help you?"

He was probably in his mid-forties, a little overweight and starting to lose his hair. He had a quick smile, though, and seemed friendly enough. *Though you'd expect that*, thought Nelson.

"I'm Lionel Bing, and these are my associates, Nelson West and Mia Wentworth."

"Hello. I'm Father Andrew," he said, offering his hand. Lionel shook it. Nelson followed suit.

We're trying to track down one of your parishioners," said Lionel. "A Bradley Baker."

"Mr. Baker? Why? What's happened?" asked Father Andrew. "Is something wrong?"

"No, we just need to get in touch with him to help us with a problem at his work," said Nelson. "When was the last time you saw him?"

"Oh, dear," said the priest. "Let me think." He took a breath and furrowed his brow. "I believe," he said after a moment, "that Bradley was at Mass last Sunday, but I'm not sure."

"Which Mass does he usually go to?" asked Mia.

"He's usually here early for the 8 o'clock. That's my Mass. He's here almost every Sunday."

"But you're not sure about last Sunday?" asked Nelson.

"Not absolutely. You see, you get used to seeing the same faces every week—usually sitting in the same places, so I *think* I remember him being here last week, but it could be just remembering him from the time before."

"Is Father Mike usually here for the early service?" asked Mia.

"No," said Father Andrew. "One of us is usually out doing sacraments or visiting the sick—"

"Or fund-raising?" said Lionel.

"Oh, no," said Father Andrew, chuckling. "That's typically up to the archdiocese or the parish fund-raising committees. We have our church fair and bake sales, but we haven't gotten to the point where we're sending the nuns and priests out to beg funds." He laughed. "I don't think we'd be very good at it."

Lionel smiled.

"What," he asked, "do you know about the Santa Barbara Church in San Pablo?"

"The Mexican parish? Yes, I know that Bradley and Father Mike were in communication with the priest down there. Oh, what was his name again?"

"Father Ignacio?" prompted Lionel.

"Yes, that's it. How did you know that?"

"As I said, we're trying to track down Mr. Baker. Father Ignacio's name came up during the course of the investigation."

Father Andrew raised an eyebrow.

"Investigation? Is Bradley in trouble?"

"His company needs to get in touch with him about an internal matter. They haven't heard from him in a while," said Lionel. He turned and glanced back at Nelson, who nodded.

You're doing fine, thought Nelson. *Just fine.*

"That's unusual," said the priest. "Hmm. Father Mike would probably know more about it. I know that they were working with Father Ignacio to help those poor people in San Pablo."

"We heard about the accident," said Nelson.

"What a terrible thing," said Father Andrew, shaking his head. "All those poor souls—lost. The families. All the fathers and husbands. Young boys, too. The town was decimated."

"What happened exactly?" asked Nelson.

"Let's sit down," said Father Andrew. He sat down on the front pew and crossed his legs. Lionel sat down next to him. Mia and Nelson went to the pew behind.

"From what I know about it, and that's not much, there was a massive explosion caused by some sort of defect in the equipment. Don't ask me what kind of equipment. I'm no good at that sort of thing. Upwards of eighty miners died. And children, too. Some of them were still in elementary school."

"What were kids doing down there?" asked Mia.

"Working," said the priest. "I understand that nearly the entire town worked there doing one thing or another, and they do start them young. They let the children do odd jobs outside the mine, but the miners would sometimes use them to get into spaces they couldn't fit into." He paused and frowned. "It's such a shame."

"Yes, it is," said Mia, her tone clipped.

"What exactly were Mr. Baker and Father Mike doing about it?" asked Lionel. Nelson felt himself frowning. He might have approached that question a little differently. *Ask him how Baker got involved. Who knew about it first? Pin down the first contact and then ask about the money.*

"Excuse me," said Nelson, leaning forward and catching Lionel's eye. "How did Mr. Baker find out about San Pablo? Did Father Mike tell him?"

Lionel gave him a look. Nelson ignored him.

"Let me think," said the priest. "I'm fairly sure it was Bradley who brought the situation to Father Mike's attention." He paused, his lips pursed. Thinking. "Yes, I'm sure of it. I remember Father Mike saying how inspired he was by Bradley's concern. He said that it's not often you see that kind of passion."

"I actually said it's not often you see that kind of *com*passion," said a voice behind them.

They all turned. A young man stood in the nave. He was dressed in jeans and a red hoodie, and his dark hair reached down to his collar.

"Father Mike," said the older priest. "Hello."

He doesn't look very priest-like, thought Nelson. *This guy thinks he's still in the seventies.*

"I'm glad you're here," said Father Andrew, standing. He introduced everyone and invited Father Mike to sit. He plopped down next to Lionel and folded his hands in his lap.

"So," he asked, "what's going on?"

"We're trying to track down one of your parishioners," said Lionel. "Bradley Baker. He seems to have gone missing."

"Missing?" asked Father Mike. "That's hard to believe. Bradley is so—stable." He looked at Lionel. "Do you suspect foul play?"

"No," said Lionel, cocking his head as he gazed at the priest. "Why do you ask?"

"I don't know," said the priest. "Going missing is unusual, isn't it? Especially for a guy like Bradley."

Nelson watched him closely. *If he knew something, he was hiding it well.*

"Are you the police?" continued Father Mike. "I beg your pardon, but you don't seem very—well—police-like."

Lionel leaned forward.

"We're private investigators," said Nelson quickly, before Lionel had a chance to talk. *No need to give anything away. This priest was tight with Baker; odds are he knows something.*

"Who hired you?"

Nelson stood up.

"You know, Father," he said. "It might be better if we go somewhere private to talk. Maybe your rooms?"

Father Mike glanced at the other priest, who shrugged.

"Go right ahead," he said.

"Okay," said Father Mike. "Right this way."

They followed him out the side door and into the rectory, a two-story brick house. The living room seemed very cozy. A couple of big armchairs sat in front of a large fireplace. Father Mike led them into the adjoining dining room and motioned them to sit.

"So, can I get you anything? Water? Coffee?"

"No, thanks," said Lionel. Nelson shook his head. Mia smiled and said no.

The priest sat down.

"So," he asked, looking around the table, "what exactly is going on here?"

"What do you mean, going on?" asked Nelson. "We told you why we're here."

"You have to admit it's odd when a trio of private investigators come looking for a missing man at his place of worship. Especially a man like Mr. Baker."

"What sort of man is he?" asked Lionel.

"The salt of the earth," said the priest. "He's generous, thoughtful, and very religious. We've had many talks about the scriptures, God, and the nature of compassion. His faith is unshakable."

"It sounds as if you two are pretty close," said Nelson.

"He's a devoted parishioner," said the priest, "although recently he's gotten very interested in a more purist interpretations of the Bible, which I personally consider a bit extreme. He's also very interested in Mexican Catholicism, especially Día de Los Muertos."

"What's that?" asked Nelson.

"Well, it's a holiday, kind of like our Halloween and All Saints' Day, but it's really sort of a mash-up between the two cultures," said Father Mike. "When the Spanish missionaries originally came into Mexico, they tried to convert the natives but were only semi-successful. The original beliefs about death and the underworld hung on even after the missionaries taught the indigenous people their scriptures. Día de Los Muertos is, according to the native beliefs, a time when dead souls come back to visit their families. Mexicans still build ofrendas—shrines—to them at the graves of their loved ones and wait for them to return."

"Okay," said Nelson.

"Bradley was fascinated with the holiday and its history," said Father Mike, "even though it contradicts the teachings of the church." He smiled. "People don't come back from heaven—or hell—too often around here."

"Were you okay with his interest in that?" asked Mia.

"Sure. It's a free country."

Father Mike leaned back and glanced at each of them in turn.

"Should I be worried about Bradley?" he asked.

"We don't know," said Lionel. "Maybe."

Good answer, thought Nelson. *Now he's worried about his buddy.*

"Can you tell us a little bit more about Father Ignacio and San Pablo?" asked Lionel. "We think that might help us figure this out. You know Mr. Baker has pictures of that town all over his office."

"Well, Bradley's been going down there for some time now. He ran across the village during a business trip to Guadalajara and just fell in love with the place. He told me it's just beautiful—heaven on Earth. I know whenever he goes there, he touches base with Father Ignacio, whom he admires quite a bit. Bradley told me the church has had all sorts of challenges down there."

"Like what?" asked Mia.

"Well, poverty is the big one. Most of the parishioners are dirt poor," Father Mike said as he furrowed his brow. "Bradley also mentioned something about Father Ignacio having to make deals with the devil." He shrugged. "I'm not sure what he meant by that. He didn't want to elaborate."

Nelson nodded. *Maybe Father Ignacio has a little side hustle.*

"Did he mention San Pablo lately?" asked Lionel.

"Well, Bradley came to me a while ago and told me about the mine accident at San Pablo. He said Father Ignacio needed help raising funds to help the families. Mostly unsuccessfully. He asked if we could chip in. Apparently, the mine owners weren't doing anything to help. They weren't even bringing the bodies out. Family members and volunteers had to go in there to get their loved ones out. And then the owners disappeared."

"What did Mr. Baker want to do?" asked Nelson.

"Bradley wanted to help them and thought we could send some money and supplies. Food. He was very adamant about it."

"Are there any Mexican parishioners in your church?" asked Lionel.

Father Mike nodded.

"Some," he said, "but they mostly come from the Mexico City area. They didn't know anything about the accident until Mr. Baker told them, but they all chipped in for the fund."

"The fund?" asked Lionel.

"A recovery fund we started to help out the town. Once they heard about it, people started giving on their own, and then we talked Mr. Baker into managing it."

"How much was in it?" asked Nelson.

"Maybe two or three thousand dollars." Father Mike shrugged. "People here don't have a whole lot, but they do what they can."

Lionel nodded and glanced at Nelson, who shook his head.

No, thought Nelson. *A man like Baker wouldn't bother stealing a couple grand—it wouldn't be worth it. That was small potatoes for a guy like him.*

"Where's the money now?" asked Lionel.

"Wherever Bradley put it," Father Mike said, smiling. "Listen," he said, leaning forward, "I know what you're thinking, that Bradley did something with the restoration fund, but the whole idea is absurd. He's not that sort of man, and besides, that sort of money would only be pocket change for a man like him."

"Really?" asked Nelson.

The priest nodded. "Mr. Baker makes a substantial annual donation to the church—a gift that's a lot more than the amount we're discussing here. He didn't need that money."

"Do you have any idea where he might be?" asked Lionel. "Could he be in San Pablo?"

"I don't know," said the priest. "I guess. He didn't mention going there lately—not since the accident. I know most of his trips down there were for business."

"How often did he go?" asked Mia.

The priest shrugged. "Maybe every couple of months. Every six weeks. He'd be gone a few days, maybe a week or so."

"Really?" asked Nelson, leaning forward. "Did he talk about what he was doing down there?"

"I believe he said the bank had some interests in the Guadalajara and Oaxaca areas. Real estate holdings."

Nelson glanced over at Lionel, who nodded. *Funny how Reynolds Hanson never mentioned that.*

"Father," asked Mia, "did Mr. Baker ever go to confession?"

Father Mike smiled. "Yes, he did. At least once a week."

Mia smiled back.

"You know I can't divulge anything said between us during confession, Ms. Wentworth."

"Of course not," said Mia.

"I think that's all we have for now, Father," said Lionel, standing. "Unless Mr. West has anything else."

Nelson started to shake his head when Mia broke in.

"Father," she asked, "I have a quick question. Did Bradley ever use the phone here? Would you know if he ever made an international call from here?"

Father Mike frowned and took a breath. Thinking.

Good question. Is he hiding something? thought Nelson. *Covering for his buddy? Or is he in touch with Father Ignacio himself?*

"I don't think so," said Father Mike. "I don't know for sure, though. We don't handle the utility bills here. That goes through the diocese. Sorry."

Well, thought Nelson, *that should be easy enough to check out. It would be useful to have the dates he talked to Father Ignacio.*

They thanked the priest and left. Lincoln was standing outside the car when they got out, eyeing a group of teenagers across the street.

"Those kids are up to no damned good," he whispered to Nelson as they got into the car.

Nelson nodded—although they didn't look like troublemakers to him. *They're probably just neighborhood kids checking things out.* He glanced at Lincoln, who was still frowning at them from the driver's seat. *He's as bad as a cop.*

"Well," said Lionel, breaking into Nelson's train of thought. "What do you think?"

He glanced across Mia at Lionel and felt himself frowning.

"Well," he said, "I can't say for sure, but I'd be surprised if Father Mike was involved."

Mia nodded. Lionel nodded slowly.

"Maybe," Lionel said, "but he did know quite a bit about Con Union's dealings down there."

"Well, he and Baker seem to be pretty close," said Nelson. "It might have come up in conversation."

"I don't know," said Lionel. "I think that interview raised a lot more questions that it answered."

"Right," said Mia. "Like Con Union having holdings in that area." She turned to Lionel. "Did Hanson ever say anything to you about that?"

Lionel shook his head.

"No, but that fact wasn't really pertinent to our line of questioning."

Nelson nodded. That was true. They never really did get into the Mexican angle with Reynolds Hanson.

"Maybe it's time we pay Mr. Hanson another visit," said Lionel.

"Maybe not quite yet," said Nelson. "I think we need to do some homework first."

Chapter 9

MIA LEANED BACK IN HER CHAIR, stretched her arms over her head, and yawned. Nelson glanced over at her and let his eyes linger a moment before stretching himself. It was late, past 10 o'clock. They had been going over Con Union's financial statements and tax forms from the last ten years for the past three hours. After Lionel had gotten access to them from one of Hanson's assistants, he told Nelson and Mia to look for any dealings between Banco Centro and Con Union or any connections to the San Pablo area. Nelson privately thought it was a wild goose chase. He would be surprised—really surprised—if Baker left anything exposed. It would have been very easy for him to cover his tracks. So far, the only thing that turned up had been the deposit to Banco Centro.

And that one deposit sticks out like a sore thumb.

Nelson had to admit he was getting a little frustrated about the way the investigation was going. It was odd. Everything fit except the motive. All the evidence pointed to Baker as the sole embezzler, but why did he do it? He was sending money to Guadalajara—probably spreading deposits around in different institutions—most likely after laundering it, maybe through Father Mike and the church, but parts of it didn't make sense. The Mexican connection, the priest, and that $100,000 deposit didn't fit.

Why there—why to Guadalajara? Why not to an offshore account where it would be untraceable? And what was the church connection? He wouldn't be surprised if the young priest had something to do with laundering or funneling the cash—possibly without knowing it. Maybe the Mexican priest was in on it, too.

It all goes back to motive. Why would a guy like Baker take all that money? No evidence of bad habits, blackmail, or erratic behavior, which you usually found in cases like this. No, Baker wasn't that sort of guy. So why would he funnel five million dollars—maybe through his church, which he loved—and place it, at least part of it, out in the open? Criminals sometimes—a lot of times—did stupid stuff, but Baker wasn't stupid. Nelson couldn't shake the feeling that Baker *wanted* them to find the money. But that made no sense either.

"Anything?" asked Mia.

Nelson shook his head.

"No. And I can't say I'm surprised. Baker would know how to cover his tracks."

Mia leaned back in her chair.

"What about Guadalajara?" she asked. He shook his head.

"Nothing new. I didn't see any direct links between them and Hindman or that other shell, Herman and Lund. Baker must have gotten the loan money and filtered it through the two shells before they defaulted—"

"And only $100,000 of it showed up," added Mia. "Where's the other $4.9 million?'

"And why deposit that money—in his own name—to an account he didn't even bother hiding?"

"Like he wanted it found," said Mia, half to herself.

Nelson nodded. "I was thinking the same thing. But why would he want to implicate himself? I think he did this on purpose. He *wanted* us to make the Mexican connection."

But why? thought Nelson. *Unless,* he mused, *unless he wants the investigation to focus on that specific area.*

"Mia," he said. "Did you dig up anything on Con Union's holdings in Mexico?"

"No," she said, looking up at him. "I was concentrating on following the money trail to Guadalajara."

"Did anything about the mine come up from Banco Centro?"

She frowned, and then said, "No. Why?"

Nelson leaned back in his chair and locked his hands behind his head.

"Okay," he said, "we've been looking at this like a straightforward case of embezzlement, right? A normal guy goes haywire one day and starts stealing. You think gambling, drugs, women, maybe a mid-life crisis, right?"

Mia nodded.

"I mean those are the usual causes. Nine times out of ten."

"Right," said Mia, leaning forward, "but our guy doesn't have a motive to steal—not that we can find—and he's not trying to cover his tracks."

"Only in the middle," said Nelson.

"What do you mean—in the middle?"

"It seems obvious he's the one who took the money, right? I mean, even Hanson figured that out. And we followed the money into his corporate shells, but then—poof—part of it disappears until it shows up, in of all things, a foreign bank statement."

"Yeah," said Mia, nodding, "most of the money is in limbo."

"Right," said Nelson, glancing over at her. She was looking at him through those big, plastic-framed glasses of hers. Thinking.

Lionel's right, thought Nelson. *She's a sharp one.* He caught himself staring at those eyes and quickly looked back at the spreadsheet.

Man. That's the last thing I need.

"The things that stand out to me," said Mia, "are his church, the mine, and that town. Why that particular place? What led him there?"

122

Nelson nodded. *Yep. Right on the money.*

They both turned as they heard the key turn in the lock. The door opened and Lionel walked in, holding a brown grocery bag and a black briefcase.

"Hello, Nelson," he said. "Mia. How are things going?"

Nelson glanced at his watch before answering. It was 10:30.

"About what we expected," said Nelson. "We know he took the money and where some of it went, but most of it's out there in limbo somewhere."

"Where've you been, Lionel?" asked Mia.

"Around," he said, putting the bag down on the table and taking out two wine bottles. "I've been down to the archdiocese."

"Did you get anything?"

"Yes," said Lionel. "There were no long-distance calls to Mexico from St. Alphonso, so I doubt if Father Mike is involved—at least not directly through Baker. The church funds collected for the mine survivors were sent to the San Pablo church as scheduled."

"Couldn't he have gotten in touch with them some other way?" asked Nelson.

"Maybe," said Lionel, "but I just have a feeling he's not involved."

A feeling, boss? thought Nelson. *That's it?*

Lionel reached for one of the bottles and began to open it.

"What about the money deposited at Banco Centro?" asked Lionel. "Has anyone moved it?"

"No," said Mia. "It's still sitting there."

"Let's freeze it," said Lionel, turning the corkscrew. "That might flush out our Mr. Baker. Or whoever he's working with."

"Can we do that?" asked Nelson. Papers were usually necessary for something that drastic, and this was in another country. He wasn't sure what kind of pull Lionel had beyond the border.

"Sure," said Lionel, popping the cork. "It's simply a matter of getting Hanson to make a few phone calls."

"Maybe we should get somebody other than Reynolds Hanson to do that," said Nelson. "Just to be on the safe side."

He felt Mia looking at him. Lionel paused, pursed his lips, and nodded.

"I agree," he said. "That's a good call, Nelson."

Nelson nodded. *Standard operating procedure. That's all it is.*

Lionel grabbed three glasses from the bar behind him. Nelson thought he had an odd, self-satisfied look on his face—like the cat who had gotten the canary. *What did he know?*

Nelson glanced over at Mia, who was also looking closely at Lionel.

"What did you find out?" asked Mia. "You'd better tell."

"Well," said Lionel. "After I visited the archdiocese, I happened to stop in to Con Union. Mr. Hanson had left early, but I persuaded the CFO to let me look at some of the bank's foreign assets."

He poured a glass from the bottle, held it up to the light and smiled.

"Look at that color," he said. "This a beautiful pinot."

"Lionel," said Mia, somewhat sharply.

He glanced over toward her and smiled.

"Yes, my dear?"

"What?" she said.

Lionel filled the other two glasses and brought them over to the table. He handed one to Mia, one to Nelson, and sat down.

"The Farragut Royal Company," he said, "on paper at least, owns a sixty-eight percent interest in the La Fuente Gold Mine. So, Farragut is the controlling interest in the mine."

"Oh," said Mia.

"And here's one for you. The CEO of Farragut is Reynolds Hanson's father."

Well, thought Nelson. *How about that?*

"Does Baker know that?" he asked.

Lionel shrugged. "He had to have known. The loan papers went through Con Union. His job was to handle the real estate transactions. The mine was acquired in 2022, when he was a vice president, so he was probably part of the acquisition team."

"Okay," mused Nelson. "Who else would have been in on it?"

"Some other executives," said Lionel. "And Reynolds."

"Why didn't he say anything?" asked Mia.

"Well," said Nelson, sipping his wine, "he wasn't about to give us anything he didn't have to."

Lionel nodded. "And we didn't really touch on the subject of Mexico. Only on the embezzlement."

"Are you making excuses for him?" asked Mia.

Lionel scoffed. "Him? Hardly."

"It's hard to have sympathy for a guy like that," said Nelson. "Even if he is a client."

"Is he really a client?" asked Mia. "He's not paying us."

"Well," said Lionel, "he is a friend of my father's, but that," he continued, taking a sip of the wine, "doesn't mean he's any less of a prick."

He frowned and took another sip. Nelson glanced at Mia, who merely moved her eyebrows. Lionel usually didn't swear.

"Wait a minute," said Mia. "Does Reynolds know that money is in the Guadalajara Bank?"

Lionel stared into his wine glass.

"I'm not sure if he knows about it yet, but I do think he is supposed to notice it," said Nelson, after a beat. "I think Baker wants him to notice. That's why he put it there in plain sight."

"Why?" asked Mia.

"Well," continued Nelson, "we know Baker wants to help the people there, right? That's kind of his mission. Maybe the money is a warning for Reynolds to back off."

"But it's not just a message to Reynolds," said Mia. "It's out there for anybody to see."

Nelson paused a moment. "I think he wants Con Union to go under the microscope, too. I'm not sure why."

"Maybe he's protecting someone," said Lionel.

"Could he have a personal connection down there? A girl or something?" asked Nelson.

"That wouldn't be like him," said Mia. "He seems to be a pretty straight arrow."

"What did that priest say?" asked Lionel. "That the owners of the mine weren't taking responsibility for the accident? That they weren't even helping to remove the bodies?"

"Yeah," said Nelson, nodding.

"Maybe," said Mia, taking a sip of wine, "maybe Baker's trying to force them do the right thing and help those people. It was their mine, after all. Their responsibility."

"Huh," said Lionel. "Try telling them that."

"Yeah," said Nelson, "but didn't Baker's secretary—"

"Charlotte," said Lionel.

"Yeah, Charlotte," said Nelson. "Didn't she say that Baker had been going down to San Pablo for a long time? Since before the accident? And that he was cozy with the priest down there? I don't think this started just because he felt guilty about the accident. He was in there before that—and in deep."

"If he felt guilty about the accident," said Mia, "maybe he felt guilty about the whole thing. I mean unsafe conditions, kids working in there, horrible wages."

Nelson reached over and grabbed his glass of wine.

"Jesus," he said, sipping it. "Who is this guy? Robin Hood or what?" *Damn*, thought Nelson, taking another sip. *This is good. I've never tasted a wine like this. I'm going to get spoiled.*

"I don't know," said Mia. "If Baker knew Father Ignacio from before, that might explain the church connection." She took her glass and took a sip.

"Nice," she said to Lionel, holding up her wine glass. "Oregon?"

Lionel smiled. "Yep," he said. "Drouhin from Dundee Hills."

"So," said Nelson. "Baker feels guilty—angry perhaps—because Con Union was part of exploiting the people in his favorite little Mexican village."

"Guilty," said Lionel, almost under his breath. "He felt guilty about it."

"All right," continued Nelson. "So why not go to the Board of Trustees? Why not work with the bank? I mean he was pretty important at Con Union. You think he'd have a voice."

"If I know Reynolds," said Lionel, "he wouldn't give a damn. No one in the boardroom would—not unless it was part of a PR campaign or something on that order. No. Reynolds and most of my father's friends?" He shook his head. "Altruism is not in their DNA. Neither is compassion."

He frowned and turned his glass around in his hands. Mia started to say something but stopped. Nelson felt a stillness come over his boss, as if a weight had settled on his shoulders.

"My father, however, is different. He's a good man," said Lionel softly, staring into his glass. "He's had to do some unsavory things in the past—to build his business, you understand—but that's part of the game. At heart, he's a good man. A good father."

He looked up and smiled at the two of them.

"I have to remind myself of that occasionally."

Nelson nodded. He deliberately didn't look at Mia but heard her shifting in her seat.

"What's he like?" asked Nelson. He knew he should tiptoe around the subject, but he couldn't help himself. It was the cop in him. "Your father, I mean."

Lionel looked up at him. It was a pensive, vulnerable, almost sorrowful look, the look of a frightened little boy.

"He's a good man," repeated Lionel. "A good father. He's gone to the mat for me. And more than once." He emptied his glass and reached for the bottle. He refilled his glass.

Lionel chuckled and then glanced up at Nelson. "You know I've been in trouble with the law. Dad bailed me out every time, no questions asked. He's always been there for me, no matter what. He still watches out for me. He talked me into this detective business. For my own good."

"That's a good thing," said Mia.

"For all of us," said Nelson.

"He saved my life," said Lionel quietly.

Nelson took a sip of his wine and waited. Lionel glanced out the window and then looked back at Nelson and Mia.

"You guys probably know about what happened to me and my mom," he said, looking up suddenly.

Nelson nodded.

"Yeah," he said.

"Me, too," said Mia. "I'm so sorry, Lionel. That must have been awful."

"Thanks, Mia," he said, "but that's ancient history. I only mentioned it up because it was my dad who brought me through all that. It wasn't easy. It took a lot of time and money. A lot of parents couldn't, or wouldn't, have done it. They would've given up."

He looked down at his lap and smiled slightly.

"Well, anyway," he said, "he's no Reynolds Hanson."

"I guess not," said Nelson. He glanced over at Mia, who was looking closely at Lionel. *How deep is she in with the old man?* he thought. *What's her angle with this psychotherapy thing?*

As if she'd heard him, Mia turned and looked at Nelson. Her face revealed nothing.

"Anyway," said Lionel. "I owe my dad something fierce. That's part of why I'm doing this."

"Do you like it?" asked Mia.

"Yes," said Lionel, smiling. "I do. I think we had a good day today."

"I'm sure your father will appreciate it," said Mia. "Your doing this for him, I mean."

"That's part of the deal," said Lionel, smiling slightly. "He set me up with this job and I promised to pay him back in kind. That's all fine and everything, but, you know, on some level, I'm probably still seeking his approval."

He chuckled.

"Is that what Freud would say, Mia? Do I have a father complex?"

"Don't talk to me about Freud," she said, crossing her legs. "He didn't know anything about women."

"Who does?" muttered Nelson, reaching for the bottle.

"Freud," said Mia, "and men in general, are jerks. All you think about is your penises."

"I rarely think about penises," said Lionel. "In fact, I don't think I ever do. Not my own or anyone else's. Do you, Nelson?"

"No," he said, lifting his glass. "I can't say I do. I think Mia might be—what's the psychological term—projecting, right? I think she might be projecting her thoughts onto us."

"Well, Nelson," she said, "that proves my point. Your fascination with your own junk leads you to project your desires onto me—while calling me a projector." She took a breath. "Once again, in the true Freudian tradition, the woman is being cast as the villain."

"There's some badass doublespeak," said Nelson.

"I know what you're thinking," said Mia. "You think I'm a bitch. Because I'm smarter than you."

"That would be a typical male reaction," said Lionel.

Nelson shrugged. "Nah," he said. "No more than usual."

Mia smiled and shook her head.

Lionel got up and began to open the second bottle.

"So," said Nelson. "You think Baker might have done all this because he had a guilty conscience?"

"I don't know," said Lionel. "Very possibly." He pursed his lips. "But it doesn't explain why he made that deposit. He's gone to great lengths to draw attention to the loan fraud and Con Union. It has kind of an Old Testament feel. You know, the hand of God, and all that. A sign from heaven. And he's implicated Reynolds."

Nelson felt himself frowning. He didn't really see the religious angle.

"Implicated?" he asked. "Reynolds didn't break the law, did he?"

"No," said Lionel, "I don't think so, but it does make him look stupid. And it doesn't mean he's not culpable—at least in a moral sense."

Nelson nodded. *As if,* he thought, *that means anything in the real world.*

"But he's the one who brought the fraud to your father's attention, right?" asked Mia.

"Yep," said Nelson, "and what better way to draw suspicion away from yourself?"

"Nelson," said Lionel, leaning forward. "I believe we'll go see Reynolds Hanson tomorrow and find out exactly what he knew and when he knew it."

Nelson smiled. *Excellent,* he thought. He was looking forward to meeting Mr. Hanson again.

Chapter 10

Reynolds Hanson sat at the head of the conference room table with his hands folded in front of him, glaring defiantly at Lionel, who was sitting in the closest chair.

"You're telling me that Brad Baker put $100,000 of my money into a Guadalajara bank?" he asked. "Into a customer savings account?"

Lionel nodded.

"Well, let's get it out of there," said Reynolds.

"On whose authority?" asked Lionel, rubbing at a spot on the tabletop with his finger. "How would you go about proving it's Con Union's money?"

"Well, we'd—" started Reynolds and then stopped.

"That's right," said Nelson. "We'd have to file a police report and tell all your investors and customers about how you let five million dollars slip right through your fingers."

Reynolds glared at him.

"And besides," continued Nelson, "I think you'd like to get the rest of it back. Am I right? Do you think we'd ever have a chance of finding that money if we blew the whistle now?"

Reynolds continued glaring but said nothing.

"Reynolds," said Lionel. "Did Brad Baker ever do any work for Con Union in Mexico?"

"Yeah, he went down there a couple of times to help appraise some property for our loan department."

"Why didn't you tell us that before?" asked Nelson.

"You didn't ask."

Lionel sat down opposite Reynolds and asked quietly, "Was he there when La Fuente was acquired? That mine?"

Reynolds grimaced and then glanced up at Lionel.

"He arranged the loan to the Mexican companies that owned the mine, right?" Lionel glanced at a file in front of him. "Alteca and Hermanos Gordos. Correct?"

"You're good," said Reynolds. "Better than I thought you'd be." He sighed and stared down at his hands. "Yeah," he continued, "Hindman was created to act as the holding company for the Mexican mining firm. Hermanos Gordos ran the day-to-day operations. They were a subsidiary of Alteca. Brad was part of the team. We sent him down there to do the appraisal."

"That was how long ago?" asked Nelson, taking out his notebook.

"Well, we finished the deal in 2022, so Brad was probably down there the year before, setting everything up."

Lionel leaned forward and asked, "What happened to him down there?"

Reynolds frowned. "What do you mean?"

"I mean the man has dozens of framed pictures of that little town hung all over his office. He's got a leatherbound bible signed by the priest from Santa Barbara, the San Pablo church. Something happened to him, Reynolds."

Reynolds shook his head.

"I don't know," he said.

I believe him, thought Nelson, watching Reynolds closely. *I don't think Reynolds has ever seen those pictures. He's probably never been in Baker's office.*

"Something got to him," said Lionel. "Got into his head. He never said anything to you about it? Anything about Mexico in general?"

"No," said Reynolds, "but we never talked much. We didn't have a whole lot in common."

"He didn't act any differently after being there?" asked Lionel.

"He was down there a lot," said Nelson.

Reynolds frowned. "Not on business, he wasn't. He only had to go down two, maybe three times."

"Yet something kept drawing him back," said Lionel. "What was it? Did he seem different at all after going there?"

"I don't think so. He seemed like the same old Brad when he came back. Dusty. Boring." Reynolds snorted. "He was everything you'd expect a banker to be—no, not a banker, an accountant. Quiet, mousy, kind of a pussy. You know his wife walked all over him."

"And yet this pussy stole five million dollars from your bank," said Nelson. "And got away with it. What does that make you?"

Reynolds scowled and started to stand.

"Sit down, Reynolds," said Lionel. He'd gotten that iron back into his voice. Reynolds glared at him, shot a glance back at Nelson and sat, leaning back in his chair.

"Tell us about the accident," said Lionel.

"At the mine?" asked Reynolds. He shrugged. "I don't know. I guess there was some sort of explosion and the whole thing came down. It's been inoperable since."

"Was that about the time the loan defaulted?" asked Nelson.

Reynolds nodded slightly. "A little after that," he said. "They had to default. The operation was shot."

"We heard," said Nelson, "that the equipment hadn't been properly maintained. That the explosion was caused by a safety violation. One of many."

He was extrapolating on what Father Andrew had said but needed to gauge Reynolds' sense of responsibility—and remorse, if he had any.

"Safety violations?" said Reynolds and laughed. "This is Mexico, for Christ's sake. Do you think they give a shit about standards down there? All they wanted to do was suck as much gold out of the ground as they could. Greedy bastards."

"Are you talking about Alteca? Or Hermanos Gordos?" asked Lionel. "Or was it Farragut? Your father's company. Choose one."

Reynolds stared at him.

"It's quite the coincidence your dad's company happens to own a major share of the mine and has a controlling interest in the company that operates it. The company your bank financed," said Nelson. "Is that even legal?"

"You're the cop," retorted Reynolds. "You tell me."

"Who set up the Hindman shell?" asked Nelson.

"I told you. It was Baker."

"Did you tell him to do it?"

"No," said Reynolds. "No. It was his idea. Hindman was supposed to be the loan intermediary between us and the Mexican companies. I don't know anything about this Herman and Lund."

Nelson glanced over at Lionel. *We didn't ask about Herman and Lund.*

"What happened after the accident?"

Reynolds shrugged. "The mine was dead. Hermanos defaulted on the loan. We had to absorb the loss."

"A lot of people died in that accident," said Nelson. "As majority owners of Alteca, Farragut could have been held liable."

Reynolds shrugged. "They weren't," he said.

"How much did the people get compensated after the accident? The mine workers?" asked Nelson.

"I don't know," said Reynolds. "We did the financing and helped Alteca with acquisitions. Labor wasn't our responsibility."

Wait a minute, thought Nelson, glancing over at Lionel. *Acquisitions? Was Farragut actually involved in running the mine?*

"What was the extent of your involvement in La Fuente?" asked Lionel.

Yep, thought Nelson, nodding to Lionel. *He's onto it.*

"Farragut had a controlling interest in Alteca," said Reynolds. "Con Union granted them a substantial loan for expansion. That was it."

"We know that," said Nelson. "Who ran the day-to-day operations for La Fuente? Who was overseeing acquisitions? Who was in charge of modernization?"

"I'm not sure," said Reynolds, glancing down at his hands.

"You're not sure?" asked Lionel, getting up. "How can that be? A multi-million-dollar foreign investment with a twelve percent profit margin? You know, Reynolds, I believe the average return of a mining operation is about eight percent, but La Fuente was doing remarkably well. Why was that?"

Cutting corners, I'm sure, thought Nelson.

He sat on the edge of the table and gazed down at Reynolds, who was still staring at his hands.

"Remember, Reynolds," said Lionel, "if you refuse to cooperate with us, we'll be forced to go to the authorities. Word will get out. The board of directors will probably fire you, and then you'll probably be charged as an accessory—at the very least—for embezzlement. Your stock will bottom out, and it might even mean the end of the bank. You'd be ruined."

Reynolds sat very still, staring down at his hands.

"Tell us what happened," said Lionel, "and we'll get the money back and try to keep this thing quiet."

Nelson glanced up at him, but Lionel was keeping his gaze fixed on Reynolds.

Well, thought Nelson. *I guess that's what his dad wants, but I hate to see this bastard get off.*

Reynolds sighed. "That's it. I told you. Hermanos Gordos asked Alteca to help them with the loan. Alteca contacted Farragut. They couldn't have gotten it without them. Brad and I examined the details. It looked good and we approved it. End of story."

"All right," said Lionel, standing up. "If you're not going to cooperate, we'll go right over to the DA's office. They might be interested in taking a look at your books."

"All right," said Reynolds. "Shit. Yeah, okay. All right. Farragut handled the acquisition of the new equipment for the mine. We didn't trust Alteca. You know, there's a lot of corruption down there."

"Who ran the day-to-day operations?" asked Nelson.

"That was Hermanos Gordos," muttered Reynolds.

"Who was in charge?"

"Alfredo Juarez." He shook his head. "But like I said, I didn't know any details about the operation itself. We were strictly financing. Farragut handled acquisitions. They worked with Alteca."

"What happened after the explosion?" asked Nelson.

"We had to write it off as a default," said Reynolds. "An unforeseen occurrence. You know, the cost of doing business. Or so we thought at the time. It turned out the money had never gotten past the holding company. Alteca never got the money. Brad had it the whole time. He took it all."

"So the explosion caused the default," said Nelson, looking over at Lionel. He looked back at Reynolds. "And Farragut—your dad's company—handled acquisitions for safety equipment that was never even purchased. So, let's see, Reynolds. That disaster put five million dollars into your pocket."

Shit, thought Nelson. *Maybe Baker engineered that explosion. Our little Bradley might be a stone-cold killer.*

"Not into my pocket," said Reynolds. "Talk to Brad. He's the one who arranged everything. He approved the loan. He was in charge of disbursing it. He was the one in charge. He's the one who held the money up in Hindman."

"So, when the shit hit the fan, Brad was left holding the bag?" asked Lionel.

Reynolds shrugged.

"Who expected anything to happen?" asked Reynolds. "Everything was fine until the money disappeared. Farragut sponsored the Alteca loan, we approved it, and we were set to disburse it—but then it all blew up."

"Disburse to Alteca?" asked Nelson.

Reynolds nodded. "Yeah, under Farragut's supervision."

"But then Baker decided—for no apparent reason—to hold everything up," said Nelson.

"He wanted to steal it all along," said Reynolds, smiling and leaning back in the chair. "It's a total surprise. Like I said, the guy was a nothing. A pussy. I didn't think he had the balls."

Nelson stood up and walked over to where Reynolds was sitting. He sat down and stared at him.

"What is it, detective?" asked Reynolds, smirking. "Is something bothering you?"

"You know," said Nelson, "when this is all over and we've gotten your money back and Lionel has straightened everything out between you and his dad, well, it won't really be over."

"No?" asked Reynolds, smiling. "Why not?"

Nelson smiled back, stood, and walked back to his chair. Reynolds laughed. "Are you threatening me, Detective West? Are you trying to scare me? What are you going to do? Put the cops on me?"

Nelson sat down and put his feet up on the table.

"Have you ever heard of Los Gallos?" he asked.

"Nope," said Reynolds.

"They're one of our local street gangs. Actually, they're not really local. They're national. They have clubs all over the country. They're originally from Jalisco, the Guadalajara area, and they're pretty much all related to each other. You know, one of those deals where everybody knows everybody else. I wouldn't be surprised if some of them had friends or family who died in that accident."

Reynolds had stopped smiling.

"If Los Gallos ever found out about who was really responsible for that explosion, I wouldn't be surprised if they took matters into their own hands."

"You are threatening me," said Reynolds.

"*I'm* not threatening you," said Nelson. "I'm making you aware of a possible threat to your safety. I'm warning you of a clear and present danger."

"What do you want from me?" asked Reynolds. "I've told you everything I know. I had nothing to do with that mine blowing up."

Lionel stood and buttoned his coat. "Yes," he said, "and thank you for your cooperation, Reynolds." He nodded to Nelson, who also stood and put on his coat.

"Well," said Reynolds, "what am I supposed to do about these Gallos?"

"I'm sure you'll come up with something," said Nelson. "Maybe you could ask Mr. Baker to help you."

"Goodbye, Reynolds," said Lionel. Nelson followed him out the door.

Chapter 11

"What do you think?" asked Nelson. "Is he telling the truth?"

"Some," said Lionel, "but I don't think we're getting all of it. Something doesn't quite fit."

Lionel looked out the window and then glanced down at his hands. He seemed edgier than usual.

He's either high or low, but he's always jittery, thought Nelson. He sighed. It was hard enough doing police work. Keeping an eye on Lionel's twitches on top of that was getting a little old.

"What do you mean?" asked Nelson. "What doesn't fit?"

"Why would Baker set up a second shell company?" said Lionel. "All they needed for the Alteca loan was Hindman. Baker could have disbursed the money directly from there. Why create a second shell?"

"I don't know," said Nelson. "To hide the money after he took it? Maybe to shield what he was doing?"

"Perhaps," mused Lionel and gazed out the window.

They drove in silence. Nelson saw Lincoln glance in his rearview mirror and frown. *Maybe he's worried*, thought Nelson.

"I think," said Lionel, "I'd like for you and Mia to go over a few more records. I want to find out some more about Mr. Hanson's personal finances, and I want you to make a detailed timeline of the events going all the way back to Mr. Baker's first trip to Mexico."

"Do you think Reynolds is involved with the fraud?"

"It's a possibility," said Lionel, "but I need to talk to somebody first. Then I'll have a better idea."

A beat. A pause. Nelson nodded. The boss would tell him when he wanted him to know.

"I'd also like to know more about Hermanos Gordos," said Lionel. "Who they are and how they first came to Con Union."

"Lincoln," he called.

"Yes, Mr. Bing."

"I'd like for you to drop off Mr. West at my apartment."

"Nelson, all of Con Union's records are still at my house." He glanced at his watch. "I'll call Mia and see when she can join you."

"Where is she?"

Lionel shrugged. "I'm not sure. She usually doesn't come by the apartment on Wednesdays."

"Why?"

"She insisted on having one day off a week," said Lionel. "She said she has a life of her own. I have no idea why."

Nelson leaned back in his seat. *Huh*, he thought. *Imagine that. Mia's got a secret life. What is it? A lover? A sick mom? A bad habit?*

"She will come over, though," said Lionel. "She's made concessions for me before."

"All right," said Nelson, glancing at his watch. "I'll get right on it. What are you going to be doing?"

"I have a meeting of my own to go to," said Lionel.

* * *

Mia knelt on the floor with an array of documents spread out carefully around her.

Like petals around a flower, thought Nelson and shook his head. *Jesus, West. What's the matter with you? You're getting flaky.* He chuckled aloud.

"What's so funny?" asked Mia, looking up and frowning. She wasn't happy. She hadn't said so, but Nelson had the feeling she didn't appreciate being called in to work at the last minute.

"Nothing."

Mia shook her head and turned back to rearranging the documents.

"I hope this didn't pull you away from anything tonight," said Nelson.

"No," she said, "not really. I only had tickets to see Taylor Swift at Soldier Field."

"Shit. Those are hard to get. And expensive. Why didn't you tell him?"

"It doesn't matter."

"It looks like it matters."

"It doesn't, Nelson. And who asked you? Maybe you should mind your own business."

He nodded. *All right*, he thought. *All right*. Except everybody deserved a little break now and then. He glanced at his watch.

"It's only 7:30. What time does the show start?"

"Eight."

"Go. You can still get there in time. Call your date and tell him you're on the way."

"I thought I told you to mind your own business."

"Look, Mia," said Nelson, standing up and stretching. "There's nothing here I can't handle. I have all the info I need on Reynolds' financials, and I can go ahead and finish up the timeline myself. You already have everything laid out there on the floor. You did most of the work already. Go ahead. Go. Get out of here."

She looked at him a moment, glanced at the array of papers around her, and then stood up from her cross-legged position by simply straightening her legs and rising—a quick and graceful movement.

Jesus, thought Nelson. *I wish I could still move like that. If I ever could.*

143

"Whoa," he said. "Were you a gymnast or something?"

"No," she said and walked past him into her room.

Nelson knelt down amongst the papers, groaning inwardly, and took a look at Mia's timeline—or at least the beginning of it. *Okay. All right.* It looked as if the documents were arranged left to right in chronological order. It was all ready to go. Nelson looked around for his pad of paper and saw it sitting on the table. He slowly got to his feet, went to the table, and grabbed his yellow legal pad. He started back to the papers, but on second thought, he dragged one of the chairs over.

No need to abuse my knees any more than I have to. He placed the chair amidst the papers and started documenting.

The first Alteca loan application, under the auspices of Hindman, came into Con Union on November 9, 2022. He scanned the nearby packets. After review, auditing—yadda yadda yadda—the loan was approved on March 15, 2023. The good old Ides of March. The loan was paid out on April 22, signed off by Bradley Baker.

What's next? he thought, scanning the documents. *Oh yeah, the newspaper article about the mine accident.* Dated June 23, 2023. Then, Alteca formally defaulted on the loan—because of mitigating circumstances—on August 10. During that period, five million dollars were transferred to Herman and Lund, which, according to documents signed by Bradley Baker, was formed to act as a secondary holding company for Hindman. That pretty much jibed with what Reynolds had told them.

Then the rest was all pretty much airline ticket receipts from Baker for his trips to Mexico. They started in March 2020—well before the mine acquisition—and went all the way up June 9th, 2023, two weeks before the accident.

That's odd, thought Nelson.

Nelson stared down at the papers. Didn't Reynolds say that Baker was done with La Fuente after the loan went through? Why would he go down there after that? Do they have other interests in Mexico that Reynolds didn't mention?

He leaned back in his chair and wrote Santa Barbara on his notepad and circled it. What was Bradley's personal connection with San Pablo, and when—and how—did that start? He leaned down and shuffled through the documents, trying to find some evidence—car rentals, travel vouchers, or credit card receipts—that drew a straight line between Baker and San Pablo or Father Ignacio. Nothing.

So, thought Nelson, *when he traveled down there after the loan went through, he didn't log any business expenses. And he logged absolutely everything else, so it was apparently personal. And why was he in Guadalajara in 2020, two years before the mine loan?*

He looked up as Mia entered the room. She had changed into jeans and a red t-shirt she wore under an embroidered black denim jacket. She was wearing red heels, too.

She looks like a college kid, thought Nelson.

He smiled and nodded.

"You look good."

"Thanks," she said. "You know I didn't need your permission. I was getting ready to leave anyway."

"Go out and have a good time, but don't be back too late. Remember it's a school night."

"Fuck you, Nelson," she said and sauntered out. He grinned and continued looking for any church documents.

Shit, he thought after finding nothing. *I should have asked Mia about it.*

Nelson leaned back in his chair. Could Baker be using the church—both churches—to hide the money? No, that didn't make sense. Baker wouldn't need that—he could stash the money offshore. *And it feels like the whole religion thing was on the level.* He went through Mia's papers a second time, looking for something he may have missed.

Nelson looked up as he heard the key in the lock. Lionel entered, holding a paper bag.

"Hello, Nelson," he said, glancing around the room. "Where's Mia?"

"She went to the Taylor Swift concert."

"What?" he asked, obviously surprised. "Are you joking?"

Nelson shook his head. Lionel shook his head and sighed.

"Well, I suppose it is her day off."

"Yeah," said Nelson, getting up. "She told me she had tickets—and a date, apparently—and since we were pretty well caught up here, I told her to go ahead—that I'd finish the timeline."

"Oh."

"Is that all right?" asked Nelson.

"Yes, of course," said Lionel. "As long as everything is in order." He glanced at the array of papers on the floor and frowned again.

C'mon, boss, thought Nelson. *Don't get all pissy.* Lionel placed the bag on the table and took out a bottle of wine.

"What have you been up to?" asked Nelson. "Besides buying wine, I mean?"

"I went to visit my father," said Lionel, taking a corkscrew from the portable bar. "Since we're investigating this matter as a favor to him, I thought he might be able to tell us something about Reynolds Hanson."

146

Lionel twisted the screw in, set the lever, and pulled the cork. He motioned for Nelson to get glasses from the sidebar. He did.

"You know what my father told me?" asked Lionel, pouring out the wine.

"No," said Nelson. *No need to say more.* He'd been around enough witnesses to know when somebody needed to spill. Lionel handed him a glass.

"He said that Reynolds Hanson didn't ask him for help with the default. His father did. Apparently, Reynolds wanted to take care of the matter himself. Internally. What do you make of that?"

"I'd say Reynolds Hanson might have something to hide."

Lionel took a long sniff of his glass and then sipped and smiled.

"Good old California Cabernet, Nelson. But not your usual fruit bomb."

"Fruit bomb?"

"Yes. Domestic cabs are sometimes notorious for that. They're produced to highlight super-ripe fruits and to have a high alcohol content. People love it. This," he continued, taking another sip, "is not that wine."

Nelson stuck his nose in the glass the way Mia had showed him and breathed deeply. He could smell cherry and licorice. He took a taste. Not fruity, but rich and silky smooth.

"Nice," he said. "Really nice."

"Of course it is," said Lionel. "It's from Napa."

He went over to the table and sat. Nelson followed him, sitting in the chair opposite.

"I was thinking," said Lionel, staring into his glass, "hoping, I suppose, that my father might tell me he hadn't known what we were getting into, and that he wasn't using me to sidestep the law. I should have known better."

He glanced up at Nelson.

"He knew, all right, and he put us right in the middle of it—whatever this is—deliberately."

"What did he know?"

"I think Miles Hanson, Reynolds' dad, told him that Reynolds—and the bank—were having a problem. My father knew this would not be just an instance of me tracking down a bad loan, recovering the money, and hushing things up."

"Did he tell you that?" asked Nelson.

"Not in so many words," answered Lionel, sipping his wine.

"What exactly did he say to you?"

"He said there was no possible way that Reynolds Hanson would be implicated in any criminal activity."

"Your dad thinks he's innocent?"

Lionel took a long sip of wine and glanced at Nelson.

"You have to understand, Nelson, that my father has a way of speaking that leaves absolutely no doubt as to what he wants, how he wants it, and when he wants it. If he says there is no way Reynolds is involved in this, then Reynolds cannot and will not be incriminated. It's that simple. If Reynolds somehow happened to be implicated, my father would be very displeased."

He glanced at Nelson.

"You see, Miles Hanson and my father are very old friends."

"But you think Reynolds is in on it."

"Probably," said Lionel. "And we likely won't be able to do much about it."

"We could," said Nelson. "And let the chips fall where they may."

"My dad wouldn't like that."

"Man, that's tough," said Nelson, taking a sip of wine. "We might not get paid."

Lionel looked at Nelson, laughed, and took another sip of wine.

"Well, he has threatened to cut me off before."

"I doubt if he would," said Nelson.

"What makes you say that?" asked Lionel.

Nelson paused a moment. He knew what he wanted to say but wasn't sure if saying it would be the smartest thing. They were getting along pretty well—he'd almost call Lionel a friend. *But he's still the boss,* he thought, *and I might be overstepping my bounds. Oh, well. What the hell.*

"Well," said Nelson, "you said before that your dad did every-thing possible to help after the kidnapping. He even arranged this business for you. It says a lot that he trusts you to figure this whole mess out while keeping Reynolds clean. Isn't that saying he trusts you—and that he needs you? Why else would he do this?"

"I suppose you're right," mused Lionel, staring into his glass.

"So, you think we're actually working this case for Miles, Reynolds' old man?"

"Yeah."

"Why didn't your dad say so at the beginning?"

"I don't know. Maybe Miles Hanson wanted to keep his own involvement quiet."

"He's not willing to put himself at risk, but he's ready to put his own son out there?"

Lionel smiled and nodded.

"Welcome to my world," he said.

What you don't know is that your dad is looking out for you in ways you have no clue about, thought Nelson. He took a slow sip of wine.

"So do we think Reynolds is dirty?" asked Nelson. "We know your dad does."

"I'm not sure," said Lionel. "He's arrogant and a little dumb, but I don't think he's dumb enough to let all this happen right under his nose. But maybe."

"So, you think he was at least aware of the scheme to defraud?"

"Yes, I do. This whole set-up is awfully convenient for him, isn't it? All the evidence just misses him. Yeah, he's involved."

And you're exactly right, thought Nelson. *You've got good instincts, kid.*

"Maybe you just don't like him," said Nelson.

"That wouldn't matter," said Lionel, completely serious.

"Well, your dad says Reynolds Hanson is untouchable," said Nelson. "All right. So, we leave him be for now. What do you think our next step should be?"

"Well," said Lionel, standing up and stretching. "How's your Spanish?"

"San Pablo?"

"Why not? I think it's time, don't you?"

"What do you think we're going to find down there?" asked Nelson.

"I think Bradley Baker is in San Pablo," said Lionel. "He might be hard to smoke out, but he's either in that town or close by. Probably somewhere near that church."

"Could he claim sanctuary?" asked Nelson. The thought had suddenly—unpredictably—popped into his head.

"Maybe," said Lionel. "But that doesn't mean we couldn't try to talk to him. I've got a few questions for him."

Nelson nodded. *More than a few,* he thought. *Why the obvious deposit in the Guadalajara bank? That'd be a good place to start.* And *what's the story behind Herman & Lund, that second shell company? And why—of all places—San Pablo?*

Chapter 12

THEY WERE LUCKY. THE PLANE to Guadalajara wasn't quite full, so it was turning out be a comfortable flight. Most flights were packed these days—or so Nelson had heard. He didn't travel much. He glanced over at Mia, who was staring out the plane window. Lionel was asleep. He didn't like flying and took pills he said knocked him out—and he hadn't been exaggerating. The minute the plane was in the air—boom, he was in dreamland.

Getting ready had been hectic, but Lionel had pulled it off. God only knew how much he had paid for tickets. *As if it matters*, thought Nelson. He had to admit he was a little surprised they hadn't taken the Bing family jet—assuming there was one, but maybe he was jumping to conclusions. Maybe the Bings weren't quite *that* rich.

Once he had decided to go, Lionel wanted to get started immediately. He had gone into a frenzy—getting tickets, packing, sending Mia shopping, and gathering up all the gear he needed took up most of the morning. Nelson tried to stay out of his way. He managed to find his passport in the back of his sock drawer. He'd gotten lucky—again. It was still good, just six weeks shy of expiration.

They piled Lionel's four big suitcases into the trunk, along with Mia's and Nelson's carry-ons, and got to the airport just in time. Lucky again.

It's been a lucky week, thought Nelson, leaning back in his chair. *I got a job—a good job, I'm working an interesting case, and I'm going to Mexico. Who'd have thought? It's probably too good to last. Something will happen. It always does.*

The good thing is that the boss and I get along. That's a pleasant change. I just have to keep it that way. He took a sip from his gin and tonic and frowned. It tasted flat, not lively. One week ago, he wouldn't have even noticed. *My God,* he thought. *I'm turning into a wine snob—right before my very eyes.*

"What's so funny?"

He turned. Mia was looking at him.

"What?"

"You were smiling."

"Was I?"

"Yes. What's so funny?"

"Nothing," he said. "I was just remembering something."

"Cougars?" she asked.

"Cougars?"

"Yes," she said, folding her hands on her lap. "I thought Marilyn Baker might be on your mind."

"Her? God, no. What makes you say that?"

"Well, you're attracted to her, aren't you?"

"No. I am not."

"You certainly seemed attracted to her."

"No," he said. "No way."

"There was a spark there," said Mia, nodding slightly. "I can tell these things."

"What about you?" he said. "You were flirting with that Lance kid."

"The little guy?" she said. "Nope. No way. He's not my type. I prefer an adult portion. No happy meals for me."

Nelson chuckled and glanced toward Lionel, who was curled up on his seat and sleeping with his mouth open. He looked like a little kid.

Thank God he doesn't snore, thought Nelson. *And thank God there's no kid behind me kicking the seat. I guess this really is my lucky week.*

"Hey."

He turned. Mia was looking at him. She gestured toward Lionel with her chin.

"What were you and Lionel talking about last night?" she whispered.

"I don't know," he said. "The case. Why?"

"He seemed distracted this morning—even more than he should have been in getting ready for the trip," she said. "And I don't think he slept very well last night. Not that that's unusual," she added, more quietly.

"Hey, Mia."

"What?"

He glanced at Lionel, who looked absolutely dead to the world.

"What was going on with that secret meeting the other day? You know, with Lionel's dad."

"Oh," she whispered. "I don't know if this is the best time for that. He's sitting right here."

"He's out like a light."

"I don't know."

"Could we go in the back?" he asked. "There's some empty seats back there."

She gave him a look.

"Really?"

"You're right," he said. "People will think we want to join the mile-high club."

She snorted. "Are you kidding? You and me? Do you know how old you are?"

"All right. Fine."

Nelson took a sip from his drink. Mia turned to look out the window.

"What do you see?" he asked.

It was late afternoon, and the sun was starting to set. He wondered what a sunset might look like from up here.

Mia shrugged.

"Mountains. Desert. A few lights here and there."

"Is the sun going down?"

"It set down there already," she said. "You can see the shadows behind the mountains—that's their night. We've got a few minutes yet."

Nelson leaned over to get a look but couldn't see much out the tiny porthole. Just mountains with darkness crawling across them. The sun was almost down. He leaned back in his seat and glanced at Lionel. Out. A little drool was running out the side of his mouth. Nelson leaned out of his seat and looked toward the back of the plane. There were a few rows of open seats.

"Hey, Mia," he whispered. She was still gazing out the window.

"What?"

"There're seats in back. We can talk there. Let's go."

She glanced at Lionel, looked at Nelson, pursed her lips and sighed.

"All right."

He got out of his seat and stood in the aisle as Mia wormed her way around the sleeping Lionel. Nelson led the way to the back of the plane. Mia slid in and he followed, trying not to spill his drink.

"So, Mia. Talk to me."

"What do you want to know?"

"What was the deal with Lionel's dad the other day? I thought your job is being Lionel's assistant, but I guess not. Are you spying on him for the old man?"

"No, I'm not spying on him."

She glanced out the window. Nelson waited.

"What did Mr. Bing tell you?" she asked without looking at him.

"He said he recommended me for the job, and that part of my duties—besides doing detective work—are to make sure Lionel stays out of trouble—sort of like a bodyguard I guess—and that this is all some sort of therapy."

"So, what do you want to know?"

"I want to know what you know. Where do you fit into all this? Did you set up the meeting between me and Lionel's dad?"

"No," she said. "He did it. Don't worry, though. That's standard procedure for him." She glanced out the window.

"What do you mean standard procedure?"

"Look," she said, turning towards him. "I'm not supposed to talk about this. The two of us are supposed to be working independently. We're supposed to be compartmentalized."

"Well, that ship has sailed."

"All you need to know, Nelson, is that you're here to protect Lionel, along with being his partner—and mentor."

"What's your job?"

"I'm Lionel's assistant. You know what I do," she said.

"Not all of it. There's more. What else?"

"I can't tell you," she said.

"Because of Lionel's dad?"

"No," she said, leaning back in the seat and folding her arms over her chest. She sighed. "Because of HIPAA."

"HIPAA? The medical privacy thing?"

She nodded.

"What are you talking about?" he asked. "You're not a doctor."

"You don't think so?" she answered. "What do you really know about me, Nelson?"

He leaned back in his seat. *What the hell is this?*

"Look," he said. "This whole weird thing, whatever it is, affects me, too. I have a right to know what's going on—everything that's going on, especially if this starts to get dangerous."

"I can't. I signed a non-disclosure agreement."

"All right," he said. "Should I ask Lionel?"

"He doesn't know anything."

"Then I'm out. As soon as we land, I'm going to get on the first flight home. I'm not going to risk my life without knowing what the hell is going on."

He stood up and started edging into the aisle.

"Nelson, wait."

He stopped. Mia was looking up at him. She took a deep breath. "Sit down."

He sat.

"I'll tell you, but you have to promise not to tell anyone, especially Mr. Bing. I'd get fired—and sued—if he found out."

"All right."

"I told you one of my degrees is in psychology. It's actually clinical psychology. Last year, I got a call from Lionel out of the blue—just like you did, offering me a job as a part-time investigative consultant and assistant. After I interviewed with him, I went home and found the Rolls Royce in front of my apartment. One of Mr. Bing's men came out and told me he wanted to talk to me." She shrugged. "I knew who he was—I'd just interviewed with his son—so I got in. Guess what he told me?"

"That he was responsible for getting you the job. That he picked you out himself."

"Yeah, basically, except in my case, he said he wanted me to work with Lionel's psychiatrist on a new sort of therapy to help with his PTSD."

"What sort of therapy?"

"It's sort of a hybrid between psychotherapy and exposure therapy."

"What's that?"

"Psychotherapy, or talk therapy, is when an analyst helps guide a patient through a traumatic experience. They typically cover the incident itself, the feelings it arouses, and work on helping the patient deal with their guilt and fears."

"Sure. Lie on the couch and tell me about your mother."

"It's sad," she said, "that a stupid comment like that doesn't surprise me anymore."

"What about this exposure therapy?"

"That's when a therapist will attempt to work with the patient to recreate the trauma, to relive it, and by doing so, gain insight into their actual role in what happened."

"What role? Aren't most of them victims?"

"Yeah, of course, but victims often tend to blame themselves. I've seen rape victims beat themselves up for years for supposedly bringing it on themselves—you know, dressing too sexy or flirting. The same happens with battle trauma. Soldiers blame themselves, thinking they could have done more to help their dead buddies."

"So," said Nelson slowly, "Lionel is blaming himself for what happened to his mom."

"It's very possible," said Mia, "but we don't know for sure. There's still a lot he doesn't remember. That's part of what Dr. Ribot is trying to do."

"I know that name," said Nelson. "Lionel called him the other day."

"He's Lionel's therapist."

"He's been in therapy all this time?"

"Off and on," she said. "It's done some good, but Lionel still displays a lot of trauma symptoms. You know, sleep problems—nightmares mostly—trouble maintaining relationships, substance abuse, and aggressiveness. He had a couple incidents with suicidal ideation. Sometimes he gets physical reactions—you know, shaking, the sweats, and nausea. You saw it the other day."

"No flashbacks?"

"Dr. Ribot says he remembers nothing about the kidnapping itself, but those memories are still in there. He thinks Lionel is repressing them."

"All right," said Nelson. "So, you were brought in to help Lionel get over his PTSD."

"I'm still an investigative assistant, but part of my job—like yours—is to observe Lionel and try to guide him—very subtly—through the exposure therapy without him knowing it. The trick is keeping him in the dark. If he knows this whole detective thing is part of his therapy, that's the end of it."

"Why can't he know?"

"Dr. Ribot thinks that experiencing success as an—", she said, making air quotations, "'agent of justice' will act as a catharsis and help him cope with the trauma."

"So, this whole Baker thing is a charade?"

"No," she said. "That part of it is real. Both Mr. Bing and Dr. Ribot thought Lionel would see through any sort of set-up, so Mr. Bing decided to start this detective business for Lionel. He said he could definitely find enough indiscretions and scandals in his circle to keep Lionel busy."

"And this Con Union fraud just happened to pop up at the right time?"

She shrugged. "I guess so. Mr. Bing just handed it to Lionel a few days ago. Personally, I think these indiscretions, as it were, happen more often than you might think. The one percent is just good at keeping it under the radar."

Nelson nodded. *Well, I was right. I am playing nursemaid to a rich kid and his nerdy friend.*

If he didn't know better, he might have thought Mia was scamming him—but that didn't make sense. She didn't have anything to gain. It seemed nuts, but what did he know? Maybe this Dr. Ribot really did know what he was doing with this exposure therapy. Who knew what had happened to Lionel and his mom after they'd been taken? They'd chopped off her finger. The coroner said she'd been sexually assaulted—brutally assaulted. Did he see that?

He glanced up. Mia was staring at him. He leaned back in his seat, took a drink, and nodded to himself. *Well*, he thought. *What do I have to lose? If this is on the up and up, I'll be on Lionel's staff. If not, I'll find work. I'll survive.*

"Well?" asked Mia.

"Well, what?"

"Are you happy now?"

No, I'm not. This was a whole other layer of crap to work through. I have to be sure not to let anything slip. It's going to be like walking on eggshells.

"All right," he said, glancing over at Mia. "I'm happy. I'm the happiest fucking camper in the tent."

He got up to go back to his seat. Mia followed. She wormed in past Lionel, who was now drooling onto his shirt. They sat, and Nelson exhaled.

Boy, he thought. *This had been a lucky week. Up until now.* He glanced at Mia, who was looking out the window again. He settled back and closed his eyes, determined to get some sleep while he could. This could be a long trip.

Chapter 13

Even with Lionel's four giant suitcases, they got through customs relatively quickly, went to the Avis counter, and picked up their rental. It was a red Ford Focus. Nelson was surprised and a little disappointed. He thought Lionel would've gotten something a little bigger or more fun, like a Jeep or a Mercedes, but it had been a last-minute trip. There probably hadn't been much choice. Still, he figured Lionel would've gone for something a little flashier or more comfortable. After they loaded up, Lionel got in the back. Nelson looked at Mia.

"What?" she said.

"Do you want to drive?"

"No. I don't have a license. Neither does Lionel."

Nelson nodded. It figured. He climbed behind the wheel and started the car.

"Does anyone know where we need to go?" he asked.

"Yes," said Lionel, peering at a map on his smartphone. "It's about an hour drive. You need to pull out of the lot and turn right onto Mexico Highway 44 and drive for about twenty miles or so until you get to the Macrolibramiento del Sur."

"What's that?"

"A bypass around the city," said Lionel. "It's also called GUA 10. I'll tell you when you need to make the next turn. It's a toll road, too. Mia, could you get the change ready?"

Nelson followed the signs out of the airport and pulled onto the highway.

"This looks really modern," said Nelson.

"Were you expecting a burro path?" asked Mia.

"No," said Nelson, "but this is great. Better than some of the roads at home."

Traffic was relatively light, and they reached the turnoff in about fifteen minutes. Nelson turned onto the freeway. *Beautiful*, he thought. *Four lanes of driving pleasure.* When the first tollbooth loomed in the distance, Mia counted out the pesos. Nelson handed them over, thinking the tollbooth workers looked just as bored as those in the States.

He glanced around at the countryside as he drove. It was beautiful. Majestic, green mountains dominated the western skyline as they crossed through miles of lush farmland and green valleys.

Not the Mexico I imagined. I guess I've seen too many Hollywood Westerns.

After about half an hour, Lionel instructed Nelson to turn onto Highway 70 and then almost immediately onto another highway. They soon came to a small town and then turned onto Carratera Ameca, a small, two-lane highway that soon began twisting its way through dusty brown mountain foothills punctuated with patches of green. As they climbed higher, they were soon snaking their way through overhanging trees and dense vegetation. Patches of fog nestled between the distant, green mountain peaks. As they came over ridges, the views of the valleys below were spectacular.

"This is beautiful," murmured Mia.

"Yes, it is," said Lionel. "I haven't been to Mexico since my college days. We spent our spring break in Cancun, and it didn't look anything like this."

"What was it like?" asked Mia.

"Flat," replied Lionel. "Kind of barren looking. I mean parts of it were green, but not like this. The truth is, I spent most of the time in the bar."

As they went around a curve, Nelson caught sight of a steeple peeking between two hills. He pulled over to the shoulder.

"Is that it?" he asked.

"Yes, it is," said Lionel, leaning over the front seat. "That's La Iglesia de Santa Barbara. We're coming up on San Pablo."

"Do you think Baker has any idea we might be coming?" asked Mia. "If he's even there?"

"I don't see how," said Nelson, glancing back at Lionel, "but it might look suspicious if a carload of gringos drives up out of the blue. It'd help us to have the element of surprise. And a good cover."

Lionel nodded. "Agreed," he said. "I wonder how many tourists they get out here."

"Is there another town nearby?" asked Nelson. *It might be a good idea to consolidate. To make a plan.*

Lionel consulted his map. "Yeah, here's another town. Hidalgo. It looks big enough to have a hotel."

"Where is it?"

"Go up about three miles and turn left on—" Lionel peered at the map, "Calle Allende."

"Okay," Nelson pulled out and drove slowly up the winding road, looking for the turnoff. A small green and white bus with a skull painted on the front came careening around a curve in front of them. The driver leaned on the horn as they sped past.

"Oh-oh," said Mia. "You better get it together, Nelson. That driver's probably already put out a gringo alert."

Smart ass, thought Nelson, taking his time on the narrow road. *Why don't you drive if you're so damned smart?*

"Right there," said Lionel, pointing to an intersection ahead. "Turn left."

The road was worn and dotted with potholes. The jungle opened around them as they started down a long slope. In the distance, Nelson could make out a few buildings. As they came closer, he could see the square—the plaza—with some stores and a church. *That must be Hidalgo*. He stopped in front of a small restaurant.

"You guys hungry?" he asked. He was starving. They hadn't had a chance to eat after they landed this morning. They'd had a long layover at the Mexico City airport the night before, but nearly all the airport food shops were closed. All he'd had was a bag of chips.

"Yes, I am," said Lionel. "That's a great idea."

They piled out of the car and walked into the place. There was no door, only an open archway. The place was empty. About a dozen tables, covered with plastic red and white checked tablecloths and flanked by multi-colored resin chairs, were scattered around the room. None of them had been set yet. The place was older but looked clean. The front entryway was open to the outside, and there was no glass in the windows.

"Hello," called Mia.

They waited. After a moment, they heard someone pattering through the kitchen. A youngish man, probably just into his twenties, came bustling in.

"Hola," he said, smiling. "How are you?"

He speaks good English, thought Nelson. *Good. Maybe can give us the lowdown on San Pablo*. The man reached out his hand and Lionel shook it. "Welcome to Hidalgo. You are welcome. Would you like something to eat?"

"That'd be great," said Nelson.

"Here, sit," said the young man and motioned them to a table off to the side. They sat. He trotted off toward the kitchen and disappeared. Nelson could hear him talking to someone in the back, and then he reappeared with a tray of water bottles, place settings, and some menus tucked under his arm.

"I'm sorry we weren't ready for you," he said, "but there's usually not much of a crowd until lunchtime."

"That's fine," said Lionel, smiling. "It's early. We just drove in from Guadalajara."

"I am Luis, and I will be serving you today. What would you like?"

"Coffee," said Nelson and Mia simultaneously. Lionel smiled slightly.

"Señor?" asked Luis.

"I'll have some coffee, too."

"Gracias," said Luis and disappeared.

"Pretty nice place," said Lionel, glancing around the room. He flinched as a small bird flew close overhead.

"Open-air dining," said Nelson. "You gotta love it."

"Yeah," said Mia. "This is great. A good undercover opportunity. We can blend right in with the wildlife."

"I like it," said Nelson. "Down to earth. I like that."

He glanced at Lionel, who was studying the menu. Nelson looked at his own menu. From what he could make of it, the specialty of the house seemed to be "Enchiladas Mineras." *Whatever that is,* thought Nelson. There was also a wide selection of tostadas, gorditas, tacos, and ceviche available—and a breakfast menu. *Now you're talking,* thought Nelson.

"You know," said Lionel, still reading the menu. "I saw a hiking trail sign on the way in. We should ask Luis about the best trails around San Pablo."

Nelson nodded. "Good idea," he said. *But we need to be careful,* he thought. *We don't want to spook this kid with too many of the wrong questions. He might say something to the wrong people.*

Lionel had been doing well up to now, but Nelson didn't want to see the case—or his boss—or himself—jeopardized because of a misstep. *And this could turn ugly. There are cartels operating around here, and we don't know what Baker might have gotten himself into. He might be in a lot deeper than we think.*

He leaned over and spoke quietly to Lionel.

"Do you want me to talk to him?"

Lionel shook his head. "No, Nelson. I'm good."

Nelson nodded and leaned back into his chair.

"What are you getting?" asked Lionel.

"I think I'm going to have the huevos rancheros," said Mia.

"Good choice," said Lionel. "I'll get that, too. What about you, Nelson?"

"I'm not really sure what's on here. Do they have regular breakfasts?"

"Regular for here, yes," said Mia. "Did you mean do they have American-type breakfasts?"

Nelson shrugged. Lionel looked at him and smiled.

Okay, he thought. *When in Rome…*

"I'll try those huevos things, too," he said. "On your recommendations."

Luis came back with their coffee, and they ordered. Lionel leaned back in his chair and stretched.

"Did you sleep well?" asked Mia.

Lionel nodded. "Yeah," he said, "those pills are monsters. I was having weird dreams, though."

"Oh, yeah?" asked Mia, leaning forward on her elbows.

"Yeah. I was dreaming I was locked in a closet—a big closet with all sorts of stuff inside. Childhood stuff. Toys, bicycles, games, army men—life-size army men—and a washing machine. Weird. I was alone, but I could hear people whispering outside."

"Could you hear what they were saying?" asked Mia.

"Not really," he said, "but it seemed very familiar somehow."

"Was it frightening?" she asked.

Lionel looked at her a moment, furrowing his brow.

You're pushing too hard, Mia, thought Nelson. *Take it easy.*

"No," he said, after a moment, "not really. Why?"

She shrugged. "It sounds a little scary to me, being locked in a closet."

Lionel sipped his coffee.

"No," he said, without looking up, "not at all. It felt safe. Protected. Like a hiding place."

Mia nodded and glanced at Nelson.

"It just seemed so real," Lionel continued, "as if the people were right there."

This'll be a fun one to report to your Dr. Ribot, thought Nelson. *Had he heard me and Mia talking, maybe subconsciously, and dreamt about it? Was it a flashback? Or maybe—gasp—it had nothing to do with anything.*

Well, he thought, sighing, and leaning back in his chair. *That's not my department.*

"Are you tired, Nelson?" asked Lionel. "It was a long flight."

"I'm good. I'm used to staying up late. I did long hours—and strange hours—for years at the CPD. It doesn't bother me."

"And you, Mia?" asked Nelson.

"I slept on the plane."

Lionel nodded at her and then glanced back to Nelson. He had an odd half-smile on his face.

Does he suspect anything? thought Nelson. *He looks pretty cagey.* He resisted the urge to look at Mia.

The food finally came, and Nelson realized how hungry he was. The eggs were great. It was different having them served over tortillas, and to have refried beans for breakfast, but they were delicious.

"This is tasty," he said.

"It is good," said Mia.

"Excellent," said Lionel.

He looked up as their waiter came up to the table.

"How is everything?" the waiter asked, smiling.

They all told him how good the food was. Lionel went on to ask about the restaurant. He asked Luis how long he'd worked there, where he'd gone to school, and what the area was like for hiking. Nelson sat back and watched Lionel work. He was good. He had a way of getting people to open up to him. He seemed calmer today, too. Maybe those pills had taken the edge off. He'd been pretty wound up the day before.

Luis talked about how his family had owned the restaurant for three generations and that his mother and sisters still did the cooking and made their own tortillas. Business had been bad since the big accident in San Pablo. A lot of the miners used to come in for breakfast after the night shift, but most of them were gone—or killed—and the mine was still closed. They'd been worried about the restaurant going out of business for a while.

"How's the hiking around here?" asked Lionel. "I heard it's pretty good down by San Pablo."

"It's good there," said Luis, "but there's a great place close to here that has some very good hiking. You can see the forest and the hills, some waterfalls, and maybe some wildlife."

"Excellent," said Lionel. "Is there a good hotel in town?"

"Yes. The Hotel Montana is very nice. It is just down the street. I happen to know that there are vacancies right now."

"Sounds good," said Lionel. "I think we'll head there now."

He paid the bill, and the three of them went outside. Nelson stood in the warm sun and stretched. It had been a long day. He wouldn't mind zonking out for a couple of hours. He glanced over toward Lionel and Mia. They had walked over to the side of the restaurant and were looking up at the surrounding hills. Lionel was pointing at something. Nelson walked over.

"What's up?"

"We were just getting our bearings," said Lionel, pointing toward one of the hills. "San Pablo is back over there about two and a half miles."

"We could walk it," said Mia. "Pretend we're tourists doing a hiking tour."

"What do we know about the jungle here?" asked Nelson. "Do they have any snakes or tarantulas or jaguars or anything?"

"I'm more worried about cartel activity," said Lionel. "I had read there was some sort of territory dispute going on here a couple months ago. I never heard whether they resolved it or not."

"We could ask the concierge about getting a guide," said Mia. "That would fit in with our cover."

"Nah," said Nelson. "We don't want any guides looking over our shoulders."

"Let's check in first," said Lionel. "Then we can get settled and figure out a strategy."

"I could use a shower," said Mia.

"And a nap," added Nelson.

They drove the half-block past the banco and the central plaza to the two-story brick building adorned with a hand-painted wood sign reading "Hotel Montana." They walked into the tiled lobby and were greeted by a middle-aged man dressed in a white shirt and dark pants. Nelson took in the lobby while Lionel checked them in. The place was clean, but it was pretty run down. The white plaster walls were cracked and yellowing near the floors. It didn't seem to Nelson that there would be enough people here to keep a hotel—or even a restaurant—afloat.

Nelson wandered through the lobby and stuck his head into a smaller room with a couple of armchairs arranged in front of a small fireplace. There was a small table placed between them. *Looks like some sort of a sitting room*, he thought.

"This looks like a tearoom," said a voice at his elbow. Mia.

"Yeah, I guess," he said. "There's not a lot of space. I doubt if more than two or three guests could fit in."

"Yeah," said Mia. "Couples only, I guess."

"So," he said. "Do you think you were pressing Lionel a little hard about that dream this morning?"

"No. Why?"

"He looked a little—I don't know. Wary, I guess."

"Well, I have a suggestion," said Mia.

"What?"

"Why don't you do your job and let me do mine?"

He looked over his shoulder. Lionel was still at the desk.

"Screwing up your job can make mine a whole lot harder."

"Don't worry," she said, "I'll let you screw up on your own."

Lionel was motioning to them.

"Here we go," he said, handing each of them a key—an actual key. "We're in adjoining rooms, so—" he said, glancing at this watch. "Let's say we meet at 1 o'clock. That'll give us a few hours to rest."

They followed the concierge through a doorway and into a large, open courtyard with brightly painted walls, a few massive plants growing from huge clay pots, and a small pool that shimmered in the sunlight.

"Wow," said Nelson, under his breath.

"This is nice," said Mia.

"I didn't pack my swimming suit," said Nelson.

"It's all right, señor," chimed in the concierge. "We can provide them here."

"Okay," said Nelson. "I just might take you up on that."

They were escorted to their rooms. Nelson entered his. It was nice enough. Small, but clean. There was a window with a balcony looking out over the courtyard. Nelson stepped outside and took a deep breath. Green hills rose to his right. If his sense of direction was right, San Pablo lay beyond the middle hill. Maybe a couple of miles away. It wouldn't take much to hike there. To his left, past the restaurant, the ground sloped down steeply.

I wonder if there's an ecotour park or something around here, he thought. A tourist attraction that would give us good cover for going to San Pablo. He stretched, went back into his room, and lay down. *I'll just close my eyes a minute*, he thought. *Just a minute.*

Chapter 14

SOMEONE WAS TALKING TO HIM from a distance. Somebody he knew.

"Nelson. Wake up."

He opened his eyes. Mia was standing next to his bed with her hands on her hips, looking as exasperated as usual. She was wearing shorts and a t-shirt.

"Oh," he said, sitting up. "What time is it?"

"Time for our meeting. Come on. Lionel is waiting." She turned on her heel and left.

He stood up and went into the bathroom, splashed some water on his face, and went out into the hall where Mia was waiting.

"Come on."

They went into Lionel's room, where he stood over a table covered with a large map.

"There you are," he said, frowning slightly as he glanced at his watch.

"Sorry. I was really out."

"No worries," said Lionel. "I think I have a plan of action."

Nelson and Mia walked over to the table.

"Okay," said Lionel. "This is a map of the area—a hiking map that Ivan, our concierge, gave to me. You can see," he said, pointing to a dot on the map, "that we're right here. San Pablo is here, about three miles away. There's a good number of trails between here and there. I think Mia and I should be able to walk into town without setting off any alarms."

"So, we just go wandering into San Pablo and ask for Baker?" asked Nelson. "Is that the plan?"

"No," said Lionel. "We're going to have eyes on the town—hopefully we find Baker before we get there." He turned toward Nelson and smiled.

"I'd like to put you up here," said Lionel, pointing at a spot halfway up a hill on the map. "You'll have a bird's eye view of the whole town from there, Nelson. I'd like for you to see if you can spot Baker or anything unusual—you know, somebody taking supplies into the jungle, or anything odd like that. At the very least, you can get a feel for the town."

"Okay," said Nelson. "It's been a long time since I've been on a stakeout, though."

Not a bad plan, he thought. *Having a young—youngish—couple hike into town as tourists would look better than all three of them traipsing in. And I'll be able to get a feel for the big picture and see things they can't. But will the two of them be able to handle themselves?*

"What kind of surveillance equipment do we have?"

"I have some binoculars I brought with me," said Lionel, opening up one of his big suitcases, "and a scope and telephoto lens. What would you prefer?"

Nelson walked over and looked in the suitcase.

"I guess the binoculars and that spotting scope would be good," said Nelson. "Maybe the camera to get documentation—if we need it," he added, glancing over at Lionel.

"We might," he said. "At this point, we're just looking to get the money back, but it can't hurt to have some evidence in our back pocket."

Good call, thought Nelson. He nodded.

"What's the terrain like up there?" he asked, going over to the map. "Can you tell from this map?"

"Mia looked at Google Earth. I think she has an idea of the terrain."

"Yeah," she said, walking over. "There's a lot of mature trees and vegetation in the area. Brush and vines, I guess, and some rocky outcrops. That's what this'll be," she said, pointing to the marked spot on the map. "A flat rock."

"Yeah, that would be a clear sightline," said Nelson. "If I stay low, I should be able to stay out of sight, too."

"Well, I think the frontal vegetation should provide good cover," said Mia, "and this is on a flat ledge. You should be able to lie on it, be unseen, and still have a great view of the town."

And bake in the sun all day. Well, if Mia's right, there should be some cover. I'll figure it out.

"Will there be any shade up there?" he asked.

"Probably," said Lionel. "You might have to improvise a little bit."

"Wear a hat," said Mia. "And hydrate."

Thanks, Mia, thought Nelson. *That's brilliant.*

"Are there any native species I should worry about?" he asked.

"Well," said Mia. "I Googled it, and yeah, you have rattlesnakes, Gila monsters, Mexican beaded lizards, coral snakes, scorpions, fer-de-lances—that's another snake, a nasty one—black widows, Chilean recluse spiders, and mosquitoes."

"Wonderful," muttered Nelson.

"She's messing with you," said Lionel. "Mostly. Coral snakes are on the other side of the country. The Chilean recluse is very shy, the Gila monster is in the northern deserts, fer-de-lances live in the jungle, and we have bug spray for the mosquitoes."

"All right," muttered Nelson. "Won't I be going through the jungle?"

175

"Stay on the path," said Lionel.

"Just keep your eyes open and don't reach into any dark places," said Mia. "Rattlesnakes are probably your main concern. They like to sun on stone, so keep your eyes open."

"You good?" asked Lionel.

Oh, yeah, thought Nelson. *Rattlesnakes and beaded lizards? I'm fucking great.*

He nodded.

"Okay," said Lionel. "We still have the afternoon. Should we get going?"

"Yeah, I don't have hiking boots, though," said Mia. "Just running shoes."

"Let's see if we can pick up some in town here," said Lionel. "If not, we'll try to find something in San Pablo. Can you make running shoes work for today?"

Mia nodded. Nelson looked down as if he were examining the spotting scope.

Really? he thought. *Back in the day, we didn't need special shoes to hike or exercise or play basketball. All I needed was my Converse high tops.* But he didn't say anything.

Why poke a hornet's nest? he thought. *And she actually looks like that girl in that book "The Girl Who Kicked the Hornet's Nest."* Despite himself, he chuckled.

"What's so funny?" asked Lionel.

Nelson shook his head.

"He does that a lot," said Mia, giving him a sidelong look. "I think he thinks we're funny."

"Funny how?" asked Lionel.

"I'm not sure," she said.

Nelson shook his head. "Sorry, guys," he said. "I'm just wool-gathering."

"Hmm," said Mia.

Nelson glanced at Lionel, who was giving him an odd look.

"It's nothing, Lionel," said Nelson. "Really. I was just thinking about Marilyn Baker and that Lance Malkowitz. Mia thought I was hot for her."

"For Mrs. Baker?" asked Lionel. "Really, Mia?"

She shrugged.

"I know," said Nelson. "It struck me as ludicrous, too. Of course, I pointed out that I thought Mia had a thing for young Lance."

"All right," said Mia, standing up. "Enough. We should get going."

"You see," said Nelson. "She's avoiding the subject."

"No," she said quickly. "I'm avoiding you."

"All right," said Lionel. "Let's go."

* * *

Nelson lay on the outcrop of flat rock which he had checked out for reptiles beforehand—and edged further into the shade of the scraggly bush growing there. It wasn't much, but it was some cover. He peered through Lionel's scope. It was a Celestron, a premium piece of equipment, but that didn't surprise him—not anymore. Lionel having anything less than the best would be a surprise. The guy didn't spare any expense.

And he picked out a prime observation position, too, thought Nelson. He had a clear view of the town but was screened by the forest below him. It was perfect. There were mosquitoes around, but Lionel had packed—of course—some high-intensity deep woods-level repellent, and they weren't bothering him at all. But he still was keeping his eyes peeled for snakes. *And fucking scorpions.*

Nelson peered through the scope at the dusty central plaza of San Pablo. Nothing unusual. A mother—or grandmother—was sitting on the gazebo steps watching her two kids play in the dirt, just as she'd been doing for the past hour or so. A man dressed in white was leading a scraggly horse behind what Nelson assumed was a tavern, a building with a faded hand-painted sign reading "La Casita" hanging over the door. One of those little blue and white signs he had seen in the photos at Baker's office hung on one corner of the wall. He couldn't quite make out what it said from where he was.

A few men had wandered into La Casita during the heat of the day but hadn't come out yet. Nelson panned the scope over to the church. Quiet. The doors were open, but there wasn't much traffic—just a few old ladies, the ones who probably came to Mass every day, just like back home. Father Ignacio hadn't shown himself yet. Nor had anyone who could possibly be Baker. Seven or eight younger people—college kids, probably hikers—had wandered in and out of town, mostly stopping at the little café next to the bar, but that was about the extent of it.

There wasn't much else there. A long block of one-story white stucco buildings, divided by a narrow cobblestone street, stretched to the left of the church. An official-looking building occupied the opposite side of the plaza from La Casita. *Maybe municipal offices*, he thought. That seemed to be about it. Some small stone buildings, once painted white, stretched down a slope behind the church. *Houses, probably.* A few stables were tucked in behind them, and one or two dusty chickens wandered in and out of the road. The street on the right side of town stretched up the slope of the mountain and disappeared into the jungle. A couple of college kids came trudging down a trail to the left of it.

Yep, they're wearing hiking boots, too. They all are. I guess you can't use anything else on the trails. Nothing works except those phenomenal $200 dollar boots.

What a scam. It was worse than the guy who convinced a nation—the world—that bottled water was healthier than tap water—that it in fact was necessary for survival. What a crock.

Well, thought Nelson, scanning the plaza again, *if Baker's down there, chances are he'll be coming up for air sooner than later.* He probably feels pretty safe here. In Nelson's experience, a typical suspect wouldn't think twice about eating at the café or joining the local boys for a drink, but Baker was smarter—more cautious. Not your garden variety perp. He's most likely thinking somebody might be coming down to look for him and would be keeping a low profile. We might not see him until he goes to church.

Nelson scanned back up the trail toward Hidalgo to see if he could get a glimpse of Lionel and Mia coming in. They should be showing up any minute. He hoped so. He didn't really enjoy sitting up here on the hill, baking in the sun. It was uncomfortable and boring—like any stakeout. The town was quiet. No tour buses or day trips to see old Mexico. No crowds. In this environment, he'd be able to spot an undercover cop—or a federale—a mile away. But still, Nelson had a nagging feeling there was more than met the eye down in San Pablo—that they were missing something. Things weren't quite right.

Lionel had held out on him. He hadn't shared his plan for flushing out Baker until their meeting, which—so far—had been unlike him. Until then, Lionel been up front about strategy with Nelson, but then he just sprang the stakeout thing on him of nowhere. Not that Nelson was complaining. Surveillance was a good idea—it's just that he would have liked to have known about it beforehand. Lionel didn't know procedure—he didn't have the experience to go off half-cocked, and Nelson didn't want them exposed by any half-baked ideas his boss might have. He'd been good so far, but given his freaky tendencies, Nelson couldn't be too careful. He needed to know what else Lionel might be up to.

If he has a plan at all. Maybe he's playing it by ear. Which would be dangerous.

He was worried Lionel was biting off more than he could chew. It might be more than a crooked banker and the friendly neighborhood priest waiting for him down there. The kind of money involved could bring out all sorts of vermin. He'd feel better once they knew exactly what they were dealing with. Nelson took a deep breath. It was his job to keep Lionel safe. He never should have let him go down there alone. He should be closer. Nelson stretched and took another glance around his rock.

So far, so good. No critters. It was hot in the sun, but there was a little bit of a breeze. It wasn't too bad. He saw a couple of figures emerging from the forest and homed in on them.

Yep. It was Lionel and Mia, looking all the world like a young couple enjoying the Mexican countryside. They stood and looked around a minute, like any gringo couple would, and proceeded to the café, where they sat down. Mia got up and walked toward the bathroom, glancing up in his general direction. He waited. It took about a minute for his phone to ring.

"Hey," whispered Mia. "Anything?"

"Nope. Other than the nest of rattlesnakes I had to kill, everything is completely normal. No sign of our friend or the priest."

"Okay. I'll let Lionel know. Be careful."

She hung up before he could say anything else. Nelson lay back down, inched forward to the edge of the rock, and focused in on the square again. Mia was on her way back, and Lionel was sitting at the table with a couple of beers in front of him. Nelson scanned the rest of the square and stopped abruptly at the door to La Casita.

A couple of guys he hadn't seen before were leaning on the wall of the building. They were dressed in silk—or polyester—button-down shirts and slacks. *Definitely not from around here.* The guy wearing an orange shirt was smoking a cigarette, and the other one with a patterned black and white shirt just stood there with arms folded. They looked as out of place as gold teeth on a nun. He hadn't seen where they came from, but he knew they hadn't been there five minutes ago. He quickly scanned the area. No cars. Good. If he'd missed a car coming into that little town, he'd have to retire. He reached for the camera and snapped a couple pictures of the two men.

No, he thought. *They've been here for a while, hanging out in the bar or one of the other buildings. Something, or somebody, brought them outside.* The one with the cigarette leered as Mia walked past him.

Careful, asshole. She's a friend of mine.

Mia went back to the table and sat down. She exchanged a few words with Lionel and then looked up as the waiter came to their table. They ordered and Lionel turned, casually looking toward the church and the entrance to La Casita, where the two guys were standing. He turned back nonchalantly—like a good gringo—and continued his conversation with Mia.

Nelson had a bad feeling about those two. It was obvious—even from his perch—that they had pistols in their waistbands, and the way the townspeople avoided looking at them spelled bad news. They were known here, and they were feared.

They're local thugs, or maybe enforcers. Probably cartel, thought Nelson. *Their sudden appearance on the square might have something to do with Lionel. Or it could be sheer coincidence. But I don't believe in coincidences.*

He glanced up. The sun was still high in the sky but edging down toward the western mountains. It was still hot. Nelson mopped his brow and edged closer to the scrawny bush growing on the edge of the rock. It wasn't much shade, but it was better than nothing. He homed back in on Mia and Lionel.

Their food came, they ate, had another beer, and talked. All the while, the two amigos didn't move. No phone calls and no interaction with other people. A couple of older men avoided going into the bar, and the few that came out walked hurriedly past them without making eye contact.

The waiter came with the bill, and Lionel paid. He stood and stretched. Mia picked up her backpack. One of the thugs, the guy with the cigarette, took a cellphone out of his pocket and made a call. He said a few words, nodded, and then leaned over and spoke to his cohort, who nodded back. Lionel and Mia started wandering around the plaza. Lionel pointed at one of the buildings and started talking, no doubt explaining finer points of architecture and history to Mia. The amigos watched them. They weren't focused on any of the other hikers or townspeople.

They're keyed in on Lionel all right, thought Nelson. *They might not know who he is or why he's here, but somebody knows something. Or suspects it. Who tipped them off? Baker? Maybe. After putting that money in the bank, he must be expecting somebody. Which means he's nearby. But why Lionel? He's not the only gringo here. Maybe Father Mike has been in contact with the local priest—or with Baker himself.*

Nelson scanned the buildings of the square quickly, hoping to catch someone else watching. Nothing. He returned back to Mia and Lionel. They were slowly making their way to the church. As they passed La Casita, the two amigos casually stepped away from the building and followed them.

Nelson took a deep breath. He should be down there, but it would take a good twenty minutes for him to reach the plaza. If he called Mia, the amigos—and whoever had sent them—would probably guess that they were being watched, too.

The best thing to do is to sit tight. Nothing else I can do. He watched as Mia and Lionel walked into the church, and were then, shortly afterwards, followed in by the amigos.

Nelson's phone rang abruptly. He fished it out of his pocket and answered.

"Nelson," whispered Mia. "We're in the church and we've—"

The line went dead.

Chapter 15

NELSON WAITED FOR DARKNESS to settle onto San Pablo. After the lights came on in La Casita and the church, he decided it was time to start down the mountain. There was still enough daylight on the mountainside to see, so he'd be able to navigate well enough to avoid running into anything—or anybody—unfriendly. He packed up his equipment, hid it under the scrawny bush, and started down the trail.

I'll cut around behind the buildings on the square and make my way over to the back of the church, he thought. As far as he could tell, Mia and Lionel were still in there with the two amigos. Nobody had left the building since they'd gone in. Nelson wished he had a weapon, but Mexico had strict gun laws—he wouldn't have been able to get one even if they'd tried.

He walked slowly down the trail, careful to make as little noise as possible. Whoever had sent the amigos down there could very well have established a perimeter around the town, too. Chances were they had a home base nearby. Nelson stopped every fifty feet or so to listen—and to smell. One of the amigos was a cigarette smoker. He waited. Nothing. Everything was quiet.

Nelson continued on until he came to where the jungle met the edge of town. He edged around behind the buildings to where a cobblestone street, flanked by a series of stone walls, ran down to the plaza. He could see the rear of Santa Barbara outlined by the lights from the square.

Nelson watched and listened. He could hear music playing somewhere in the distance—some traditional Mexican ballad. From

La Casita, most likely. He crouched down into the shadows and began moving slowly toward the church, careful that his shoes made no noise on the worn stone. Nelson kept half an eye on the road to make sure he didn't stumble on the uneven surface—that would be the last thing he needed.

He heard a thump and stopped, noticing a small wooden door set into the wall. The door creaked and started to open slowly. Nelson stepped back into the shadows as a stooped figure stepped onto the street. It closed the door and started making its way toward the town. Nelson couldn't make out exactly who it was. It was too dark, which was good. If he couldn't see it, it couldn't see him.

The full moon was just beginning to peek over the eastern hills. It would be bright as hell when it rose in about twenty minutes. Nelson knew he'd be as easy to see as a neon light on a country road when it did. He couldn't dawdle.

He took one last look down the street and walked more quickly toward the church, keeping to the shadows of the walls lining the narrow way. He moved quietly, but not as quietly as he would have liked. He saw some people in the distance, moving across the plaza beyond the church. He stopped and waited. They were going the other way. Still no sign of the amigos. He kept going and finally reached the back of the church.

It was dark. No light shined directly on the building, and the moon wasn't fully up yet. There was a massive wooden door at the back of the church. Nelson reached up and gently pulled the handle. Locked. He scooted over to his left and poked his head around the corner of the building. *No one there.* There was a smaller, more modern door about halfway down the wall. He walked over and turned the knob. It opened. Nelson took a deep breath and slowly pulled the door open. A narrow, dimly lit hallway stretched in front of him. Light seeped into the end of the corridor. Nelson thought he could hear faint voices.

He crept slowly down the hallway, one hand feeling along the wall ahead of him, the other resting in the pocket where he kept his blackjack. *My little helper*. If push came to shove, he could whack one amigo from behind and then have a fair shot at the other guy. He wasn't counting on Lionel to help. Who knew what he'd really do in a fight? He and Mia might be tied up, anyhow. He couldn't count on either one of them.

The voices were louder now. One was lower, a man's voice, speaking quite softly with a strong Spanish accent. Nelson couldn't quite make out the words. Then Lionel started talking.

"I don't know who you think we are," he said. "But for the millionth time, we came to San Pablo to hike. That's it."

Nelson crept toward the voices. A slightly opened door stood to his right. The voices were coming from behind it. Nelson moved slowly toward the door and tried to look through the slightly opened crack. He couldn't see much. The amigo in the orange shirt was sitting on a leather couch with his feet up on a coffee table.

"Don't insult my intelligence, señor," said the other voice. "I know why you came here. You're here because of La Fuente. The gold mine."

"We don't know anything about a gold mine," said Lionel. Nelson couldn't see him from where he stood, but he sounded okay. The amigo on the couch stood up and stretched and said something in Spanish. The other voice said something back, and the first amigo started walking toward the door.

Nelson stepped back and took out his blackjack. With a little luck, he could take this one out and sucker the other guy outside. The door opened suddenly, and the amigo stepped out. He glanced down the hall, away from Nelson, who raised the blackjack and stepped toward him.

"That won't be necessary," said a voice behind him. Nelson and the amigo turned at the same time. A spindly man with white hair stood there, smiling at him. The smile faded suddenly, and he said sharply, "No lo galpeas."

Nelson turned. The guy in the orange shirt had come up behind him, ready to whack him. He sneered at Nelson and stepped back. Nelson glared back at him and slapped his blackjack into his open palm.

"Don't worry about Manuel, señor," the man said to Nelson.

Nelson turned. The skinny old guy was standing there with his hands in his pockets, cool as a cucumber.

"Who are you?" asked Nelson.

"I am Father Ignacio."

Nelson took him in. The priest was wearing a plaid, cotton button-down shirt, blue jeans, and fancy boots. He sure didn't look like a priest.

"Where's your collar?"

"Ah," said Father Ignacio, "that is the beginning of a long story." He stepped past Nelson and stood in the doorway with his hand on the knob. Manuel took a step back to give him room.

"Please," said the priest. "Why don't you join us?" He walked through the doorway.

Nelson didn't see that he had a choice. He slipped the blackjack into his pocket and stepped toward the open doorway, keeping half an eye on Manuel. He followed Father Ignacio inside.

The second amigo got up from a chair next to the couch and took a step toward Nelson when he entered, but he stopped when the priest raised a warning hand.

"No te preocupes, Jose."

Jose nodded and sat back down. Nelson glanced around the room. Lionel and Mia were sitting on a dirty, beige couch across from him. Neither one was bound. A middle-aged man wearing sunglasses was sitting on a wooden chair directly opposite them. He turned and looked at Nelson and then slowly stood.

"Whom do we have here, Father?" asked the man. It was the voice Nelson had heard outside.

"I'm not sure," said the Father. "I met him in the hall. I have a feeling he might know these two."

"Is that so?" asked the man, walking closer. The overhead light glinted off his slicked-back hair. Nelson could sense Jose stirring in the chair behind him. He resisted the urge to look at Lionel or Mia. The man with the sunglasses got to within a few inches of Nelson's face.

"Who are you, señor?" he whispered, grinning, and leaning toward Nelson. "Quien eres?"

Nelson crashed his knee into the man's crotch as he simultaneously reached for the blackjack in his back pocket. The man moaned and crumpled to the ground, his sunglasses skittering on the floor. Nelson crouched down low as he turned to face Jose and Manuel. Jose sat frozen on the chair with his mouth hanging open. Manuel stared a moment and then cannonballed into the room. As Nelson caught him on the side of the head with his blackjack, he felt someone moving behind him. He heard growling—a guttural animal sound.

Manuel teetered and took a step back before going down hard. Nelson glanced behind him. Lionel was on top of Jose, battering him viciously and yelling at the top of his lungs. His fists were a blur. He looked out of control—berserk. Nelson had seen cops lose it like that during arrests. It was ugly. Jose had given up fighting Lionel and was just trying to cover up. The man Nelson had kneed in the crotch lay on the floor moaning.

Nelson looked back at Manuel. He was on all fours trying to get up. Nelson hit him again for good measure. He stayed down this time. Lionel was still on top of Jose, pummeling furiously. Jose's face was a mess of blood. He was trying to cover up from the furious onslaught, but Lionel had one of his arms pinned down with his knees. Jose was moaning and crying. Lionel stood and somehow pulled the man to his feet. He grabbed him around the throat and slammed Jose's head against the brick wall. He leaned forward, snarling, and bit Jose on the ear. Jose screamed. Nelson lunged toward Lionel.

Mia was on his other side, pulling Lionel's arm, and shouting. Jose continued screaming. Lionel's face had turned a dark, congested red. He leaned back suddenly, holding a chunk of Jose's ear in his mouth. Blood ran down Lionel's chin as he continued beating Jose.

"Stop," shouted the old priest. "Stop this right now."

Lionel continued slamming his fists into Jose as if he hadn't heard the priest. *Maybe he hasn't*, thought Nelson. *He's gone berserk.*

Nelson could hear Mia pleading with Lionel to stop, but he never took his eyes from Jose.

"Stop it," said the father, coming over to Lionel. The priest grabbed him by the shoulder. Lionel turned around and grabbed the priest by his lapels. Nelson dove between the two to stop him. He managed to pry Lionel's fingers from the priest's collar.

"Lionel," he shouted. "Back off. Back off. I've got him. Back off. I've got him."

Lionel looked at him with unseeing, glassy eyes.

Mia got behind Lionel and started pulling him back.

"Stop it, Lionel. Stop it."

Nelson finally felt Lionel's hands loosen. His breathing came in short, ragged gasps. He blinked, took a deep breath, dropped his head, and turned away. Mia followed him as he collapsed on the couch. Nelson took a quick look around the room. Jose had taken off, leaving a trail of blood spots on the floor. The man with the sunglasses was still lying on the floor and moaning.

Nelson leaned down and rolled over the guy on the floor. No gun. He turned to Manuel, who was getting up. He was clean, too. He got up. Father Ignacio stood in front of him, both arms extended.

"What is the matter with you?" said the priest. "Why did you do that?"

"These guys work for you?" asked Nelson.

The man with the sunglasses sat up, breathing hard, and then slowly stood, covering his crotch with his hands.

"You shouldn't have done that," he hissed. Nelson felt his fists curling.

"Enough," said Father Ignacio, stepping between them. "Enough. You," he said to Nelson, pointing at the beige couch, "sit there with your friends."

"You," he said to the man with the sunglasses, pointing at the leather couch where Jose had been, "sit there."

The two eyed each other warily as they made their way to their seats. Nelson sat next to Mia, who was rubbing Lionel's back as he sat bent over, his head between his knees. There was blood on her hands. A pool of vomit steamed on the floor. Nelson gave Mia a look. She shrugged, swallowed, and continued rubbing Lionel's back.

Nelson glanced up. Father Ignacio was standing with his hands on his hips, glaring at Manuel, who was rubbing the back of his head.

Manuel said something to him in Spanish. Father Ignacio said something back that sounded like, "Shut up." Manuel nodded and walked out the door.

Father Ignacio started speaking to the man with the sunglasses. He shrugged and gestured to Nelson, saying something that sounded like, "He started it."

Which is true, thought Nelson. He had started it. And for good reason.

"So," said Father Ignacio. Nelson looked up. "What is wrong with you? Why do you come into my church and start a brawl?"

"I was defending myself," said Nelson, glancing over at Lionel. He was sitting up now, breathing heavily—but he seemed in control of himself. Mia stared at Father Ignacio, probably trying to figure out who he was.

Jesus, Lionel, thought Nelson. *What was that? He'd gone crazy. Like some sort of fit.*

Lionel glanced at Nelson and nodded as if to communicate he was all right.

You're pretty fucking far from all right, thought Nelson.

"It looked to me as if you struck first," said Father Ignacio.

Nelson looked at him a minute. What was the story here? A priest with bodyguards?—which was too nice a term for these thugs.

"Yeah, that's true," said Nelson, standing up. "I did. Because there's something very weird here. Why are guys like these hanging around a church? Who is this guy?" he asked, pointing at the man with the sunglasses.

"That is Diego," said the priest.

"Hello, Diego," said Nelson.

"Fuck you," he said. "You're lucky to be alive." Diego stood up.

"I knew you'd say something like that. That's why I hit you." He smiled. "Call it a pre-emptive strike."

"Bastard," hissed Diego.

"Boys," said Father Ignacio. "Sit down, please. Please."

Nelson sat back down. Diego slowly sat on the other couch.

"Who are you? Do you know these people?" asked the priest, gesturing toward Lionel and Mia.

Nelson glanced at them. Lionel looked pale and still a little out of it. Mia looked at Nelson but made no sign of recognition.

Well, thought Nelson. *I guess it's up to me. How much do I tell this priest? He could be hiding Baker or even working with him.*

"Yes," came a raspy voice on his right. "He's with us. We came down here to find Bradley Baker." "My name is Lionel Bing and this is Nelson West."

Nelson turned. Lionel was staring at the priest, waiting for an answer. His face was pasty white and still streaked with blood, and he was shaking. Lionel's breath came in short, ragged gasps.

Father Ignacio frowned.

"Who sent you?" he asked.

"Marilyn Baker," said Lionel. "His wife. Her husband left without word. She's worried."

Nelson took a breath. *Hopefully, the father doesn't know much about the wife. If he did, the story wouldn't hold water. It was a gamble, but a solid one.*

"His wife," said the priest, almost smirking. "Well, I have to tell you I don't know any Bradley Baker." He stood up as if to go.

He's lying, thought Nelson. *And he's pretty good at it. He knows Baker. And he knows about the wife.*

"Father," said Lionel, standing up. It looked to Nelson as if he was recovering from whatever the hell had happened to him.

"We know," he said, "that you know Bradley Baker and that you have been working together through your respective churches. We know that Mr. Baker cares deeply about the people of San Pablo and that he is helping them get over this horrible tragedy they've gone through. We saw his Bible. The one you signed."

The priest crossed his arms and cocked his head.

"Go on," he said.

"We know he wanted to help the people here any way he possibly could."

"Why do you believe he is here in San Pablo?"

Lionel shrugged. "Everything leads here," he said.

"Why did he leave home?" asked the priest. "Is he in trouble?"

Lionel paused.

"We don't know," said Lionel. "Not yet. He left suddenly, without a word. Not even to his wife. We're here to find him."

Nelson nodded to himself. *Not bad, boss. Not bad at all.*

The priest looked at Lionel a moment and rubbed the bridge of his nose.

"I do know Mr. Baker," he said, finally. "We have, as you said, worked together for the people of San Pablo. That accident was a terrible thing. I'm sorry I didn't tell you the truth just now. I didn't want to tell you without knowing what it was you wanted."

"Have you heard from him recently?" asked Nelson.

The priest stood with his hands clasped in front of him. He glanced back and forth between them, frowning.

"Don't tell them nothing, Father," said Diego.

Nelson glanced at him. He'd almost forgotten the guy was there.

"Diego, please," said the priest.

"Father, I have to remind you that Don Francisco doesn't want anyone talking to outsiders. Especially gringos."

Father Ignacio turned to face Diego.

"This is church business, Diego. Don Francisco would also not appreciate it if you got between me and my church."

Diego scowled, took a quick look at Nelson, stood up and turned to go.

"I will," said Diego, "have to inform the Don of this." He left.

Nelson half-thought about following him but decided against it. Better to get the lay of the land. Father Ignacio sat down on the sofa that Diego had recently vacated. He leaned back, crossed his legs, and gazed at the three of them on the couch. Nelson glanced down at the priest's boots. They were made of leather, dyed sky blue, decorated with extravagantly detailed embroidery, and had a very pointy toe. Nelson had seen a few guys sporting them at the airport.

"I see you like my boots," said the priest.

"Not exactly my style, but they look good. Very well-made," said Nelson.

"*Trival* boots," said Lionel.

"That's right," said the priest. "I see you know something about Mexican culture, senor."

Lionel shrugged. "A little. Father, could I trouble you for some water?"

"Of course," he said. "Excuse me a moment."

He left the room. Lionel let out a big breath and looked at Nelson.

"What's going on?" he whispered. "Who are these thugs?"

Nelson opened his mouth to answer, but Mia jumped in.

"They might be with the Rosales Cartel," she said.

Lionel nodded.

"The cartel?" said Nelson. "What the hell would they be doing in a church?"

"That's a good question." Nelson turned. Father Ignacio stood in the doorway.

"Sorry, Father," he said. "Nothing personal."

The priest smiled and even chuckled a bit. "What, indeed?" he said, in a rueful sort of way. "That is a good question. What would a man like Don Francisco want with a small church like this? If he were indeed a member of a cartel? If he was such a man, young lady, you would be right."

"Mia, Father. My name is Mia."

The priest nodded. Nelson glanced at her.

Father Ignacio handed the water bottle to Lionel and sat down on the couch opposite the three of them.

"I should say that Mia is partly right," he said. "Some people connected with a certain organization are indeed concerned with the church. They want to protect it."

"Are they shaking you down?" asked Nelson. The priest looked at him quizzically.

"I think Nelson means to ask if they're extorting you, Father," added Lionel.

"Oh," said the priest. "Okay," he said, chuckling. "No, no extortion," he said, holding up his hands. "Nothing like that. You see, many members of that—um, organization—are originally from this area. Some are from the city of Guadalajara, but many come from farms and ranches around here. They are country people. Some grew up in this very town and came to Santa Barbara Church. A few of them were even altar boys."

Mia nodded. Lionel took a drink of water.

"The Catholic Church has a very strong influence here," continued the priest. "Much stronger than in the United States. Many Mexicans stay with it their whole lives. Even criminals find comfort in the church—and perhaps they need it more than anyone." Father Ignacio studied his fingernails a moment before continuing. "Many who grew up in the church want to give back to it. Those who do well, who make money, want to donate to it. They also want to protect it."

"Was Diego an altar boy?" asked Nelson.

Father Ignacio smiled. "No, not Diego. He's not from around here, but he does work for Don Francisco, who grew up on a ranch only a few miles from here."

"Francisco Rosales," said Mia quietly, almost under her breath.

"Yes," said the priest. "He is a very wealthy man, a very powerful man, and he is very supportive of this church." He smiled. "And of me."

"How?" asked Lionel. Nelson noticed the color had returned to his face. Mostly.

"Over the past few years, he has given a number of donations to the diocese—to this church in particular."

"Is he a religious man?" asked Mia.

"Well, I think we are all religious in our own way," said the priest. "Don Francisco does feel a need to connect with his church and to God, and presently he does that through his generosity."

"So," said Nelson. "You take donations from a drug dealer? A killer? How do you sleep at night?"

Father Ignacio shrugged. "I sleep well enough. If taking his money can help the poor and the handicapped, shouldn't it be used for that rather than big cars and guns? Refusing it would help no one. Besides, even the most evil man has a soul."

"That's—" began Nelson, but Lionel held up his hand.

"That's neither here nor there," Lionel said. "We're interested in finding Mr. Baker and restoring him to his family. That's why we're here."

"Hmm," said the priest, staring at his fingernails again. "And suppose Mr. Baker does not want to be found? What if he is happier living here in Mexico?"

"Is that the case?" asked Lionel.

Father Ignacio shrugged. "Maybe," he said, raising his eyes. "I know he loves the people here very much."

"So, he is here," said Nelson.

The priest smiled.

"Could we speak to him?" asked Lionel.

"That is for him to decide," said the priest, standing up. "I will let him know you are here and that you would like to talk to him. If he wants to get in touch with you, I will tell him how to find you."

Lionel stood. Mia and Nelson followed suit.

"Thank you, Father," said Lionel. "I hope to see you soon." He reached out and shook the older man's hand.

"I will get word to Don Francisco that you are friends of this church and will not interfere with his business," said Father Ignacio. "He will not bother you. You see, I am a little worried that Diego might be warning Don Francisco about you this very moment, telling him you are a threat."

A threat to what? thought Nelson. *What's he afraid of?*

"Thank you," said Mia. "We do appreciate your help."

"You are welcome," said the priest. "If Mr. Baker agrees to see you, I will contact you when the time is right."

"We're staying at the hotel in Hidalgo," said Lionel.

The priest nodded. "I know."

Nelson nodded. He didn't like it, but there didn't seem to be much choice. The priest sighed and put his hands in his pockets.

"I wish I could be of more help," said the priest, "but you must understand that we are in a ticklish situation. There is a reason that Mr. Baker is so hard to find. You see, I am not the only one interested in his welfare."

Chapter 16

"Well, that was interesting," said Nelson. They had taken the only taxi in San Pablo, a 1967 Volkswagen van, back to Hidalgo.

Nelson was reclining on the hotel bed, watching Lionel pace the floor. He seemed to have fully recovered from his fit—his episode, frenzy, or whatever you wanted to call it.

Except for the blood on his shirt, you wouldn't suspect he had tried to bite a man's ear off a half hour ago.

Mia sat in a straight-backed chair and was staring out the window at the plaza.

"To say the least," said Lionel. "Well," he said, stopping a moment. "At least we know Baker's here."

"In hiding," said Nelson. "But from who? Don Francisco? That's what the padre implied, but I don't know what the cartel would want with him. The money?"

"Think of it, Nelson," said Mia, turning away from the window. "Baker's a banker. The cartel might see him as a very handy money launderer with connections to American and foreign banks."

"Yes," said Lionel, nodding. "That was my thought, too."

"By the way, Mia, how do you know so much about the Rosales Cartel?" asked Nelson.

Mia looked back at him.

"Research," she said. "That's what I do. I thought it might be helpful to know what we were walking into. Common sense, really."

"And so it was," said Lionel, stopping his pacing for a moment. "Thank you, Mia."

"Sure," she said.

"So, what do you know?" asked Nelson, sitting up. "Enlighten me with your brilliance."

"Well," she said, crossing her legs, "they're involved in the usual. Drugs. Cocaine, marijuana, and lately, fentanyl." She paused. "They've also been getting involved in the produce market, strong-arming smaller farmers."

"What's their deal with the church?" asked Nelson.

"It's pretty much like Father Ignacio said. Some cartel guys are heavily involved with their local churches and parishes. They donate to them directly, and in some cases, they build shrines for loved ones or even finance patron saint days."

"Trying to buy a ticket to heaven?" asked Nelson.

"I don't know," said Mia. "Maybe. I think it's more of a cultural thing. You know, almost everybody down here is Catholic. And I think for some of these guys, it's a way to support the community— you know, hearts and minds—like Hezbollah in Lebanon. Or the Black Panthers doing free breakfasts in neighborhoods."

"The Black Panthers weren't a cartel," said Nelson.

"No, but they were definitely a fringe organization and a threat to the establishment," said Mia. "They were trying to support the community in their own way. I think that's part—maybe a small part—of what Don Francisco is after, too."

"I don't know why they need to persuade anybody," said Nelson. "Scaring the hell out of people is pretty damned effective."

"And they are excellent at that," said Lionel.

"And at buying their way into heaven," muttered Nelson.

"So do half the people that go to church," said Mia. "Remember, Nelson? Treasure, talent, and time. It's part of the doctrine."

Nelson grunted in reply. It was true. His church—and the school, too—were always doing some kind of fundraising. Church fairs, auctions, spaghetti dinners, or pancake breakfasts. *I guess in some ways Don Francisco is just like any other wealthy donor*, he thought. *Mostly.*

"So, let's collate," said Lionel. "Let's review." He sat down. "We know Baker came down here, but do we really know for what? We're assuming he fled because of the fraud and was afraid of being discovered. Is that an accurate assumption?"

Nelson stared at the ceiling, thinking.

"When did they find the discrepancy?" he asked. "When did your father get hold of you?"

"A day or two before I hired you. My father said he was contacted as soon as they discovered the discrepancy—that same day, apparently."

"And Baker's wife said he'd already been gone, right?" asked Nelson.

Lionel nodded.

"That means Baker took off right around the same time your dad was contacted," said Nelson. "Maybe a little before." He thought a moment.

"How did Reynolds find out about the discrepancy?" asked Nelson.

Lionel frowned. "My dad told me Reynolds said it was brought to his attention. He didn't say by whom."

"If Baker was trying to get away," said Nelson, sitting up in the bed, "If that's the reason he came down here, he would have to have known they found out about the fraud. But he left a couple of days before your dad got hold of you. So how would he know Reynolds—or anyone—was onto him? Did he suspect he was about to be discovered?"

"I don't know," said Lionel, "but he didn't leave any loose ends to tie up. He must have been planning on coming down here no matter what."

"And Reynolds said he happened to discover the fraud a couple of days after he left. Right. That's quite a coincidence."

"It's possible," said Mia.

"But not probable," said Lionel.

"Yeah," said Nelson. "I don't like coincidences. And that's a big one."

"So," continued Lionel, "let's assume Baker was planning on coming down here beforehand. The embezzled money had already been moved from Herman and Lund to parts unknown. Most of it is still missing except for that $100,000 in Banco Centro, which sticks out like a sore thumb. Why did Baker put it there?"

"Mia and I talked about this," said Nelson. "We were thinking that Baker definitely wanted somebody, maybe us—maybe the cops—to see that money. He knew it was going to happen. Sooner or later, somebody would be going through his accounts."

"Yes," said Lionel. "I would say he wanted the loan fraud to come to light."

"But it didn't," said Mia. "Your dad called you in to keep things quiet."

"My father said he called on behalf of Reynolds' dad," said Lionel, almost to himself. "As a favor."

"So why would Baker implicate himself by putting it into the Banco Centro account?" asked Nelson.

"Maybe not himself," said Mia. "Maybe he wanted to take someone else down. Especially if he thought he was going to be left holding the bag."

"Reynolds Hanson," said Lionel.

Nelson nodded.

"I was thinking about this," said Lionel. "Reynolds helped Alteca with financing the mine. The mine blew up, and the owners defaulted on the loan. The money disappears—except for one hundred grand. Baker is on the hook for the entire amount. I wonder if some of that money was supposed to end up in Reynolds' pocket—and if it did."

"Okay," said Nelson, "but if that was the case, you'd think Reynolds would be eager to cover the whole thing up. So, who got this ball rolling?"

Lionel looked up and smiled. "That's a good question...a very good question."

Chapter 17

"WHAT DO WE DO NOW?" asked Mia. They were sitting in the Hidalgo café having breakfast. "Do you want to go hiking?"

Lionel smiled and shook his head. "Not today," he said.

Nelson yawned and stretched. He was still stiff from the stakeout and his little workout with Manuel the previous day.

"Wait, I guess," Nelson said. "We've been told to stay put."

"Not in so many words," said Lionel, "but you're right."

Lionel looked none the worse for wear from his episode the day before.

It's funny, thought Nelson, *that he hasn't said anything about it. Maybe he doesn't even remember.* He cleared his throat.

"The padre made it clear that Don Francisco wants to find Baker, too," said Nelson. They're probably watching us to see if we go to him."

"So how do we contact Baker without alerting them?" asked Mia.

"We let him find us," said Lionel.

"If and when he wants to," said Nelson.

"He'll want to," said Lionel, taking a sip of his coffee. "We're his ticket out of here."

"If he wants out," said Mia.

"He will," said Lionel, sipping his coffee.

Nelson nodded. Lionel was right. Baker probably hadn't counted on the cartel being part of the bargain. He may not have known Don Francisco was this close to the church, or that he would be so interested in his banking skills. He was probably scared shitless at this point.

He's caught between a rock and a hard place, thought Nelson. *He needs Father Ignacio to hide him from the authorities and the cartel, but now that he knows the padre is tight with Don Francisco, he won't know who to trust. We might look like the only option.*

"You really think he wants out?" asked Mia. "He went to a lot of trouble to hide out here."

"I'd think so," said Nelson. "I don't think he counted on Don Francisco being part of it."

"You think he'd know," she said. "It's not his first time at the rodeo."

"I don't know," said Nelson. "It depends how tight he is with the locals. And he was probably counting on some insulation from Father Ignacio. Who'd guess that he and Don Francisco are in bed together?"

"That's not an altogether fitting metaphor," said Lionel, "but you're right."

"Why didn't Father Ignacio warn him about Don Francisco?" asked Mia.

Another good question, thought Nelson. *Did the church have anything to do with the embezzled loan money? Does the padre know? Or maybe he needs Baker to negotiate with the cartel.*

Lionel looked up over Nelson's shoulder. Nelson turned. A young girl, maybe seven or eight, stood there staring at them. She was wearing a ruffled, turquoise dress. Her hair was pulled back with a shiny white bow.

"Hola, chica. Podemos ayudarte?" asked Mia, smiling.

The girl looked from her to Lionel to Nelson and then back to Mia. She stepped closer to the table and handed Mia a folded piece of paper, then turned and ran away. Mia unfolded the paper and handed it to Lionel.

"It's for you."

Lionel took the paper, read it, and then handed it to Nelson.

It read: "Will arrange meeting. Ask Ivan for details. B."

Nelson glanced up at Lionel, who nodded.

"Our boy is reaching out," he said, handing the paper back to Lionel. "I think he needs our help."

Lionel motioned with his head toward a spot behind Nelson. He turned. The two amigos had come into the café and were sitting at a table next to the exit. *Our friends Jose and Manuel.* Jose had a huge bandage taped to the side of his head. He was scowling at Lionel.

I don't blame you, Jose, thought Nelson. *That was quite a beating you took. I'd be pissed, too.*

Manuel got up and walked slowly over to their table. Lionel slid the note from the girl off the table and out of sight. Manuel got to the table and stopped. He hooked his thumbs in his waistband and glared at Lionel. Nelson glanced over at Jose, who hadn't budged.

"Can we help you with something?" asked Lionel pleasantly. He took a sip of his coffee and smiled at Manuel, who didn't move a muscle.

Nelson leaned forward in his chair, placing his feet directly underneath the seat.

"The paper," said Manuel softly. "Give me the paper."

"What paper?" asked Lionel.

"I saw that girl give you a paper. Give it to me."

Lionel shook his head.

"No. You're mistaken. She didn't give me anything."

Manuel frowned and leaned on the table. "You lie, senor. You are a liar. I saw her give you a paper. Now you give it to me."

Nelson started to stand but stopped when Lionel shook his head slightly. Mia shifted slightly in her chair.

"I have no paper. Look."

He stood up and emptied his pockets. The hotel key, some tissues, change, a Swiss Army knife, a bulging wallet, and a couple of business cards. But no note.

Lionel finished, smiled slightly, but never took his eyes off Manuel.

"Enough of your gringo tricks," said the amigo. "Give it to me. Now."

"You know, Manuel," said Lionel. "Father Ignacio told us that the Iglesias de Santa Barbara watches over us. All of us."

"I don't follow orders from that priest. He is not my jefe."

"I wouldn't push it if I were you," said Lionel. "You know your jefe has a lot of respect for Father Ignacio. And besides," he said, smiling. "You know what happened last time we tangled."

Manuel scowled. Nelson kept his eyes on the man's hands. He was wearing a knit polo shirt that fit him snugly. It was obvious he didn't have a gun, but that didn't mean he wasn't carrying a knife in his back pocket. Nelson wasn't about to underestimate him.

"We'll be leaving now," said Lionel. "And you won't be bothering us anymore."

Mia got up and stepped back from the table. Nelson rose slowly. Manuel turned to face him, his hand going toward his pocket.

"Don't even think about it," whispered Nelson.

"Manuel," called a voice across the restaurant. Manuel turned. Nelson looked. He saw it was Diego.

"Venga aqui. Ahora mismo!"

Manuel frowned, glanced over his shoulder, and swore under his breath. He glared at Lionel, took a step back, turned, and started walking toward Diego. Diego stood at the table next to Jose with crossed arms, staring at them, but remained where he was.

Well, thought Nelson. *It looks as if the Don does listen to the padre. Lucky for us.*

Lionel paid the bill and the three of them started walking toward the hotel. Nelson glanced at Lionel. That had been a pretty gutsy move with Manuel—and a little reckless. He hoped the boss wasn't going to start being a hero. *That would be all I need.*

"How did you hide that paper, Lionel?" asked Mia.

He smiled and shrugged. "Just a little sleight of hand."

"Nice," she said.

"Who is Ivan?" asked Nelson.

"The concierge at the hotel," said Mia.

"Do we know anything about him?"

"I don't," said Mia, turning to face Nelson. "How would I?"

Nelson shrugged. "You knew his name."

"He introduced himself," said Mia. "Remember? You were there."

Nelson grunted. He did remember. Sort of.

"It might not be a bad idea to do a little background on this Ivan," said Lionel.

"Well, Lionel," said Nelson. "Ordinarily, that would be a good idea, but this is a small town. And it's obviously full of Don Francisco's people. We might want to be discreet."

"Could you try?" asked Lionel.

"I could try," said Nelson. *Better than you doing it,* he thought. "But I bet that the padre is behind this meeting, and I would guess Ivan is someone he trusts. It had to be the padre who got hold of Baker—if this is really Baker."

"It's him," said Lionel. "Nothing else makes sense."

"Unless it's a trap," said Mia.

"Why bother with a trap?" asked Nelson. "They can take us anytime they want. They own this place."

Lionel made a sound, frowned, and stared down at the ground as they walked.

"No," continued Nelson, "they don't want us. They want Baker, and they want us to lead them to him."

"To be their new bookkeeper," said Mia.

"Yeah," said Nelson. "Or maybe they want a slice of the pie."

"How would they know about the loan?" asked Mia. "The money?"

"I don't know," said Nelson. *But I wouldn't be surprised if Father Ignacio knows*, he thought.

They had come to the hotel. Nelson held the door for Mia and Lionel. He followed Lionel into the lobby, ready to continue the conversation, but stopped when he saw two priests leaning against the desk. The concierge—Ivan—stood at the desk, smiling.

"Welcome, my friends," he said. "You have some visitors who have come all the way from Guadalajara." One of the priests walked over to them.

"Hello," he said, in nearly perfect English. "I am Father Dom and this," he continued, gesturing at the other priest, "is Father Roberto."

Father Roberto nodded but said nothing. He was tall, sported a full beard, and looked solidly built under his cassock. There was something, something that Nelson couldn't place, that made him doubt Roberto had anything to do with forgiveness and compassion—and even less to do with the priesthood.

"Hello, Fathers," said Lionel. "It's an honor to meet you. What can we do for you?"

"May you and I go somewhere a little more private?" asked Father Dom. He was probably in his mid-thirties, wore wire-rimmed glasses, and smiled constantly—nervously. He ran a hand over his bald pate, seeming to forget he had no hair to smooth down anymore.

That one, thought Nelson, *is most definitely a priest*.

"There's a room over here," said Mia, pointing toward the tiny room with the fireplace.

"Yes," said Ivan. "That would be perfect. Please," he said, coming out from behind the counter. "Let me show you."

He led Lionel and Father Dom to the small room, seated them, chatted a bit, and then left, shutting the door. Nelson glanced at Mia, who had pursed her lips. She looked at Nelson and half-shrugged.

Nelson glanced at Father Roberto, who stood at the desk with his hands clasped behind him. He stared at Nelson, who stared right back.

Nope, that is no priest, thought Nelson. *Maybe a bodyguard. Or a bouncer. Or a cop. Father Bad Boy.*

He stepped closer to the priest, who didn't move. Nelson leaned against the counter.

"Howdy," he said, smiling. Nothing.

"Habla inglés?" he asked. The priest shook his head.

Mia came over and leaned on the counter next to Nelson.

"Hola," she said. "Como estas?"

The priest shrugged but said nothing.

"Eres de Guadalajara?"

He nodded.

"Por que quieres hablar con Lionel?"

Nelson nudged her. She turned to him.

"I'm asking why they want to talk with Lionel," she whispered.

Why is she whispering?

"No se," said the priest. "El padre Dom sabe de qué se trata todo esto."

"Gracias."

Mia nodded and turned to Nelson.

"He doesn't know," she said, still whispering.

"Right," said Nelson, loud enough for the priest to hear. The man didn't move a muscle. Maybe he really didn't understand English. Not that it mattered. He wasn't talking either way.

Mia left the counter and motioned for Nelson to follow her. They sat down.

"He's not very friendly," mused Mia.

"Nope."

"So," she whispered. "What do you think they want with us?"

"I don't know."

The only thing he could figure was that they were there to keep things quiet. Publicity about cartel money—blood money—going into the collection plate wouldn't be welcome at the archdiocese. Or in the newspapers. Or on television.

"They might be trying to keep a lid on things," he said. "Especially if the cartel is involved. I'm sure they don't want bad publicity."

Mia nodded. "They sure don't need it."

True that, thought Nelson. *Are these the guys keeping Baker under wraps? Could he be a prisoner of the Catholic Church?* He shook his head and felt himself smiling.

"You're doing it again," Mia whispered.

"What?"

"Smirking for no reason."

"Oh. Sorry."

He wasn't, though. It was funny. He had a reason.

Nelson glanced over at Father Roberto. He was the first bearded priest Nelson had ever seen in person. He knew some denominations required their priests to be bearded, but Nelson hadn't known it was an option—like the long-haired young priests he'd grown up with who sometimes grew their hair into Afros or ponytails in an effort to convince their flock that they were cool and hip to the problems of young people. But beards hadn't been an option back then. Or maybe Father Roberto wasn't a priest.

The door to the private room opened and Lionel came out, followed closely by Father Dom.

"Thank you," said Father Dom. He smiled at Nelson and Mia and then gestured to Father Roberto. They left.

Lionel put his hands in his pockets and glanced back toward the desk. He seemed nervous. He cleared his throat.

"I need to go upstairs for a minute to make a phone call," he said. "Why don't you two meet me at the pool in about five minutes?"

Nelson nodded. Mia opened her mouth as if to say something but quickly shut it. Lionel went up the stairs, two steps at a time. Nelson followed Mia into the courtyard. They sat down by the pool. There was no one else there. Nelson wondered for a moment if they were the only ones staying in the hotel.

"What's that all about?" he said. "Who's he calling?"

Mia shook her head.

"I don't know," she said, looking off toward the lobby.

Yes, you do, thought Nelson. "Come on," he said.

She glanced toward lobby again and then looked back at Nelson.

"I don't know. I really don't."

His therapist, maybe? thought Nelson. *That Dr. Ribot?*

He glanced at Mia, who was still sneaking looks at the lobby.

All right, thought Nelson, sitting back. *Be that way. I'll find out.*

Lionel appeared suddenly next to Mia's lounger. He seemed excited and energized.

"Let's go," he said. They followed him out of the lobby and out to the rental car. Mia and Lionel got into the backseat. Nelson slid behind the wheel.

"Where to, boss?"

Lionel unfolded a map and pointed toward the road to the main highway. "Get to the main road and turn left," he said.

"What's happening, Lionel?" asked Mia. Nelson glanced in the rear-view mirror. Lionel turned to Mia and smiled.

"We're heading to La Fuente. The gold mine," he said.

Chapter 18

Lionel explained that La Fuente was only about a mile east of San Pablo, but they'd have to take some precarious mountain roads to get there.

"Father Dom thought that this would be the best way to get up there," said Lionel, glancing up toward Nelson, who nodded. "So as to avoid attention. It's sort of a back door."

Nelson nodded. That made sense. They wouldn't be hauling truckloads of ore down a little dirt road. There had to be another more accessible route.

"Who is Father Dom?" asked Mia. "And that other priest. He was a little frightening."

"They're from the archdiocese in Guadalajara," said Lionel, speaking rapidly. "Father Ignacio filled them in about us. I'm not sure exactly how much they know. They do know we're looking for Baker, and they're aware of his involvement with the church. They came down to ask us to keep things quiet."

Nelson nodded. That's what he'd first thought, but something about the story didn't quite gel. *Why send two priests? Or, for that matter, why didn't the archdiocese voice their concerns through Father Ignacio? Didn't they trust him?*

"Is that it?" asked Nelson.

"No," said Lionel. "Father Dom told me he was also sent to set up a meeting between us and an interested party. And that there would be certain conditions."

"What sort of conditions?" asked Mia.

"You'll see."

"Who are we meeting?" asked Nelson.

"Well," said Lionel, "He didn't say specifically, but Father Dom told me the church wants to help Mr. Baker—and that they want us to hear his side of the story."

Nelson sighed inwardly. *This was not an ideal situation. Going to a remote location without backup was never a good idea, and here—in a town teeming with cartel thugs—it could be suicidal.*

"What exactly did the priest say?" asked Nelson. He tried but couldn't quite keep the edge out of his voice.

"Well, he told me that the archdiocese was concerned about our dealings with Father Ignacio and the local church. Father Dom asked me why we're here. They already knew about Baker working with Father Ignacio. He wanted to know why we're involved."

"What'd you say?" asked Mia.

Lionel shrugged. "The same thing I told Father Ignacio. That his wife hired us to find him."

"Did he believe you?" asked Mia.

"I think so."

"So why are we going to the mine?" asked Nelson. "Was that Father Dom's idea, too?"

Lionel shook his head and smiled. "No, that was set up by Father Ignacio."

"Who are we meeting?"

"I can't really say for sure."

"Why not?"

"Because I don't know for sure. But don't worry, Nelson," said Lionel, looking at him. "Everything has been taken care of."

"Really? How do you figure that? How do you know who's up there?"

"I don't, but I trust Father Ignacio."

This is bullshit, thought Nelson.

"Who did you call?"

"That call was personal, Nelson," retorted Lionel, his voice rising. "It's none of your business."

The hell it's not.

Nelson pulled over to the side of the road, which was not much more than a tire track, and turned around in his seat. Lionel's mouth was set, and he was hands were balled into fists. He was getting angry. Nelson didn't care.

"Listen, Lionel," he said. "You hired me as a consultant to help with investigations, right?"

Lionel nodded, breathing hard. He was trying to control himself.

"This whole situation is no good. It's dangerous. Unless you can tell me something to change my mind, I'm not taking you up there."

"Nelson," said Lionel, leaning forward, speaking low, carefully enunciating every word.

He's really pissed, thought Nelson, *and he can't quite hide it.*

"Nelson," he continued, "you'll have to trust me on this one. It's going to be fine."

Nelson let his breath out slowly.

"I don't blame you for worrying," continued Lionel. "In fact, I'd be disappointed if you hadn't said anything, but I can assure you it'll be safe. I can't tell you why, but I know it. In here," he said, tapping his chest.

A feeling. Jesus Christ.

"Remember, we're under the church's protection. They're the ones who set up this meeting. We'll be fine."

Not if we end up dead, thought Nelson. He looked at Mia, whose face was pinched with worry.

Well, I knew working with a rookie—especially as my boss—would be tough, but I did sign on the dotted line.

"All right, Lionel, I hope the hell you know what you're doing."

He started the car and pulled out onto the rutted road.

"Yeah," said Mia. "You'd better not get us killed."

"I think you two are being overly dramatic," said Lionel.

Nelson drove slowly. The dirt road was little more than one lane. He supposed two cars could squeak by each other, if necessary, but he didn't want to try if he didn't have to. *And God help us if we run into a bus,* he thought. The road snaked upward, rounding blind corners as it hugged the mountain. Off to the left, past the narrow shoulder, was a nearly vertical drop of at least one hundred feet.

Shit, he thought. *Just take your time, Nelson, take your time.*

After what seemed like an eternity, the road leveled out onto a broad plateau. Two low, prefab buildings clung to the edge on the far side. A mine entrance built into the mountainside stood directly behind them. It looked more primitive than Nelson had expected, like something out of *Treasure of the Sierra Madre.* The mouth to the mine was hewn out of the rock.

"There it is," said Lionel. "La Fuente."

It didn't look like much. They stared at it for a moment.

"Where did it happen?" asked Nelson. He realized he was whispering.

"On the third level," said Lionel, his voice low. "They were trapped inside."

Nelson glanced over at Lionel, who was staring at the entrance of the mine. His mouth was set in a straight line, and he was breathing heavily. A sheen of sweat stood out on his forehead. He looked away, toward Mia, and took a deep breath.

"Trapped inside," said Mia. "It must have been awful."

"Well," said Nelson. "I don't see anyone else here. No cars. Do you know where we're supposed to meet?"

Lionel nodded.

"Yes," he said. "In there."

He pointed toward the mine.

"You're kidding me," said Nelson. "You agreed to this?"

"Yes," said Lionel, opening the car door. He got out. Mia got out on her side. Nelson sighed, gripped the wheel, swore under his breath, and got out himself. *Ninety-five thousand a year is not enough for this shit. Even with health insurance.*

* * *

Nelson stood up and stretched. The aluminum chairs just inside the tunnel mouth were hard and uncomfortable. They'd been sitting there waiting for well over a half hour. Mia kept moving around the chamber, trying to raise a signal on her phone. Nothing. Not even outside the mouth of the mine. Lionel was sitting calmly in his chair, his head leaning against the wall and his hands resting on his thighs. His eyes were closed.

Who's it going to be? thought Nelson, sitting back down. *Baker? Or Manuel and Jose? That would be fun. Jesus.*

Lionel opened his eyes and stretched. *Relaxed as a cat on a radiator,* thought Nelson. *Does he know what he's doing, or is he playing a hunch? I don't know. After yesterday, why should I trust his judgement?*

And today, too. Lionel had been erratic all day. He had been hyper—giddy—after talking to Father Dom, but he was calm now. Night and day. Nelson sighed inwardly. He knew he'd need to be prepared to step in if things got ugly. He wouldn't like having to overrule his boss, but he was thinking more and more that he might have to.

Something clanged from somewhere within the mine. A door? The sound echoed hollowly in the rocky tunnel. Nelson peered into the darkness beyond the single overhead light. It was impossible to see anything, but he could hear footsteps. He stood up. Mia went over and stood beside Lionel's chair. The steps came closer, echoing loudly through the narrow tunnel. Nelson glanced back at Lionel, who sat with his arms crossed and one leg folded over the other, waiting.

Okay, thought Nelson. *Here we go.*

"Hello," a voice sounded from beyond the darkness. It was high and tinny. "Mr. Bing, is that you?"

American, thought Nelson, with a sense of relief.

"Yes, it's me," called out Lionel. "I'm here with some friends."

The footsteps stopped abruptly.

"I was told you'd be alone."

"I'm here with my associates, Nelson West and Mia Wentworth. They came down here with me from the States to help get this thing straightened out."

"Mr. West, could you step forward, please," asked the voice. It was a little whiny, almost petulant. "I'd like to have a better look at you."

Nelson glanced back at Lionel, who nodded, and stepped to the middle of the chamber. He glanced behind him and winced. The light coming through the mouth of the tunnel made him an ideal target.

I feel like a deer on the first day of hunting season.

He stood there, waiting. Nothing. Whoever was in there was taking his time. Nelson swallowed. He balled his hands into fists and tried to keep still.

"Are you armed?"

"No, he's not," called out Lionel. "You can trust us."

"I'd like Miss Wentworth to come forward, too. I need to see her, too."

Lionel nodded to Mia, and she rose and walked to where Nelson was standing. She stood behind him, slightly to one side.

Smart, thought Nelson.

"Is that everyone?"

"Yes," said Lionel. "That's it."

"All right," said the voice. "I'm coming out."

The footsteps began again. Nelson squinted into the darkness. A lighter patch of darkness was drawing nearer. He couldn't make much out yet. Then the shape began to take form. It was a man, an older man, with a full head of wild, silver hair. Einstein hair. He was disheveled, thin, wiry looking, and was wearing a dirty button-down plaid shirt and a very worn pair of jeans. As the man came closer, his piercing, cobalt-blue eyes gleamed through old-fashioned, wire-rimmed glasses.

They weren't focused on any one thing in particular but seemed to be looking everywhere and taking in everything all at once. His shirt had a patch embroidered over the breast pocket. As he came closer, Nelson recognized him.

Bradley Baker. Finally.

He felt Lionel brushing past him.

"Mr. Baker," he said. "It's a pleasure to finally meet you."

Jesus, Lionel, thought Nelson. *Calm down. He's not your prom date.*

"Hello, Mr. Bing," said Baker, smiling.

"This is Miss Wentworth," said, Lionel, gesturing to Mia.

"It's a pleasure," said Baker, bowing his head.

"And Mr. West," said Baker, walking toward him.

Nelson nodded.

"We've been looking for you, Baker," he said. "I think you have some explaining to do."

"Yes, Nelson," said Lionel, raising his hand. "Of course. But not right now. I think Mr. Baker has something to show us first."

"Thank you for coming here," said Baker, clasping his hands in front of him. "I know you must have a lot of questions, Mr. West, and I really do want to clear things up."

Lionel smiled a little and nodded. Mia glanced at Nelson and raised her eyebrows. Nelson took a deep breath.

"Good," said Lionel.

"Well, that's great," said Nelson.

"Well," said Baker, "First things first. I brought you here to see the mine—to see all of it—and to really understand what happened here. It plays a significant role in this entire incident."

He squeezed the bridge of his nose between his thumb and forefinger and grimaced.

"Are you all right?" asked Lionel.

"Yes," said Baker. "I get occasional headaches. I think it might have something to do with the air quality down here. Please," he added, gesturing toward the back of the mine. "If you wouldn't mind."

Lionel stepped ahead, and Baker swung in behind him. Mia looked at Nelson, who shrugged, and continued on.

Why the hell are we following this guy down into a hole in the ground? thought Nelson. *We should really just toss him in the car and head back home. Get the hell out of here. The cartel is after him, and I sure as hell don't want them breathing down our necks.*

A series of overhead lights switched on. Motion detectors. A large, caged elevator stood at the end of the corridor. Baker and

Lionel walked down to it and stepped on. Nelson and Mia followed them.

"It was a miracle that the elevator wasn't damaged in the blast or the subsequent cave-in," said Baker, "but it took some time to clear the rubble away from the shaft. It still works."

"What happened, exactly?" asked Mia. "We never got the whole story."

"The whole story," said Baker, leaning on the guardrail on the back of the elevator, "is that a lot of good people—innocent people—died because of greed and negligence. Over eighty miners and workers were in here the day it happened. Nearly all of them were killed. Only a few escaped. Those who weren't killed by the initial explosion were suffocated or crushed by subsequent cave-ins."

He gazed down at the elevator floor and clasped his hands together again.

"Nine of them are still down there," he said. "They're in a place that's too risky to dig." He looked up. His eyes were shiny. "You see, the third level has become a graveyard." Baker sighed. "At least until they figure out a way to clear it out," he added.

"Can it be done?" asked Mia.

"Oh, yes," said Baker. "It's possible to do it safely. But the owners have disappeared. No one knows where they are, and work can't start without their permission."

"So, what are you doing down here?" asked Nelson. "Hiding?"

"Me?" asked Baker. "Here in the mine? No. I have nothing to hide. Or do you mean am I hiding here in San Pablo? That is another no. No, I'm down here for another reason entirely. Didn't Father Ignacio tell you?"

Nelson shook his head.

"I thought he might have said something."

"Like what?" asked Nelson.

He could usually tell when a suspect was lying, but he wasn't getting that from Baker. Unless the guy was really good at bending the truth—and Baker didn't look like the type—he was being honest. So far.

"Why don't we take a look at the third level before we get into all that," said Baker. "I think we need to go below and see the impact of this horrible incident."

He looked at each of them in turn.

"Are we ready?"

Lionel nodded. Baker pressed the down button. The elevator roared to life and lurched into motion. They descended slowly into darkness. Helmets were hanging on the back rail, and Baker handed one to each of them and then demonstrated how to switch on the light.

"There's still no power on the third level," he explained.

"Are we going down to three?" asked Mia. Nelson noticed she was clutching the handrail. *Afraid of heights?* he thought. *Or depths?*

"Yes," he said. "That's where the explosion occurred."

"What happened?" asked Mia. "You still haven't said."

"An underground drill rig set off the explosion," said Baker. "A couple of the surviving miners thought it might have been a methane leak. It's not unusual that they'll hit pockets of it while getting at the gold."

Light started coming in from beneath the elevator.

"Here's level two," said Baker. "We only had a few fatalities here. Smoke inhalation mostly. Almost everyone here was able to get out."

Huge overhead globes lit up a monstrous tunnel lined with a set of tracks heading into the darkness. A huge loader stood at the far end. The elevator continued down past a wall of uneven rock.

Nelson felt a draft hitting his face. *We must be coming up on the third level*, he thought. He could sense open space in front of him, but he couldn't see a thing. It was dark here—black dark. The elevator stopped suddenly.

Baker switched on his helmet light. A feeble, yellow beam picked out rubble, boulders, pieces of clothing, lunch pails, and what looked like abandoned equipment. An enormous machine, maybe a drill rig, lay on its side. The tunnel was completely blocked off about thirty yards away from the elevator. Mia, and then Lionel, switched on their helmet lamps.

"Aren't you turning yours on?" whispered Mia.

Nelson shook his head.

"No," he said. "I can see fine."

It might be better for one of us not to be seen, he thought.

"Eighty-seven people died down here," said Baker softly, almost in a whisper. "They were stacking their bodies like firewood here on the elevator."

"We heard children worked here," said Mia. Baker looked at her, the yellow beam of his helmet swinging across the walls of the tunnel before resting on her face. "Father Mike told us that."

"You've spoken to Father Mike?" asked Baker, a surprised and almost petulant tone entering his voice.

"Yes, we did," said Lionel. "We also spoke to your wife and to co-workers at Con Union."

"We know about Hindman, Herman and Lund, and all the shuffling that went on," said Nelson.

Baker nodded, the light on his helmet bouncing over the jumbled rubble in the mine.

"That's a long and complicated story," said Baker. "And an ugly one." Nelson thought he saw the shadow of a frown crossing Baker's face.

"I can't wait to hear it," said Nelson.

"Why do you keep coming here?" asked Lionel. "To the mine, I mean."

"I'm working on something—something important. Something redemptive. Something holy. You see, there are still nine miners missing. I'm trying to locate the bodies buried here. I've found seven so far. They will all need Christian burials." He sighed in the darkness. "I knew most of them. They were all good Catholics. Good men. My father-in-law died down here that day. I'm still trying to find his body."

"Your father-in-law?" said Mia. "Marilyn's father?"

"No," Baker said. "Not exactly." The light on his helmet flipped slightly to the side.

"Do you have a wife in San Pablo?" asked Lionel.

"Well, no, not exactly," said Baker. "You met my real wife—my legal wife, Marilyn. Her father died years ago. He was not a very nice man. Ivan Reposado was more of a father to me than he ever was. He was a fine man who graciously took me into his family after his daughter and I fell in love."

Oh, brother, thought Nelson.

"What's her name?" asked Mia.

"Esperanza. It means hope."

"It also means to wait," said Mia.

"Well, I suppose they're both pretty much the same thing, aren't they?" asked Baker. "Hope happens when you're waiting. That's what happened to me."

"So, you do have family down here," said Nelson. "Sort of. Interesting."

Baker nodded. "I guess you could say they're a surrogate family, but they're more of a genuine family than my own ever was."

"What about your sons?" asked Nelson.

"Mark is a good boy, but he never wanted to have much to do with me. I had the feeling that I embarrassed him—that he was more or less ashamed of me. I haven't seen his brother for years."

No one said anything.

"Are you married to this Esperanza?" asked Nelson.

"No. Not yet."

"Does she know about your wife in the States?"

Baker sighed.

"I haven't exactly told her the entire truth. She thinks I'm a widower."

"You're right. That is a little less than the entire truth," said Nelson.

"You've been lying to her," said Mia.

"No, not really," said Baker. "I told her I couldn't marry her until I settled all my business back home. Technically, that's true."

"And that would include a divorce?"

Baker nodded. "I don't love Marilyn. She hasn't loved me for years. Mark is out of the house, so why keep living a lie? And now, because of the accident, Esperanza has lost her father, her brother, and two cousins. She needs me. Her sisters and cousins all need me. The whole town needs help."

His voice hitched.

Come on, thought Nelson. *Are you kidding me?*

Baker cleared his throat.

"Why don't I show you the full extent of what happened down here, per our agreement. Then we can go upstairs and talk," he said.

"All right," said Lionel. "Let's go."

And the sooner the better, thought Nelson. This place was giving him the creeps.

Baker pulled up the elevator guardrail and stepped into the tunnel. Lionel and Mia were right behind him. Nelson hesitated a moment before following. This still didn't feel right.

Baker says he's down here to look for bodies, thought Nelson. *That doesn't really make sense. Why is he really here?*

He glanced over at Lionel. *He and Mia are buying this stuff hook, line, and sinker*, Nelson thought. *C'mon. This guy walks away with five million bucks, and now he has these two eating from the palm of his hand. They're treating him like some poor lost soul because of this little sob story.*

Baker stopped by the overturned machine.

"This," he said, "is exactly like the drill rig that we think caused the explosion. The defective one is further down the tunnel, behind all the rubble."

He motioned toward a black box on the cab.

"You see this?" he asked. "This little device is supposed to shut down the rig as soon as any methane is detected to stop it from sparking an explosion. According to one of the survivors, the detector on the other rig, the one that blew up further down the mine, was missing."

"Why would that be?" asked Mia.

"Because the company that ran this place was too cheap to replace it," said Baker, a note of anger in his voice. "If you look around, you'll see dozens of other safety violations."

"Why weren't they reported?" asked Mia.

Baker shrugged. Nelson thought he saw the shadow of a frown in the dim light.

"Well," he said, "government regulation down here is spotty at best. There's a fair amount of corruption—you know, one hand washing the other."

Nelson nodded. Don Francisco and the cartel could be a big part of that. Maybe they helped with the financing. Maybe they had decided to take the whole operation over, blow it up, and start from scratch. That would be another reason for them to want to get their hands on Baker—to shut him up.

Especially, thought Nelson, *if he's going to turn into a whistleblower. And he's the type.*

"Follow me," said Baker. He started carefully picking his way among the fallen rocks and rubble.

"How stable is the mine now?" asked Lionel.

"It seems to be pretty good," said Baker, his headlight pointing up suddenly. "I haven't felt any sort of movements for a couple of days."

Mia made a sound in the darkness.

That's reassuring, thought Nelson. *That's wonderful.*

They made their way past the tipped-over drill auger and climbed a waist-height pile of rocks and rubble.

"There's a mobile car under there," said Baker. "Sort of like a golf cart."

They came to a larger pile of rocks and debris, including smaller separate stacks of tools, helmets, and shoes. Nelson thought he spotted what looked like a boot on top of one stack. He looked closer and realized a foot was still in it. Next to it was a sort of shelf unit with all sorts of stuff on the shelves.

Baker bent down and turned on a battery-powered lamp. Nelson saw the shelf unit was stacked with photos, flowers, and prayer cards. It looked like some sort of altar. There were dozens of framed pictures on it. Men, boys, and children all smiled up through the flickering lamplight. Cans of soda, beer, bottles of tequila, and trays of food also stood on the shelves. There was even a box of Twinkies. Personal articles like pocketknives, crosses, and lockets lay stacked in neat piles.

"An ofrenda," murmured Mia.

"Yes," said Baker. "An offering. And a tribute to those who died here."

"What is it?" asked Lionel. His voice was hushed, barely more than a whisper.

"I have placed offerings for the dead here," said Baker.

"Like Day of the Dead?" asked Mia.

"Yes and no," said Baker. "Los Muertos is a celebration of the day when the dead return to visit the living. Ofrendas are set up next to the loved one's grave, and families stay all night to wait to greet them." He looked up at them, his face shining in the half-light. "These souls never left. They are still trapped here. I am letting them know with this ofrenda that I am here, working to get them started on the road to heaven."

"That doesn't sound very Catholic," said Mia.

"No," said Baker. "It's not. You see, this situation is so unusual it called for a different kind of liturgy. I drew on the old Mexican traditions to enhance the process—to reach God."

"You made up your own religion," said Nelson. "That's blasphemy. What would Father Mike say?"

"I did no such thing," said Baker sharply. "Absolutely not. There's nothing new here. It's all been done before. And besides, I know—I know in my heart that it's all one with God. He is with me here, helping me save these victims' souls."

No one said anything. Lionel cleared his throat.

"What is this?" asked Lionel, pointing at the mound of objects next to the ofrenda.

"I've collected the survivors' effects and placed them here," he said. "When the time comes, they will take the miners up to the surface and bury whatever's left in hallowed ground. Not here, but in hallowed ground."

At the bottom of the large pile of debris stood a wooden cross. Baker shined his helmet light onto it for a moment. Nelson could read the name Carlos Garcia. Baker knelt down in the dirt, crossed himself, and hung his head. He started murmuring.

Is that Latin? thought Nelson. *He's praying.* He glanced over at Mia. She had her head bowed. Lionel had his hands folded in front of him. Nelson couldn't see his face for the glare.

Baker finished, crossed himself, stood up abruptly and brushed himself off.

"That's where Carlos is," he said, nodding toward the cross. "Most of him, at least. He was Esperanza's cousin. He was only twelve years old." The beam from his helmet played over the pile. Two more crosses were placed in different spots.

"How did you know where to find them?" asked Lionel.

"I found one of Carlos' shoes right here," said Baker, pointing. "Alejandro's helmet was half-buried near the elevator. I found part of a hand; I'm not sure whose, but I put it in a shoebox and mounted a cross near where I found it. I don't know exactly where the bodies are, but these markers are close. The crosses will guarantee they're careful when they start digging. That's what's important. Right?"

"Of course," said Mia.

"Part of a hand," mused Lionel. His voice sounded off, distant.

This is crazy, thought Nelson. *Over the top. Let them rest in peace, Baker. They're already buried, for Christ's sake.*

"They lie in unhallowed ground," said Baker, as if reading Nelson's mind. "They need to be laid to rest properly. And they will be moved."

"So," said Nelson, glancing around the tunnel. "This is what you wanted to show us?"

"What more do you want to see? Bodies? Blood?"

"You made your point," said Lionel, "but we already knew there was a tragedy here."

"Yeah, why bring us down here?" asked Nelson. "You could have told us all this on the surface."

"I wanted you to see God's truth," he said, his voice rising. "I wanted you to see the scope of what really happened. I wanted you to see this terrible place. This was hell down here—a real hell. I wanted you to see the evil that was caused by the greed and the avarice. This," he said, "is the devil's work. This is hell on Earth made possible by mortal man. And I wanted you to see my work, to understand why I did what I did and to see how I am following God's will."

His voice had taken on the lilt and tenor and volume of a preacher.

This guy thinks he's God, thought Nelson.

The beam from Baker's helmet lamp swung around to shine on Lionel. He squinted as the light shone into his eyes.

"What you won't find down here," said Baker, "is the pain and the suffering still left on the surface. You won't see the scores of families unable to make a living. Starving. You won't find the widows or the fatherless children or the grieving parents. You won't find the men who ran this mine, either. Or the owners. You won't find the evil wrought on the living up there and the dead down here."

He snorted slightly and turned around, the beam of his light flashing on the wooden crosses placed on the hill of rubble.

"You won't find the sword of justice down here, but you will find it on the surface. I've guaranteed that." His voice had risen. It echoed off the walls.

Hallelujah, thought Nelson. *He's got to testify.*

"Tell me, Bradley," said Lionel, stepping forward. "Where will you find justice for Carlos and Ivan? And all the others? Where is it?"

Bradley looked at him and then dropped his head.

"All you'll find down here is dust and rock and darkness and death," said Baker. He took off his helmet and switched off the light.

"Come with me and I'll show you God's work."

Chapter 19

THE ELEVATOR HUMMED NOISILY. Nelson breathed deeply when he saw daylight seeping through the top of the elevator shaft. *Thank God*, he thought. Fresh air. He wasn't sure whether it was the actual air quality or the closeness of the cave—or his own paranoia—that was making him anxious, but he felt his chest loosening as the sliver of light increased. He glanced to his left. Mia was also looking up at the light and smiling. Lionel was staring at his hands on the guardrail and frowning.

Is he having another anxiety attack? thought Nelson, edging toward him slightly. Lionel turned his head and glanced over at him. Nelson saw him half-smiling in the gray light. He seemed fine. The elevator was almost at the main level. Nelson squinted as the light streamed into the open car.

"Okay," said Baker, pulling up the guardrail. "We're here." He stepped off the elevator.

"Mr. Baker," said Lionel, following him. The man turned. "We've humored you by following you down into the mine," said Lionel. "We've seen what happened, and we appreciate what you've done, but I'm afraid we need some answers now."

Baker looked at him, smiling. Mia stepped off the elevator, and Nelson followed.

"What happened to the money?" asked Lionel. Nelson glanced at him. He wasn't smiling now. His face was set, getting close to angry.

"The money," said Baker. "As if that's what's important."

"Some people would say five million dollars is pretty important," said Lionel.

"People like Reynolds Hanson, I suppose," said Baker, putting his hands in his pockets. "He's the one who sent you down here, isn't he?"

Lionel crossed his arms. Nelson glanced toward the open mouth of the mine. He'd rather they had this discussion somewhere else. Being in the open like this was risky.

"What makes you say that?" asked Mia.

"Money is Reynolds' life. That's all he cares about," said Baker.

"How did he find out you took the money?" asked Nelson. "What tipped him off?"

"He knew from the beginning," said Baker. "It was all his idea. It was his money—the money he stole. That I took."

"Can we get out of here?" asked Nelson. Anyone could walk right in and corner them. They were too exposed standing here.

Lionel looked up at him and frowned. He seemed irritated at being interrupted.

"It's not safe here, Lionel. Anyone could waltz right in here."

"Oh," said Lionel. He glanced at the mine opening and nodded.

Clueless, thought Nelson.

"All right," said Baker. "We could go back to my place. Would that do?"

Lionel glanced at Nelson who nodded—reluctantly. He'd rather be on neutral ground, where there'd be less of a chance of being ambushed. He glanced over at Mia, who was staring at Baker over the top of her sunglasses. *She doesn't like it either*, he thought.

They walked out into the bright sunlight, shading their eyes. Nelson did a quick scan. *Nobody here*—at least no one he could see. They got into the car. Baker sat in the front seat next to Nelson and directed him out of the main driveway, down the mountain, and onto the main highway. After about half an hour of driving, Nelson could see the shimmering surface of water in the distance.

"That's Lake Chapala. We're almost there."

He directed Nelson down a dirt road and up to a flat area, where a small, yellow, brick and stone house stood. A horse and a burro stood at a hitching post to the left of the door. Baker got out and trotted to the door. Nelson left the car running. He got out and stood behind the open driver's side door and motioned for Mia and Lionel to stay in the car. If they had to, he could jump in and get out quick.

As Baker approached the front door, it burst open, and a group of children came tumbling out. They ran to him, jumping and shouting and wrapping themselves around his legs.

"Well," said Nelson, glancing back at Mia and Lionel, "I guess we're okay here."

* * *

They sat around the small kitchen table, sipping horchata. Nelson liked it. It sort of tasted like liquid rice pudding. A young woman stood by the stove with her hands clasped together under her apron. She was pretty, young—a little south of thirty—and very polite and gracious.

"This is Esperanza," said Baker, gesturing toward the young woman. "She's my fiancée."

Mia nodded. Baker said something to the girl in Spanish. She nodded and smiled. Baker said something else, but the girl shook her head and blushed.

"She's working on her English," he explained, "but she's too embarrassed to speak it in front of strangers—especially Americans."

"We don't bite," said Mia.

Baker smiled. Mia smiled back.

"So this is your spread," said Lionel.

"Yep. Well, it's not mine. Esperanza inherited it from her mom's family."

Nelson looked around. If Baker had the money, he sure wasn't throwing it around. This place was nice and presentable, but it sure didn't cost anything close to what was taken from the bank.

"Are those your kids?" Mia asked.

"God, no," said Baker. "I don't have that kind of energy—or time. And besides," he continued, suddenly looking serious, "we're not married yet."

"Does the original Mrs. Baker know about your pending marriage?" asked Nelson. He glanced over at Lionel, who sat with his arms crossed across his chest, just staring.

"Not yet," said Baker, glancing at Esperanza. "I'll be serving Marilyn the divorce papers in about a month." He reached over and grabbed Esperanza's hand. The girl blushed again.

Oh brother, thought Nelson.

"Whose are they?" asked Mia, smiling at a little girl standing next to her at the table. Esperanza had already shooed most of the kids outside.

"Esperanza watches them for three of her cousins. They're off working in town." He frowned. "Because of the accident."

"The accident," said Lionel, nodding. "Because of the mine accident," he repeated softly.

"Yes," said Baker. "These children all had fathers, uncles, or brothers who worked there. They didn't make it out. Now their moms have to work."

Lionel nodded. Nelson took a deep breath. He had never seen anyone be this polite to a suspected felon before. The cop in him started bristling.

"So, Mr. Baker," said Nelson, leaning back in his chair, "we would like to know what happened at Consolidated Union. They seem to be short a little money."

Baker sighed and said something to Esperanza, who nodded and took the little girl by the hand and led her outside.

"Yes," he said. "About five million dollars, I believe."

"Where is it, Mr. Baker?" asked Nelson, leaning forward.

"It's in a safe place."

"Why did you take it?"

"He didn't," said Lionel. "At least not initially." He put his hands on the edge of the table and pushed his chair back. "Did you?"

Baker smiled at him—the smile of a believer. A chosen one.

Lionel stared at him, then then glanced at Nelson.

"Reynolds Hanson was behind the original loan fraud," said Lionel, "wasn't he, Mr. Baker?"

Baker nodded.

"Yes," he said. "Reynolds thought the mine would be a great investment. You probably know by now that his father's company, Farragut, had a controlling interest in it. Con Union had been working in this area for some time, doing various investments. Real estate, mostly." He paused and took a drink. "Reynolds brought La Fuente to my attention a few years back. He told me that he thought modernizing it would make it twice as profitable and that it would be a great investment for the local community. He told me to come down and do some feasibility studies. I did." He took another drink. "I did."

"What happened?" asked Mia.

"It all checked out. The investment looked great. Not as huge a moneymaker as Reynolds thought, but solid."

"So Reynolds Hanson financed this La Fuente improvement with bank funds."

"He told me to set up the loan through Hindman, the shell company," said Baker, "so his name wouldn't be involved—that was because of his father's involvement with Farragut. I don't know if that was strictly legal, but it wasn't ethical." He looked at Lionel and shrugged. "I thought it would help the town."

"What happened?" asked Nelson. "Why did it default?"

"I think we might be getting ahead of ourselves," said Lionel. "Tell us what happened with the acquisition."

Baker sighed.

"Okay," he said. "Reynolds brought me into his office one morning and told me he wanted to invest in the mine but that his father couldn't drum up the financing. Which turned out to be a lie. He told me to set up the loan through the bank. You know, Regulation O makes it really tough for bank executives to extend credit for personal advantage. Reynolds didn't want to chance getting caught, so he told me to set up Hindman."

"You knew this was illegal," said Nelson.

"Unethical," said Baker. "There's a difference."

"Tell us about it," said Nelson.

"There is a significant gray area in the law. Reynolds assured me it wouldn't be a problem."

"Not for him," said Lionel. "He knew you'd be the one holding the bag if things went sour."

"Yes. Reynolds told me that the loans would not only improve production, but that new safety measures would be taken. You should have seen the mine when I first got down here. The breathing apparatus was antiquated, there were only a few methane detectors, and there was barely anything else from the twentieth century."

"So that was the first time you came to San Pablo?" asked Mia.

"No," said Baker, smiling. "About three years ago, I was in Guadalajara for a couple of weeks closing a land deal. I was here alone, so I had to find ways to entertain myself on the weekends. One Sunday after church, I decided to take a drive to get out of the city. I got lost and was trying to find a place to get directions when I saw a church steeple in the distance. I followed it and ended up here in San Pablo."

He smiled and gazed down at his empty tumbler.

"I stopped at the hotel, where I found out that no one spoke English here except Father Ignacio, so I went to the church. Mass had just started, so I sat in back. It was beautiful. There was something in that church—something, a feeling, that I'd never felt before. I felt closer to Jesus, to God, than I ever had before."

Nelson gave a sidelong look toward Lionel. He was looking at Baker and nodding.

Is this legit? he thought. *Or a royal soft sell?*

"I went up to Father Ignacio afterwards and thanked him. We got to talking and had lunch together. You've met him?"

Lionel nodded.

"You know, then," said Baker. "He's got the gift."

Mia leaned forward, putting her elbows on the table.

"Did you know the mine was here at that time?" she asked.

Baker shook his head. "No, I didn't," he said. "Not then. I found out later, when I got to know the people here. That was part of the miracle of it. God led me here to San Pablo, Father Ignacio, and then to La Fuente. It was no accident."

"Why?" asked Mia. "Why do you think God led you here?"

"So I could help the people," said Baker. "At least that's what I thought at first. When Reynolds started talking about La Fuente, I knew that my having already been there was more than a coincidence. It was God's will."

Nelson shook his head. Baker sighed.

"I know it sounds naïve and a little ridiculous," he said, "especially to a non-believer, but that's what happened."

"Okay," said Lionel. "You were convinced that fudging a little bit on the Con Union loan would be helpful for the people here?"

"Yes."

"Even though it was illegal?"

"Unethical," said Baker.

"Illegal," returned Lionel. "That gray area is not that gray, Mr. Baker. And you know it."

Baker shrugged.

"If you want to split hairs."

"The Chicago DA's office loves to split hairs," said Nelson.

"So let's take this from the top," said Lionel. "You wrote the loan, got it approved, and then what happened? Did any of the money make it to the mine?"

"That's where things got strange," said Baker. "The money was supposed to go directly to Alteca, the parent company, and then to Los Hermanos Gordos, the company that ran operations for upgrades. But there were all sorts of delays and complications between the loan approval and the disbursement from Hindman. Reynolds told me it had to do with international regulations, which was odd."

"Why?" asked Mia.

"We'd done a lot of transactions here before. These delays were very unusual—so unusual that I made some inquiries outside normal channels and found out some irregularities in the transfer to Alteca."

Baker coughed and cleared his throat.

"The transfer had gone through to Alteca on paper, but they never got the money. It stayed in Hindman, the holding company Reynolds created through Farragut. That was right before the explosion."

"So it looked like Alteca had the money," said Nelson, "except they didn't."

"Right," said Baker.

"The loan was in Farragut's name. The company owned by Reynolds' father," said Lionel.

"Correct," said Baker. "You see, Reynolds Hanson was planning on stealing that money all along." He smiled slightly. "That's the first time I ever actually said that. It feels good. Reynolds was going to take the money after the default. He figured everyone would assume Alteca and Los Gordos had defaulted because of the accident. I'm sure there was a payoff involved." Baker smiled and looked down at his hands. "But once they defaulted, Reynolds would have the lion's share."

"Do you have proof?" asked Nelson.

"He didn't leave much of a trail," said Baker. "I don't know if I could prove it, but I know that's what he was up to. That money was supposed to improve the mine and these people's lives, and Reynolds tried to steal it—but I stopped him. When I figured out what he was up to, I moved the loan money to Herman and Lund, the other holding company I'd set up. Of course, the accident made the loan default easy. It looked as if Alteca and Los Gordos had already spent it."

"Where's the money now?" asked Lionel.

"It's safe," said Baker.

"Of course, you know what we're here for," said Nelson.

"To take me back to stand trial," said Baker. "I'm ready. I'm not ashamed of what I did, and I'm not apologizing for it."

"Don't play the martyr, Baker," said Nelson. "You're no saint, no matter what you might think. You're nothing but a liar and a thief."

"Well, while I think Mr. Nelson's wording might be a little harsh, he's correct, Mr. Baker," said Lionel, standing up and walking to the window, "but I'm not a cop. I'm here because my father sent me on behalf of Con Union. All the bank wants is its money back. The law doesn't necessarily have to be involved."

Baker stood up and put his hands in his pockets. No one said anything. Lionel turned away from the window.

"Con Union wants this to go away," said Lionel quietly. "That's why we're here. Personally, I don't care what happens to you, Mr. Baker. We're here for the money."

"I'm afraid I can't help you with that," said Baker. "It's gone."

"We know $100,000 of it is in a Guadalajara bank," said Mia.

"Yes," said Baker, smiling a little. "I want Reynolds to pay for what he did. That's why I planted that little clue. I knew it would bring people here. But the rest of the money is spent, Mr. Bing. It's now being used to aid the miners' families and everyone else hurt by Reynolds Hanson."

"Mr. Baker," said Lionel. "That accident was not an accident, was it?"

Baker shook his head.

"I don't know," he said. "I don't think Reynolds could do something like that, but I don't know."

There was a cry outside. Before Baker could reach the door, it swung open. Diego, Manuel, and Jose stood there, framed by the bright sunlight streaming in behind them. Diego held a pistol in his hand.

"You," said Diego. "Baker. All of you. Don Francisco wants to see you. Ahora mismo."

Mia got to her feet. Nelson followed, not making any abrupt motions. Lionel remained standing with his hands in his pockets.

Don't do anything stupid, boss.

"What does Don Francisco want with us?" asked Lionel.

"You will find that out very shortly, Mr. Bing," said Diego. "Let's go." Lionel slowly walked over to the table. Diego took a long look at Mia and then glanced at Nelson.

"Ah, señor," he said, walking toward him. "We meet again."

Somehow, Diego looked bigger in the small kitchen. Nelson braced himself. *This guy wants payback.* Nelson couldn't blame him. *After all, I did kick him in the nuts.*

Nelson glanced down at the nine-millimeter leveled at his gut and then looked back up at Diego. He smiled.

"How are you doing?" he said. "I hope things are okay down there. I'd hate to have ruined your love life."

Diego smiled and turned back toward the others. He started turning back toward him just before Nelson saw the blur of his arm. He tried to duck, but the gun barrel caught the side of his head. Everything flashed white for an instant and then went blurry. He staggered sideways a moment and caught a short glimpse of Diego's smiling face before the world flashed white and everything went black.

Chapter 20

NELSON FELT A THROBBING IN HIS head and raised his hand to the pain before he opened his eyes. It started coming back to him. Baker's house. Diego. He reached up and tentatively felt the side of his head. It was tender. Sticky. He blinked his eyes to get rid of the blur. Yeah, he'd gotten whacked pretty good.

"Lie still," said someone. A woman's voice. He tried to focus. Mia hovered over him and started dabbing a washcloth on his head. It stung like crazy.

"Jesus," he said, pushing her away and trying to sit up. "What are you doing?"

"Cleaning you up. You're kind of a mess."

He took a look around. They were in a cavernous room. Lionel and Brad Baker were sitting in a couple of leather armchairs at a huge table. Diego sat at the other end with his pistol on the table in front of him. Manuel and Jose stood just behind Lionel and Baker. Nelson was lying on a leather—it looked like calfskin—couch. Mia was sitting next to him.

"Welcome back, señor," said Diego. "I hope you are feeling better."

Nelson sat up and swung his legs to the floor. Mia moved to sit beside him. He still felt a little foggy. His ribs felt a little sore, too.

How many times did that little bastard whack me? He remembered two. *Did he kick me when I was down?*

Nelson took a deep breath and glanced at Lionel and Baker, who looked a little nervous. Baker kept smoothing back his hair.

Well, thought Nelson, tentatively touching the side of his head. *He has good reason to be scared. Don Francisco was jefe of the local cartel. It was hard to say what he wanted from Baker. Or the rest of them. Maybe a piece of the action. Maybe more. Who could tell? And they'd get it. These guys have no rules*, thought Nelson.

The sound of heels clicking on stone echoed down a corridor. Someone was coming. Nelson glanced around the room. Manuel and Jose were both glaring at him. Diego smiled at him, his hands on the top of the table, right next to his Glock. *Well*, thought Nelson. *I guess we're surrounded.* He leaned back on the sofa. Mia leaned forward toward the sound of the footsteps.

Another man walked into the room. He was small and slender, dressed in a black suit and white button-down shirt with no tie. His black hair was slicked back, and he had an air of sophistication decidedly lacking in Diego and friends.

"Mr. Baker," he said. "Could you please follow me and bring Mr. Bing and his associates with you?"

Baker rose and gestured to Lionel, who rose and walked over to the couch. Manuel and Jose started to follow him, but the new guy waved them off. Lionel leaned over to help Nelson up. He grabbed him under the arms and whispered, "Let me and Baker do the talking. There's been a complication."

"Hey," said Diego. "No talking."

"He was just helping him up," said Mia.

"You, señorita," he said, "can talk as much as you like. We can have a private discussion anytime you like." He smiled and chuckled.

"Fuck you," she said. Diego laughed.

"So much spunk," he said. "Such a shame to waste it."

Nelson rubbed the side of his head to keep himself from looking at Diego. That was two he owed that bastard.

"C'mon, Mia," said Lionel, taking her by the arm. "Let's go,"

They followed the dapper little man down a marble-paved hallway. They passed alcoves hung with paintings and adorned with sculptures. Some hallways split off to other rooms that looked as gigantic as the first. *Jesus*, thought Nelson. *This is a fucking palace.*

As they walked through the corridor, Nelson noticed the walls were hung with tapestries that looked old and valuable even to his untrained eye. Lionel looked up at one and nodded.

"That one is an original Boucher," said their guide, seeing Lionel looking at the piece. "It is valued at over two million dollars."

"Excellent," said Lionel. "Don Francisco has impeccable taste."

The little man smiled.

"Yes, he is very serious about his collection. Do you indulge, sir?"

"No," said Lionel. "Not in tapestries. My passion is wine."

"Ah," said the little man. "Excellent. Don Francisco would greatly enjoy showing his cellar to you."

"I'd be honored."

"Allow me to introduce myself," said the little man. "I am Armando, Don Francisco's valet."

"Lionel Bing." He held out his hand and they shook. Gesturing, "This is Mia Wentworth and Nelson West, my associates."

"Pleased to meet you. Perhaps Mr. West might like some medical attention?"

"No, I'm fine," said Nelson. He glanced behind him. "I just need some air."

"Just so," said Armando. "In due time, sir. Let's continue. Don Francisco is waiting."

They came to a set of huge black walnut doors. Armando knocked. A young man in a button-down shirt answered, opened the door, and led them into a large room. Nelson glanced up. The ceiling had to be at least twenty feet high and was lined with dark wooden beams in the old mission style. Windows lined one side of the room. Three men armed with AK-47s stood guard at that wall. One never took his gaze from the windows. Nelson frowned to himself. *Are they expecting trouble?* he thought. *Or is this all for us?* Of course, he had no idea what the perimeter of the building looked like—he'd been out like a light. Armando turned and dismissed Diego and the others.

A mahogany desk stood in the middle of the room. A woman was getting up from behind it. She was tall, almost six feet, and was wearing a dark blue dress and heels. Her hair was dark and hung down to her shoulders. Her eyes were the color of melted caramel. She was beautiful. She walked up to Nelson.

"Are you all right, señor?" she asked. Her English was excellent. "Perhaps you need some medical attention."

"I'm fine," said Nelson, resisting the urge to touch his face. "Thank you. I just ran into an old friend. Diego."

"Hmm," she said, frowning. "Diego will be dealt with by my father for his actions. You were not supposed to be harmed."

"Well, Diego and I have a little history. I don't know if I wouldn't have done the same thing."

She nodded without smiling and turned to Baker.

"Mr. Baker, I have heard much about you from Father Ignacio."

The priest? thought Nelson. *Odd bedfellows.*

"Hello," he said. "You must be Paola. It's a pleasure to meet you. I've heard a lot about you, too. You have quite the reputation for your business acumen."

"For a woman, you mean?"

"I didn't say that."

"Well, Stanford School of Business will do that for you. I understand you went to Booth. Another great school."

"I didn't know this was alumni week," said Mia. "Perhaps we should come back later."

Paola turned to look at Mia. She smiled slightly. Mia crossed her arms. The two women stared at each other a moment until Lionel stepped forward and said, "Hello, my name is Lionel Bing. These are my associates—"

"Nelson West and Mia Wentworth," said Paola, smiling slightly. "Of course, I know of you, Mr. Bing." She shifted her gaze to him. "It is a pleasure." She held out her hand. Lionel shook it, smiling.

Nelson glanced at Mia, who was staring at Lionel. Baker stood next to her, his hands behind his back. He had a slight smile on his face. *Who is this woman? Don Francisco's daughter? His girlfriend? She wasn't just some bimbo working the front room.*

"Please," said Paola. "Follow me." She turned and walked toward the rear of the room. Lionel followed with Baker close behind. Mia glanced at Nelson, shrugged, and fell in line. Nelson glanced at the guards behind him and followed Mia. Paola stopped at an oaken door, opened it, and motioned Lionel through. He went in without hesitation.

Great, thought Nelson. *Well, what else could they do? There wasn't much choice at this point.*

Baker and then Mia followed as Paola held the door. Nelson glanced at her as he walked by.

"I'll be right behind you," she said.

"What about them?" asked Nelson, gesturing toward the guards.

"There is no need to worry," she said. "They never leave their posts."

Nelson stopped at the doorway. A flight of stone stairs led down a narrow passageway lit by two bare bulbs. He could just see Mia turning the corner to the right. He started down the stairs. Resisting the urge to turn around, he heard the door creak shut behind him and then the clicking of Paola's shoes as she began following him down.

He entered a brightly lit room that looked at least 200 feet long and two-thirds that wide. The entire expanse was covered in hardwood flooring. The place was as big as a ballroom. Bigger. A half-court basketball court stood at the far end. Four pool tables, an air hockey game, a ping-pong table, various pinball machines and video games—including Pac Man—lined the walls. *Well*, thought Nelson, grinning to himself. *Don Francisco's rec room*. Mia, Baker, and Lionel stood directly in front of him.

There were two men leaning on cues and talking at the nearest pool table and two more men sporting AK-47s standing near the door.

"Will you look at this?" asked Lionel. "This is wild."

"Don Francisco likes to have a place to unwind," said Paola. "He put this room together as kind of a getaway."

"A man cave," said Lionel.

"Yes," said Paola. "I suppose you could call it that." She gestured toward a door halfway down the room on their left. "He has a screening room behind that door, where he can watch television or some of the latest movies."

"My father has one of those at his house," said Lionel. "He's got a state-of-the-art sound system and a 100-inch flat screen. It's like being in a theater."

"This is an actual theater," said Paola. "It can seat one hundred people."

She smiled and walked up to the two men. As they turned, Nelson saw that one of them, the smaller man, was Father Ignacio, who was, as seemed to be his pattern, out of uniform. He was wearing a Taylor Swift t-shirt and Levi's, along with his turquoise boots.

The other man was only slightly taller than the priest. His curly, black hair was parted at the side and combed over. He had a narrow, bony face flanked by well-groomed sideburns. His mouth was set into a hard, cold line, like the barrel of a gun, and his eyes, the same color as Paola's, held none of the warmth or invitation of hers. They were as cold and hard as agate.

Nelson took a breath. There was a vibe around this man that made the hairs on the back of his neck stand up. He'd run across a few guys like this when he'd been a cop—they were always trouble. This had to be Don Francisco.

"Hello, my friends," said Father Ignacio, placing his cue on the table and coming toward them. "It's a pleasure to see you again."

"Father," said Lionel. "This is a surprise."

The priest simply smiled.

"I would like to present to you Don Francisco, who is an important part of the local parish. He wanted to meet with you and asked me to arrange a meeting."

Don Francisco leaned on his pool cue and stared at them. He nodded to Paolo, who turned and left.

"A simple invitation would have sufficed," said Lionel. "It wasn't necessary to kidnap us."

"My apologies for that," said Don Francisco. His voice was raspy and somewhat high. "I asked my men to fetch you, but I didn't mention that you were to be my guests." He shrugged. "They were only doing their job." He took a long look at Nelson. "Apparently, they were doing it a little too zealously."

"What is it you wanted to see us about?" asked Lionel.

Easy, Lionel. Don't get pushy, thought Nelson. *Don't piss this guy off.*

"Ah, you are a man of action. I like that. Please," said Don Francisco. "Let us sit." He motioned to a large, round table to the right side of the pool tables. Nelson glanced around the room. There only seemed to be the one exit, unless there was another way out of the home theater room. Not that it mattered.

They sat. Don Francisco motioned to one of the men sitting near the door and told him to bring some refreshments. The man disappeared up the stairs.

"I understand you were sent by the authorities to fetch Mr. Baker."

"Well, not exactly," said Lionel. "We were sent by the Chicago bank that Mr. Baker works for."

"I see," said Don Francisco. "But you are here about the missing money. This is about the loan default. Am I right?"

"Yes," said Nelson. Don Francisco shifted his eyes to Nelson.

"Nelson West," he murmured.

Nelson nodded.

"Mr. West," he said, gazing at him and smiling slowly. "Your reputation precedes you."

Nelson leaned back in his chair.

"I have friends in Chicago who say you are very good at what you do and very difficult to—let us say—work with."

"Thank you—I guess," said Nelson. *No need to give this guy any more than he already had.*

"And you, Miss Wentworth," he said, smiling. "Are just as beautiful as my men have said."

Mia nodded, smiled a little, and folded her arms across her chest. The Don turned to Lionel.

"And our Mr. Baker," he said, shaking his head. "What a lot of trouble you've turned out be."

Bradley Baker smiled sickly and swallowed.

"I must confess I am a little puzzled by your involvement in all this, Mr. Bing," he said, turning to Lionel. "You are a very wealthy man. I'm not sure why you would trouble yourself with this matter."

"Let's just say I'm helping out a friend."

"I see," said Don Francisco. "Ordinarily, I wouldn't trouble myself with these things, but whenever my church is presented a problem, I make it my problem. And I solve problems."

The man returned with a tray of drinks. Lionel and Mia declined. Father Ignacio took a beer. Nelson grabbed a bottle of water and sipped it. His head had started throbbing again.

"Thank you," said Don Francisco and waited until the man left before speaking.

"I grew up in this area," said Don Francisco, "just a few miles from here. I attended Santa Barbara when I was a boy. You might say I was raised by the Catholic Church."

Boy, thought Nelson, *would your parents be disappointed.*

"It is still very important to me," the Don continued, "and I support it however I can."

He gestured toward the priest.

"Father Ignacio and I have worked together on a number of projects, including a shrine to my dead mother in her hometown not so very far from here. I also provide resources to the church to help them complete their mission to God."

Nelson saw Mia smirking out of the corner of his eye. He felt like kicking her under the table.

"When Father Ignacio told me that he had been in touch with Mr. Baker and that he was working with the church to help with the accident at El Fuente, I was of course interested. As I said, if my church is involved, I am involved."

Nelson glanced at Father Ignacio, who was gazing at Don Francisco and half-smiling. *Strange bedfellows, indeed*, he thought. *How does Father sleep at night knowing he's taking money from a killer? From a drug kingpin?*

"I know many of the families whose fathers and brothers were trapped in the mine," the Don continued. "It was a terrible thing."

"Do you know the owners of the company who ran the mine?" asked Lionel.

Don Francisco nodded. "Yes," he said. "I knew them. Guillermo and Alberto Albacete. They were the owners of Los Hermanos Gordos."

"What happened at the mine?"

The Don shrugged. "I don't know. Mining is not my business. I can't really say. Some who know what happened say that the Albacete brothers cut corners, and that their negligence was the cause of the explosion and the cave-in."

"Where are the Albacetes now?" asked Nelson. "Were they ever arrested or charged?"

The Don shrugged. "They seem to have disappeared. I'm sure they were frightened by the possible consequences of their actions and fled."

He took a small cigar out of his shirt pocket.

"Do you mind if I smoke?" he asked, smiling.

No one said anything.

"Thank you."

Father Ignacio cleared his throat.

"To help the community, Don Francisco has graciously volunteered to take over operations of the mine and will reopen it as soon as possible."

"Don't the original owners still have control?" asked Lionel.

Don Francisco shrugged. "As I mentioned, they have disappeared, but the remaining family members have agreed to sell the mine to me."

Nelson leaned back in his chair. He didn't know Mexican law, but that hardly seemed right. In the States, the mine would have stayed closed until an investigation was completed.

"Yes," added Father Ignacio. "Señora Albacete, Guillermo's wife, is a parish member. She wants to do right by the church and the community."

"A fine woman," added the Don.

"So, with all due respect, Don Francisco," said Lionel. "What does this have to do with us and the money stolen from Con Union?"

The Don smiled and leaned his elbows on the table.

"According to what Father Ignacio has told me, you're here to recover the money that you believe Mr. Baker took. Correct?"

Lionel nodded.

"First of all, I don't believe a man of God like Bradley Baker would ever steal," said the Don. "Especially money that was earmarked to be invested into La Fuente. Do you, Father?"

Father Ignacio slowly shook his head and gazed at them evenly.

He doesn't even have the grace to look away, thought Nelson, meeting his gaze.

"No, I don't," said Father Ignacio. "The money may have been stolen, but not by Bradley. I believe he discovered the surplus, but rather than have that money go into the wrong hands, to be the fruits of sin, as it were, Mr. Baker helped divert it to help the families of the miners."

Baker nodded, glancing nervously from Father Ignacio to Don Francisco.

Yeah, Mr. Baker, thought Nelson. *You'd better get this one right.*

"So, Father," said Mia, leaning forward, "let me get this straight. Are you saying your church is laundering stolen money? And then using it to help these people?"

"No," said Don Francisco in a harsh voice. "That is not correct. As the Father said, we don't know if that money was stolen, and if it was, by whom. You see, no one here engages in illegal activities."

He smiled. Nelson smiled back. He hoped he didn't look too sick. He glanced over at Lionel, who was frowning. He started drumming his fingers on the table.

"What is the matter, Mr. Bing?" asked the priest.

"Well, I'm not sure how the Catholic Church can accept stolen money," said Lionel. "It's not exactly moral, is it?"

"Well, as we said," said the priest, "the church did not accept the money. And we're not even sure it's stolen. We merely, well, diverted it. You see, we believe it came from an anonymous donor. We are using it to help the people of San Pablo."

That's certainly splitting hairs, thought Nelson.

Lionel leaned back and continued drumming his fingers on the table. Thinking.

"Who's got the money?" asked Lionel finally. "I give up."

"It was donated anonymously and turned over to a trust set up by Mr. Baker here," said the Don. "A trust formed to ensure the well-being of the people of San Pablo. We are not sure who actually donated the money. They prefer to remain anonymous."

"So," said Lionel, putting his hands on the table, "let me get this straight. Don Francisco and Father Ignacio. You refuse to give this money back even though you are aware of the fact that it's stolen?"

Don Francisco had stopped smiling. A coldness had swept over his face. "How can we give back money that was donated to the church?"

"It's stolen money," repeated Lionel. "We're all aware of that."

"So you say," said Don Francisco. "We prefer to believe otherwise. The money was donated by an anonymous donor."

"But you just said—" began Mia. She stopped when Lionel held up a hand.

"In that case," said Lionel, "we should probably take Mr. Baker back to the States with us. To explain things."

Father Ignacio glanced at Don Francisco, who was gazing down at his hands. He sighed.

"You wish to take Mr. Baker back to stand trial for a crime he didn't commit?" The priest leaned forward. "He did not steal that money."

"He originated the loan," said Lionel. "He diverted it to a holding company after it was stolen."

"Perhaps he should explain this himself," said Father Ignacio.

"We already heard Mr. Baker's story," said Lionel, leaning forward. "He puts it all on Reynolds Hanson, which may or may not be true. You know, Father, this Robin Hood bit is not going to fly with the authorities. If the prosecutors get hold of this information, you'll be investigated and—"

"This will not happen," said Don Francisco. His voice was flat and emotionless, as cold as a cube of ice. "Father Ignacio and the church will not be implicated. This investigation is over."

"What about our problem?" asked Lionel.

"It is your problem," said the Don. He shrugged. "As we have already said, the money was donated to the church anonymously, perhaps by the very person who took it, perhaps by an interested party. No one knows. We do know that Mr. Baker is innocent. He is, in fact, under the protection of the church which, is—" he smiled, "under my protection."

Baker crossed his arms, leaned back in his chair, and smiled.

Lionel smiled slightly and nodded. Don Francisco smiled back. Nelson took a deep breath and slowly glanced to his left. The two guards stood at the wall gazing at them.

Well, thought Nelson, *this could be what they call a Mexican standoff.*

"I'm sorry we're not able to help you," said the Don, "and I'm afraid that Mr. Baker will not be able to accompany you back to America."

He leaned back in his chair. Lionel gazed at him, still drumming his fingers on the tabletop.

"Well," he said, leaning forward. "We seem to be at an impasse."

The Don nodded. Father Ignacio glanced from him to Lionel. He frowned.

"This will not stand," said Lionel.

The Don looked at him without changing his expression.

"I need to bring the money, Mr. Baker, or have a very good reason why I can't do that."

Don Francisco smiled slightly.

"Many things could possibly prevent you from fulfilling your duties, Mr. Bing. An accident, a car crash, or some other misfortune," he said. "We would hate to see anything unfortunate befall you."

Lionel started to stand up.

"Wait," said Father Ignacio. "I believe Mr. Bing deserves to know the whole story. I think that might be enough to satisfy him."

Don Francisco glared at the priest, who didn't turn a hair. Nelson felt himself tensing up. For all his lip service about loyalty to the church, he wouldn't put hurting a priest beyond Don Francisco.

"Don Francisco," said the Father. "Please."

Francisco looked at him a moment and nodded.

"I believe," said the Don, turning to Lionel, "that the explosion at La Fuente was done deliberately. When the mining operation was crippled, it forced Hermanos Gordos into default. And then the money went poof," he said, raising his hands. "Gone until our friend Mr. Baker found it and placed it in a secret account. He is now giving it back to the families of the people who died for it."

Nelson nodded to himself. *That fit in with what Baker had said. Reynolds had ensured the default.*

"Maybe what we are doing is not strictly legal, but it is the right thing to do," said the priest. "We are righting a wrong. We are correcting an injustice. We know it can never replace the dead or repair the families, but it will help."

"Yes," chimed in Baker. "Along with rebuilding the mine, we're going to build a new school..." His voice petered out as Don Francisco fixed him with a stare.

"I suggest you go back home," said the Don, turning to Lionel. "Your guilty party is there. You will find him, but you will never find the money. Perhaps your friends will be satisfied with that. I suspect, Mr. Bing, that if you look too hard for the money, you may disappear, too."

Lionel glared at him, his face becoming pinched.

"However, I do have much respect for you and your family. I know you have traveled a long way to complete your mission, and I don't want to see you leave here with nothing."

He took a puff from his cigar.

"I am prepared, said Don Francisco, "to offer you something in return for your inconvenience and—oh, let us say your understanding in this matter." He took another puff from his cigar.

"I have heard about the unfortunate incident you experienced as a child, Mr. Bing. You and your mother were kidnapped, no?"

Lionel said nothing. He glanced down at his hands.

"Your mother was tortured, raped, and murdered by criminals," continued the Don. "And you were brutalized, too. Correct?"

Lionel had gone as still as a stone. Nelson leaned forward, ready to grab him if tried anything foolish.

"Yes," Lionel whispered. "That's all true."

"I understand the perpetrators were never caught."

Lionel nodded. "That's so," he said.

"I have many friends in the United States," said Don Francisco. "And many in Chicago. I believe I can help you bring these killers to justice." The Don shrugged. "Either your country's justice or whatever justice you may personally see fit to implement. That would be your choice. But I would do my best to help you find closure."

"What do you know, Don Francisco?" asked Nelson.

"Always the policeman," said the Don, smiling slightly. "I'm sorry, Mr. West. This matter is between Mr. Bing and myself."

He turned to Lionel. "This is my proposal, Mr. Bing. You find a solution that will please your clients without implicating Mr. Baker, and I will help with this other matter."

Don Francisco took a deep breath. He glanced at his watch.

"If you excuse me, I must be going. Father Ignacio, will you help our guests find their way home?"

The priest nodded. They all stood. Don Francisco nodded and left. Nelson watched as his two bodyguards followed him. *He doesn't take many chances.*

"Come," said the priest.

They followed him out the giant rec room and up the stairs. They walked through the vast promenade and past the ancient tapestries without saying a word.

Nelson glanced over at Lionel, who was frowning slightly as he walked alongside the priest, hands in pockets. He stared at the ground as he walked.

Well, thought Nelson, *That's that. I don't think we're going to be able to pull this one off.* Lionel muttered something under his breath, something Nelson couldn't catch, but the priest glanced sharply at him.

He's freaking out, thought Nelson. *Confused. He wasn't expecting the kidnapping to come back. Jesus, I hope this doesn't push him over the edge. This would not be a good place for him to snap.*

Mia cleared her throat. Nelson glanced over at her. She opened her mouth to speak, but Lionel turned to the priest and spoke first.

"Father," he said. "Could you come by the hotel?"

"I think this matter is closed, Mr. Bing."

"Yes," said Lionel, his tone clipped. "It certainly looks that way. Still, would you humor me and come by tomorrow about 9 o'clock?"

They had reached the doorway. The priest sighed, shrugged, and nodded.

"Thank you," said Lionel. Father Ignacio watched as the driver ushered them into the car and drove away.

Lionel stared out the window, nodding to himself, muttering under his breath. He began rocking back and forth. The driver either didn't understand English or didn't care. Mia sat next to him, never taking her eyes off Lionel. Nelson stared at the back of the driver's head and wondered what the hell was next.

Chapter 21

THEY WENT TO THE CAFÉ AGAIN that night for dinner. Luis had suggested his grandmother's chicken molé recipe, which, Nelson had to agree, was excellent. Lionel was quiet, but he ate well. Mia, on the other hand, barely touched her food but downed three beers during dinner. She looked like a nervous wreck. There wasn't a whole lot of conversation.

No wonder, thought Nelson. *Don Francisco has left us with a whole lot to digest.*

The investigation was done—they knew where the money was and how it had gotten there, but the problem was going to be getting it back, which would be extremely difficult—impossible. Not only would they have to get Baker away from Don Francisco, but they'd also have to worm the money out of him. And that was never easy with a zealot on a religious mission.

And, thought Nelson, *Baker is that. He's a believer. He thinks he's one of the chosen, that he's seen the light, that he's the Lamb of God. Whatever.*

He glanced at Mia, who was still rearranging the food on her plate. Lionel had finished his meal and was staring off into the distance. Nelson took a sip of his beer. He supposed they could try to bring Baker back, although to do so would be tricky. And dangerous. That might satisfy Lionel's father, although Nelson wasn't sure if Mr. Bing would be happy with him if he put Lionel in that sort of situation.

And then there's Don Francisco's proposition, thought Nelson. *Where's Lionel with that?*

"So," said Mia, her voice splitting the silence like the sound of breaking glass, "where do we go from here?"

Lionel took a long drink of his beer and put it down softly. He smiled slightly and looked at Mia.

"What do you think, Mia?" he asked.

Classic, thought Nelson. *Put the question to a subordinate. The question was what Mia would prioritize—Lionel's therapy or their safety.*

"I think we're done here," said Mia slowly. "We traced the money and found out who took it."

"Allegedly," said Nelson. "There's no proof that Reynolds Hanson took it. Only Baker's word."

"I think his story fits in pretty well with the route the money took," said Lionel slowly. "And it seems to fit all the details we know. If Baker took it, why would he implicate himself by depositing that money in the Guadalajara bank? He wants Reynolds to be caught."

"Or maybe he wants to frame him," said Nelson. "Baker is bulletproofed right now, and he knows it. Nothing short of an army is going to get him out of San Pablo."

"The question," continued Mia, "is how to check Baker's story. He says that Farragut, his father's company, originated the loan for Alteca and Los Gordos with the approval and urging of Reynolds. Baker did all the legwork and pushed the loan through, but when he noticed irregularities, he started looking into who was doing what."

She paused and took a sip from her beer bottle before continuing.

"Right around that time, the mine blew up and Los Gordos defaulted on the loan. That's when Baker said he knew Reynolds was trying to defraud the bank."

Nelson shrugged. "Baker could have done all of that. He could very well be trying to set up Hanson."

Lionel cleared his throat.

"I think it's pretty obvious that Baker has an emotional investment here. He feels like he belongs—like this is his family. Why would he destroy that?"

"Unless that's all a front," said Nelson.

"You are a cynical man, sir," said Lionel. Nelson smiled.

"Well," said Mia, "if he's telling the truth, we should be able to see how the money is being used down here. What did he say? New homes? A school?"

"It sure didn't look like they were rebuilding the mine," said Nelson.

"Not yet," said Mia.

Lionel nodded and said nothing for a moment.

"Well, Mia," he said, "I think that's a really good idea. I wanted to ask Father Ignacio for a tour of the town tomorrow. That should give us a good idea of what's happening. Priests love doing that stuff, anyway."

* * *

Nelson leaned forward in his seat, put down the portable tray table, and took the drink from the flight attendant. He took a sip of the gin and tonic. Yesterday had been a long day. They'd rustled up Father Ignacio, who—accompanied by Manuel and Jose, their old friends— had taken them on a tour of the new school that was being built for San Pablo. It was a few miles away from the town, near the house where Don Francisco had grown up. The priest told them that the school would be the first building with internet WiFi in the area and would be state-of-the-art in every respect.

He then took them to see the day care center that had been set up in Hidalgo to take care of the children of the dead miners while their mothers worked or took online classes—tuition paid for out of the trust. It all looked brand new.

Father Ignacio explained that renovations on the mine would begin once plans to create a safe and modern facility were completed. Apparently, a Guadalajara engineering firm was presently working on it.

"We are not supposed to go inside the mine yet," said Father Ignacio. "It's not safe." He smiled and shook his head. "But that hasn't stopped Bradley Baker. He's been in there searching for the missing and marking their graves. He feels it is his duty after everything that happened. He feels responsible. We will bring them out when it is safe."

It adds up, thought Nelson. *Maybe a little too neatly.*

Lionel had nodded and said nothing. When they got back to town, he told Father Ignacio they would be leaving that next day, which was news to Nelson. Lionel mentioned he had booked the flight right after they'd returned from Don Francisco's house. He asked Nelson and Mia to go back up the mountain and retrieve the stakeout equipment while he tied up some loose ends.

They had dinner together later that night. Nobody said much. Lionel spent most of the evening wrapped up in that faraway look of his. Mia was quiet, too. Afterwards, they all went to their rooms.

After he packed, Nelson went to stand out on the balcony. It was a beautiful night. The full moon was rising over the mountains and cast a pale blue light over the deserted square. A few patrons were still inside the bar, but it was generally quiet. Nelson took a deep breath. It was a shame this had been a working trip. He would have liked to have gotten to know the place a little better.

A movement at the hotel entrance below caught his eye. Someone was coming out. The person paused at the door and turned left. Lionel.

What the hell is he up to now? He turned, ran down the stairs and out the door. Lionel was halfway across the plaza, heading toward the church. Nelson followed at a distance. He wanted to see what his boss was up to but paused when his attention was caught by one of the blue and white placards spread throughout the town. He leaned over and read "En Memoria de Los Mineras de San Pablo. FUHR." *Whatever the hell than means.*

Lionel walked to the edge of the plaza near the church and sat on one the stone benches there. Nelson noticed some slight movement inside La Casita. *That could be Jose or Manuel—who might be tempted get back at Lionel for the beating he took.* Lionel crossed his legs and stared across the plaza, seemingly oblivious to everything around him.

Well, I'd better keep an eye on him.

He walked into the plaza, crossing Lionel's line of sight.

"Hey, boss," he said. "What're you doing?"

Lionel blinked his eyes and looked at him blankly for a moment. *It's like he doesn't even recognize me.* He waited until Lionel smiled.

"Sorry," he said, "I was thinking." Nelson sat down next to him and glanced over at La Casita. Quiet.

"I couldn't sleep," said Lionel quietly.

"Me either," said Nelson. "It's been a long couple of days."

"Yes, it has. And this case has taken a very strange turn."

Nelson nodded slightly. *Let him talk it out.*

"You know," continued Lionel, "I thought this was going to be a lot easier—a lot more clear-cut than it turned out to be. You know, swoop in, get the bad guy—Baker—and get out. But it's gotten to the point where I have no idea who the good guys are anymore."

"Yeah."

"I know that probably sounds naïve to an ex-cop. You've probably seen a lot of cases like this."

"No, believe me. I haven't."

It was true. He'd never usually gotten this deep into a case as a cop. For the most part, his perps weren't that smart and not that hard to catch. Those cases were more like wham-bam-thank-you-ma'am. This was different. This case was as tangled as a plate of spaghetti.

"Was it easier?" asked Lionel.

"I guess. Most murders were pretty easy to figure out. It was usually somebody who knew the victim, like a husband or a wife or a jealous boyfriend. Those were pretty obvious. Sometimes it was a drug thing. Business. You rarely found the killer, but you knew what happened and why."

"What about crimes that weren't really crimes?"

"What do you mean?"

"Well, crimes that could be excused—rationalized."

"You think this is one of those?" asked Nelson.

Lionel shrugged.

"I don't know if what Baker did was wrong. He stole money that had already been stolen and used it to rectify the damage it had caused."

"He stole," said Nelson. "That's a crime."

"He stole from a thief and used the money to make things right."

"Not for Con Union," said Nelson.

"Are they so innocent?" asked Lionel. "They approved the loan for Farragut without doing their due diligence. They indirectly caused the deaths of those miners."

"It was all legal," said Nelson, glancing over at him.

"Yeah," said Lionel, "legal."

He stared off into the distance. Nelson glanced over at La Casita. Quiet. He didn't see Manuel or Jose. Just some locals.

"You know," said Lionel softly, "for a long time I was convinced that there was no justice in the world—that no matter what we did, the thugs would eventually take over everything."

"Yeah," said Nelson. "There were days I felt that way, too."

"My mother and I were kidnapped in broad daylight. We were confined. I don't remember much, but I know she was tortured. They cut off one of her fingers."

He glanced over at Nelson.

"I don't remember that," he said. "I've tried to remember. I learned about it afterwards. That and she was gang raped. I do remember when they found her body."

Lionel stared down at his hands.

"They told me there was nothing I could have done. That I was only twelve. But I should have remembered, Nelson." He turned to him, tears brimming in his eyes. "I should have remembered their faces."

"It wasn't your fault."

"We were out shopping," he said dreamily, as if he hadn't heard Nelson. "For me. I wanted a new game system. A Nintendo 64."

"It wasn't your fault," repeated Nelson. He doubted if Lionel could hear him.

"I've killed those guys a thousand times in my mind," said Lionel. He smiled. "Every way you could imagine. But it never does any good."

"They never had any idea who did it, did they?"

Lionel shook his head and leaned forward, his hands clasped. They sat in silence.

Jesus, thought Nelson, gazing at Lionel. *He's still beating himself up, even after twenty years.*

"I'm still trying to remember it—to see them," said Lionel, "but I can't. It keeps getting harder and harder. Am I like Baker? Or worse? Am I a victim, or am I the coward who let the men who killed my mom get away? At least Baker did something."

"Baker can forgive himself," said Nelson. "Hell, he's even congratulating himself, which is rich for somebody as religious as he says he is. He's a thief, an adulterer, and a liar, Lionel. That's three commandments right there." He stood and stretched.

"Baker's going to get away with it," Nelson continued. "Father Ignacio forgives him, the law can't get at him, and Don Francisco is protecting him. Nothing short of a commando raid will get him out of here."

Nelson stood in front of Lionel and put his hands in his pockets.

"We lost, Lionel. There's nothing we can do."

Lionel nodded.

"Maybe not here," he said, "but we still have Reynolds Hanson." He stretched. "And," he said, "I have Don Francisco's proposition."

* * *

Yeah, thought Nelson, leaning on his tray table. *We still have Reynolds.*

Something nudged him. Mia.

"What?"

She was staring at him intently.

"What?" he repeated, glancing past her to Lionel, who was out of it, zonked on meds again.

"What happened last night? I saw you two out on the plaza."

"Yeah, we were out there."

"What did Lionel say? He was so focused this morning."

Nelson shrugged. "We talked about the case. And he talked about what had happened to him. You know, the kidnapping."

"What did he say?"

"I don't know. He talked about his mom and the stuff they did to her. He still feels guilty about it. And he's frustrated about this case. About not fixing it."

"I don't think it's such a loss," said Mia.

Nelson looked at her.

"What? We have Reynolds Hanson. He's the one who defrauded the bank."

"If we can prove it. Right now, it's Baker's word against his."

"I don't know if we have to," said Mia. "This won't be a court of law. We're doing this for the bank. If Con Union is convinced, we're fine."

"And Baker gets off scot-free?"

"He did the right thing, Nelson. He did."

He snorted.

"He should be in jail," he said. "They all should be in jail, Father Ignacio included. He's probably the worst of the bunch."

"You're right. They broke the law, all of them, but hundreds of people are being made whole again with money from that crime. It could be worse."

She sighed. "Tell me what else Lionel said."

He told her as much as he remembered. She took some notes in her little leather notebook. *Fucking therapy*, thought Nelson. *What good will it do?*

When he finished, she thanked him and leaned the chair back. After a while, she fell asleep. A little after that, her head came to rest on his shoulder. He let it stay there.

Chapter 22

THE INTERESTED PARTIES WERE sitting in the CEO boardroom at Con Union, waiting.

As soon as they arrived at his house, Lionel had called his father and arranged for the meeting at nine the next morning. He told Nelson he wanted them there early. They arrived about 7:30. While Mia set up the AV, Lionel sat and started poring over his notes. Miles Hanson, CEO of Farragut Enterprises and Reynolds' father, arrived first. He was a burly man who almost took Nelson's arm off when he shook his hand. Reginald Bing arrived at 9 o'clock on the dot. Nelson nodded and smiled as Lionel introduced his father. He had to keep reminding himself the two of them had never met.

And so there they were. The seat at the head of the table, Reynolds Hanson's chair, was empty. Reginald Bing sat directly to the right of it. Miles Hanson sat next to him. Lionel was sitting directly opposite his father. Mia sat next to him, and Nelson sat at the end. He was closest to the door. Hanson's assistant, Heather, the young woman who had buttonholed Lionel a few days before, stood at the door. The girl fidgeted nervously with her hands. They were waiting for Reynolds Hanson.

Nelson glanced at his watch. Fifteen minutes late.

Maybe he bolted, thought Nelson. He glanced over at Lionel, who was going through the case files. Mia was watching him and glancing over at Mr. Bing occasionally.

Miles Hanson looked at his watch.

"You know I don't have all day, Reginald," he said. "I have a business to run."

"It's your son who's making us late," murmured Mr. Bing, glancing over at him. "Maybe you should go in there and give him a good talking-to."

Nelson looked into his lap and smiled slightly.

"I'm so sorry, everyone," said Heather, making a frowny face. "I'm sure Mr. Hanson will be here any minute."

"Be quiet," said Miles. "We don't need your yammering, young lady."

Lionel looked up at him a moment. He didn't quite frown. He opened his mouth to say something but then continued with what he'd been doing.

Reginald Bing leaned back in his chair, watched Lionel for a second, and then turned his gaze to Mia, who nodded slightly. He then looked over at Nelson, who looked back. He thought he saw Mr. Bing smile a little bit. Maybe.

The door swung open, and Reynolds Hanson entered, strutting like a rooster. He brushed past his assistant, plopped down in his chair, and faced the room with a scowl on his face. He nodded to Heather, who immediately left.

"This had better be good," he said. "I have a board meeting in five minutes."

No one said anything. Lionel continued rearranging the papers in front of him. Nelson gave Reynolds a slight smile. Lionel tapped the sheaf of papers on the table to straighten them.

"Well?" demanded Reynolds. "What's this all about?"

"You might want to reschedule or even cancel your meeting, Reynolds," said Lionel. "I think we have quite a bit of ground to cover."

"Did you find Bradley Baker?"

"We did indeed," said Lionel, leaning forward with his elbows on the table.

"Well, you caught him. It's over, right?" Reynolds stood up. "So, I can go."

"Sit down, Reynolds," said Lionel. He spoke quietly, but there was an edge behind his words. Reynolds frowned and sat back down.

"I'll start from the beginning," said Lionel, "for the benefit of those who aren't quite up to speed."

Nelson glanced at Miles Hanson, who was staring at his son and frowning.

"My father called me a little more than a week ago and asked me, as a favor, to look into some discrepancies in a particular Con Union account. Apparently, a five-million-dollar loan that had been issued to a holding company named The Hindman Group had disappeared. My team and I, Mr. West and Ms. Wentworth here, looked into it and discovered that some very interesting manipulations were made after the loan was granted."

Lionel glanced over at Reynolds.

"Mr. West and I interviewed Reynolds last week, and for some reason, he was less than forthcoming about who The Hindman Group was created for. Would you like to enlighten us, Reynolds?"

Reynolds leaned back in his chair and scowled.

"I have no idea what you're talking about."

"All right," continued Lionel. "If that's the way you want it. It turns out that one of Hindman's guarantors was Farragut Enterprises."

"What?" said Miles. "Farragut is my company." He thought a moment. "That's impossible. We have no business with any Hindman."

"Yet there it is," said Lionel, sliding a paper over to him. "Farragut is listed as one of the guarantors on this loan application. The money was supposed to be transferred to a Mexican company called Alteca. Alteca owned a small mining outfit called Los Hermanos Gordos, which managed a gold mine named La Fuente near a little town called San Pablo, just outside of Guadalajara. It's a very pretty area."

"I don't understand," said Miles, glaring down at the paper. "Who authorized Farragut's involvement?"

"We don't know," said Lionel. "You might ask someone with access to your records. A member of the Farragut board, perhaps."

Miles Hanson glared at his son, who was staring at Lionel. His father slid the paper over to him.

"Explain this, Reynolds," he growled. "How did you not notice this?"

Reynolds stared at the paper a moment and slid it back.

"I don't know how this happened. Brad originated this loan, and I assumed that everything was on the up and up. I don't know how he brought Farragut into this. Hindman was supposed to be the sole originator and holding company."

"You're on the Farragut board, and your signature is on the application, Reynolds," said his father. "Didn't you read this?"

"I trusted Brad," said Reynolds.

The two of them glared at each other. Lionel cleared his throat.

"The loan," he continued, "was approved and issued to Hindman, with Farragut as guarantor. It was already in the process of being transferred to Alteca, Hermanos Gordos' parent company, when the money was quietly diverted to Herman & Lund, a shell company. While Alteca was waiting for the money, there was an accident at the gold mine, causing it to shut down. It was a disaster.

Almost ninety miners died. This forced Alteca and Hermanos to default on the loan."

A silence settled over the room.

"Who," Miles finally asked, "is behind Herman and Lund?"

"We don't know," said Lionel. "Obviously someone who had access to the loan process."

"Why did they divert the money?" asked Mr. Bing.

"After the accident, when Hermanos Gordos defaulted," said Lionel, "the money was apparently still being held by Hindman. It hadn't quite made it over to Alteca or Gordos. It was in a sort of financial limbo."

"So, they defaulted before they even had possession of the funds," said Mr. Bing.

"That's right," said Lionel. "Hindman stalled the transfer, and then Herman and Lund diverted it. That's when it disappeared. It turns out they're a shell company. Nobody knows who or where they are."

"And the money?" asked Mr. Bing.

"Gone," said Lionel. "Probably offshore somewhere. Untraceable. The bank was defrauded."

"Baker took it," said Reynolds. "He managed the loan. He manipulated this whole thing."

"Well, I think it was supposed to look that way," said Lionel, "but that theory doesn't really hold water."

"What are you talking about?" said Reynolds Hanson, standing up.

"Sit down," said Nelson. "Lionel isn't done yet."

"Fuck you," said Reynolds, pushing back his chair. "I've had enough of this bullshit. I'm leaving."

Lionel stood up, nearly knocking over his own chair. He faced the younger Hanson and hissed, "Sit down, Reynolds."

Lionel had transformed. In a split second, his face had grown deathly pale, and his fists were clenched so tightly his knuckles had gone white. He stared at Reynolds, his eyes bulging, then staggered slightly. He put his hands on his temples and pressed. Nelson rose and sidestepped behind Mia's chair, ready to jump in if things got ugly, but Reynolds stepped back slowly, never taking his eyes from Lionel's face.

"Jesus," said Reynolds. "What the hell is wrong with you?"

Sudden emotional outbursts, thought Nelson. *Uncontrollable violent impulses. Well, Lionel. It looks like you're showing the whole PTSD catalog here.*

"All right, son," said Mr. Bing, leaning forward. "Take it easy."

Mia had risen, and she started whispering something in Lionel's ear. A sheen of sweat had broken out on his forehead. At first, he seemed not to hear her, but then he finally nodded and sat down.

Nelson wondered what had triggered the attack. Maybe Reynolds' demeanor had sparked a memory. *Who knows? He probably doesn't know himself. The answer was buried somewhere deep in Lionel's head, so deep only hints of it shot out—like today.*

"What's wrong with him?" asked Miles. "Is he having a fit?"

"I'm fine," whispered Lionel. "Just a little anxiety attack. I'm sorry."

"Maybe we should reschedule," said Reynolds. "You look like you need a doctor."

"I'm fine," repeated Lionel. "We're not done yet, Reynolds."

He cleared his throat and glanced around the table. Reginald nodded to him. Lionel glanced at Mia and then looked over to Nelson, who nodded.

"On Reynolds' recommendation, we investigated Mr. Baker, a vice president and one of the loan officers here at Con Union. According to Reynolds, the loan originated with him. The records bore that out. Baker arranged the particulars with The Hindman Group, not yet knowing that the loan was targeted to go to Los Hermanos Gordos for modernizing La Fuente, the gold mine. He only knew about Alteca at that point."

Lionel paused and took a drink of water. He seemed to have recovered most of his composure.

"You see, Brad was familiar with La Fuente and San Pablo. He'd been down there on business a few years ago and fell in love with the place. Photos of it are all over his office. In fact," he said, turning to Reynolds, "he told you all about it, didn't he? He talked about the town, the people, the beautiful country, and told you there was a gold mine nearby."

Reynolds shrugged. "He may have mentioned it. I never paid much attention."

"Bradley traveled down there on his own quite a bit," continued Lionel. "In fact, he planned to leave his wife and move down there."

Reynolds snorted.

"Mr. Baker also established quite a strong connection with Santa Barbara, the Catholic Church in San Pablo, and the priest there, a Father Ignacio. Bradley Baker is a very religious man and a very conscientious man. We were told that he attends Mass at least once a week."

Miles Hanson squirmed in his chair and glanced at his watch.

"This is all very fascinating, Lionel," he said, "but I do have business to attend to—"

"I think you'll want to hear this." Lionel glanced around the room. "I think everyone needs to hear this."

"My team and I had been working under the assumption that Brad had defrauded the bank and taken the money. He certainly had the opportunity—the means—but we were having a hard time pinning down a motive. He had no outstanding debts, no secrets, and no gambling or drug problems. He had a very nice nest egg set up. So why take the money?"

"During our interview with Marilyn Baker, Brad's wife, she showed us a deposit that had been made to a checking account in a Guadalajara bank for $100,000. This just didn't make sense. If Mr. Baker had taken the bank's money, why would he have made a deposit like that out in the open? He must have known we—or the police—would have found it."

"It's as if he wanted it to be found," said Mr. Bing.

Lionel nodded. "That's what we thought. It was like a big, red arrow pointing to San Pablo, Mexico."

"Why would he do that?" asked Miles. "That's idiotic. Did he want to be caught?"

"Another good question," said Lionel. "We went down there to find out."

"What happened? Did you find him?" asked Reynolds.

Lionel leaned his elbows on the table and ignored Reynolds.

"Among other things, we discovered that the accident—the explosion—at La Fuente happened a short time after the loan was supposed to have gone through. We took a tour of the mine. Apparently, defective equipment played a role in the accident. Some evidence suggests that there was deliberate sabotage."

Mia looked up and straightened her laptop. Nelson hid his surprise. They'd discussed that possibility, but evidence? *Is this a bluff? What the hell is Lionel doing?*

"If that's the case," continued Lionel, "then this is no longer just bank fraud. It involves wrongful death, and possibly murder."

Miles glanced at his son, who was glaring at Lionel.

"We also met Father Ignacio, with whom Mr. Baker had been working closely after the accident. By all metrics, he has been doing a great job of helping the surviving miners and their families to get through this crisis. Brad Baker has been helping out, too."

"What exactly are they doing?" asked Miles.

"Mia?" asked Lionel. "Would you like to answer that?"

"Sure," she said, opening her laptop. "We contacted Father Ignacio late last night, and he agreed to join us on a videoconference."

She clicked on a few keys, waited, and then clicked a few more. Nelson leaned over to look. In a moment, the Zoom screen appeared on the laptop with her face on it. Then they waited a few moments for the priest to login. Nelson stole a look at Reynolds, who was poking furiously at his cellphone.

Who's he texting? Who should be worried?

"Hello. Hola."

Father Ignacio had come through. Nelson could see the image of the skinny old man on Mia's laptop from where he was sitting. He was sitting in the same room where the four of them had first met. Father Dom, one of the priests who had come to visit Lionel, sat off to the side.

"Hello, Father Ignacio," said Mia.

"Hello. Hello. Can you hear me? How are you?"

"Good. Yes, we can hear you. I'm here with Lionel and Nelson and some other people who have an interest in the La Fuente affair."

"Hello, everyone," said the priest. "Hello."

"Hang on," said Mia. "We're going to put you on a big screen so everyone can see you."

She reached to the middle of the table and hooked in a wire. The monitor on the far wall came to life, the image came into focus, and the priest's face seemed to fill the room.

"So, Father," said Mia. "Could you tell us what's been going on in San Pablo since the accident at La Fuente?"

"Yes," he said. "Forgive me. I need Father Dom to give me a little technical assistance. This technology is far too confusing for an old man like me."

The young priest moved in and tapped a few buttons to begin the screen sharing. In a moment, the screen changed to a video of a busy construction site.

"Is it on?" Father Ignacio's voice rang out. "Is it working?"

"Yes, Father, it's on," answered the young priest.

"And yes, we can see it, Father," said Mia.

"All right, then. What we are seeing is the building of a new school for the San Pablo community. This school will have state-of-the-art technology and internet capability, as well as a laptop for every student. There will also be a wing for adult education to help retrain the displaced miners and to help the widows of those killed in the accident get job training. The school administrator hopes to establish programs for medical training, paralegal coursework, and even pre-college courses. We are also building a daycare center so the little ones will be taken care of while the mothers are in school."

"Very nice, Father," said Miles. "Very nice. But what does this have to do with us?"

"I'm not sure," said Father Ignacio. "You'll have to ask Lionel that question. I only know that Mr. Baker has been kind enough to help administer the funds necessary to make this happen."

"What funds?" asked Reynolds. "How much money?"

"You would have to ask Mr. Baker that," said the Father, smiling, "but I believe that Don Francisco is responsible for a significant part of the funding."

"Don Francisco who?" asked Miles.

"Francisco Uvalde Hidalgo Rosales."

"El Cuchillo," murmured Reynolds.

"What?" asked his father.

Reynolds turned to Mia. "Can you mute this for a second?" he whispered.

"Father Ignacio, we're going to put you on mute for a minute. We need to work something out."

"Fine," said the priest, nodding. "I'll be right here." Mia silenced his feed.

"He's off," she said.

"Jesus, Lionel," said Reynolds. "Do you know who this Don Francisco is?"

Lionel looked at him and smiled.

"Do you?" continued Reynolds. "Jesus, this man is one of the most vicious drug lords in Mexico. He's murdered dozens of people. He decapitates people. He sells cocaine, fentanyl, heroin. My God, Lionel. He's a cartel chief."

"And apparently, he's also a good friend of the Catholic Church," said Lionel.

"What?" asked Reginald.

"We spent a fair amount of time with Father Ignacio and a couple of other priests from Guadalajara. Apparently, Don Francisco is very closely affiliated with the church," said Lionel. "He grew up near San Pablo. Santa Barbara was his parish. Despite his career choices, Don Francisco is still involved with his parish. He donates money to help with their All Saints' Day festivals, he has helped renovate the building, and he has built a shrine to his mother, with the blessing of the church, in his hometown."

"But he's a criminal," said Reynolds. "My God."

"So, the church is supposed to turn its back on him?" asked Mia. "That goes against the spirit of the Christian faith."

"He's a fucking killer!" exclaimed Reynolds.

"Father Ignacio holds out hope for his redemption," said Lionel. "And who knows? He might be right. Stranger things have happened."

"You know what they say," said Nelson. "To err is human—."

"Shut up," said Reynolds.

"Don't tell him to shut up," said Mia.

"You shut up, too, bitch!"

"Reynolds!" exclaimed Miles. "That's enough."

Nelson glanced over at Lionel. He was staring down at the papers in front of him, but he seemed calm. At least there were no outward signs of a further freakout.

"People," said Reginald. "Please, let's take it easy. Let's relax." He waited until he had everyone's attention.

"Tell me," he said, turning to Lionel, "how does this information pertain to our loan problem?"

Lionel looked up and smiled.

"We believe that the defrauded money has been—with the help of Don Francisco and the local cartel—channeled into the La Fuente recovery funds."

"What about the church?" asked Miles. "Is it involved?"

"It's hard to say," said Lionel. "It's impossible to trace the money at this point. After Herman & Lund appropriated it, the money pretty much disappeared. It could be offshore. It could have been laundered. It might be buried under a rock somewhere."

"But you believe it's being used to rebuild the mine," said Reginald.

"And to help the town."

"But there's no way to prove it," said Reginald.

"How is Baker involved?" asked Reynolds.

"We believe he shepherded the loan to the point where it reached the shell company. Once it was moved, there was no straight line between him and the missing funds."

"Let me get this straight," said Reginald. "Do you think the people behind this planned on defaulting all along?"

"Yes," said Lionel. "And I think that explosion was deliberately set so that the collapse of the mine would cause Alteca to default. And it would have worked, except the money had already been spirited away at that point. Apparently, somehow, the saboteurs were not aware of that."

"Why are you so sure it was planned?" asked Reynolds.

"As I mentioned previously, Mr. Nelson and I found several key pieces of evidence in the mine."

"Yes," said Nelson. "It's obvious it was no accident."

"Baker did it," said Reynolds.

"Doubtful," said Mia. "He's been spearheading the rebuild, even going into the mine to find bodies. That behavior doesn't jibe with a stone-cold killer."

"Maybe he's got a guilty conscience?" asked Miles.

Lionel shrugged. Reynolds sighed.

"All right," he said. "So basically, you investigated this loan defraud and came up empty. Is that right?"

Lionel smiled.

"Not quite. I think we've worked out an arrangement that might be to everyone's advantage."

"Like what?" asked Reynolds.

"Okay," said Lionel. "Let's look at the big picture. Con Union issued a loan under suspicious circumstances. The loan was used for criminal purposes and resulted in the wrongful deaths of dozens of innocent people. When—not if—the media breaks this story, it'll come out that Farragut Enterprises was one of the guarantors of the loan. They'll put you under the microscope, Miles, and make Farragut look responsible for the deaths of dozens of innocent people, including children."

Lionel stood up and started pacing the floor behind the table. "Knowing the level of public trust in corporate America, people are going to be angry. They are going to want justice."

Miles shifted uncomfortably in his seat. Reginald Bing nodded slightly.

"If public opinion believes Farragut had a hand in blowing up that mine," continued Lionel, "there will be a major backlash. Your stockholders will bolt. Shares will take a hit. Profits will suffer." He shrugged. "Charges could be filed."

He stopped a moment, looked at Reynolds, and smiled.

"But we could avoid all that with a pre-emptive strike. If Farragut would acknowledge its culpability in the loan default, apologize for its negligence in being named as a guarantor—without its knowledge, of course—and then get behind this effort to rehabilitate San Pablo and put people back on their feet, the company would still take a hit, but it wouldn't be nearly as bad as getting caught in a coverup."

"Bullshit," said Reynolds.

"Be quiet," said the elder Hanson, glaring at his son. Reynolds glared back at him.

"Wait a minute," said Miles. "If we admit culpability, wouldn't we be liable? Couldn't they charge us with blowing up the mine?"

"I don't think so," said Lionel. "There's no direct link between your company and what Alteca did. And you said earlier that you have no idea how Farragut showed up on the loan applications. If you happened to find out how that signature got on, the public would be that much more inclined to forgive and forget."

"That's right," said Mia.

"I think maybe you find out who was behind it and serve up that responsible party. That would demonstrate your good intentions to the courts and to the public."

A silence settled over the room.

"Oh," said Mia. "Father Ignacio is still on the line. We don't need him anymore, do we?"

"I don't think so," said Lionel. They signed off with the priest.

Reginald Bing stood up.

"Thanks for all your work on this. Miles, could I speak with you a moment?"

The two men left the room. Reynolds leaned back in his chair, shook his head, and snorted.

"Something on your mind?" asked Nelson.

"I was just thinking about the shit job that the three of you did. I send you down to get back the money and you tell me it's being used to build schools and boys' clubs and shit." He stood up.

Mia crossed her arms and leaned back in her chair.

"Jesus, Reynolds, you are just about as stupid as they come. Don't you see what Lionel just gave you? Gift-wrapped for you?"

"What are you talking about?"

"We know what you did, Reynolds," said Lionel quietly. "You were behind the default. You knew all along that money was never going to be used to modernize the mine. You told Bradley Baker to originate the loan for your Mexican associates. You created Hindman as a holding company, but, as insurance, you made the paperwork point back to Brad—so if anything went sour, you could always point the finger at him."

Reynolds sat back down.

"When Brad stumbled onto your scheme, unbeknownst to you, he created Herman & Lund, which became the new trustee for the money. So, when the time came for you to pay Alteca their share of the cash, it was nowhere to be found. You didn't tell them, and believing the money would show up, they went ahead and blew up the mine anyway."

"What bullshit," said Reynolds, although more quietly this time. "You can't prove a thing."

"No one's asking us to prove anything," said Lionel. "Con Union wants its money back. That's why my dad called me. Your father was the one who asked him to look into it, wasn't he? Since he's a board member of Con Union, he was concerned about the default. He knew nothing about the Farragut involvement, did he?"

Reynolds didn't say anything.

"It's kind of odd he didn't call you," said Mia. "You'd think he'd trust you, his own son, to get to the bottom of this."

"So, what about the money?" asked Reynolds.

"You tell us," said Nelson. "You're the one holding the bag."

"What about Baker?"

"As far as we're concerned, he's off the hook. He might have made some questionable decisions when he diverted everything over to his shell company, but he didn't steal the money. Someone else did that. He's simply making sure it's being used to make things right."

"We believe that the bank will be able to absorb the loss," said Mia, "but someone will probably have to pay for allowing this to happen."

"Baker," said Reynolds.

"No, asshole," said Nelson. "You. You signed on your father's company as a guarantor. You made the deal with Alteca. You hired the operative who blew up the mine."

"No," said Reynolds. "Bullshit. There's no way you can prove it."

Nelson shrugged.

"We don't have to," said Nelson. "Nobody wants to take this to the cops, much less to court. Except maybe me."

"That's right," said Lionel. "Con Union doesn't want the publicity. Neither does Farragut. The only people we have to convince are the CEO of Farragut—your dad—and the board of directors here at Con Union. My dad said he can take care of them."

"What about the money?" asked Reynolds.

"You have a four-million-dollar performance bonus as CEO coming," said Mia. "Undeserved as it is, that'll take care of a good part of it."

"And there's that hundred grand in the Guadalajara bank," said Nelson. "That'll help."

"The rest," said Lionel, standing up and leaning forward, "is up to you. You can work out a payment plan with my father if necessary."

"Fuck that. You're not taking my bonus."

"Yes, we are," said Miles as he walked in with Reginald. "I just got in touch with Harrison over at Farragut. We asked him to do a little digging. He told me that new kid—what's his name—Erickson had done the paperwork for the loan. The kid said you told him to do it. Apparently, you had some information about his opioid habit and threatened to reveal him."

Miles stood at the table, staring at his son.

He looks angry, but there's an element of—what—in his face? thought Nelson. *Sorrow? Pity? Well, who could blame him? His own son tried to rip him off.*

"You will forfeit your bonus, make up the rest of the balance of the fraud, and submit your resignation to Con Union, effective immediately," said Miles, his voice flat. "I want you out of your office by closing time today."

Reynolds sat back in his chair. He looked shrunken, defeated. Nelson almost felt sorry for him.

"You're lucky, son," said Miles. "In different hands, this may very well have been a criminal prosecution. You could've gone to prison. You probably *should* go to prison."

"What about Baker?" asked Reynolds. "Does he get off scot-free?"

"Mr. Baker will be working with Father Ignacio and the church, and—umm—their associates in San Pablo to help oversee the mine reclamation," Lionel said.

"But he robbed us," said Reynolds.

"No," said Lionel. "He brought the crime to our attention. Without his help, you may very well have gotten away with this. When Mr. Baker deposited that money, it told us exactly where to go."

"After the mine is repaired," said Miles, "Brad Baker will coordinate our efforts to rehabilitate the town of San Pablo. He will be our liaison there."

"You're not going to fire him?"

"Let's say it's a mutual agreement to preserve the status quo," said Reginald. "He stays there, does what he loves doing anyway, in exchange for his silence. Reynolds will remain nameless in this terrible accident."

"What about the people who died down there?" asked Nelson. "Who pays for those murders?"

"Their families are being compensated," said Reginald. "And I understand that the owners of Los Gordos Hermanos have fled—disappeared, as it were."

No one said anything. Nelson glanced at Mia, who nodded slightly.

"What about Alteca?" asked Reynolds.

Miles shrugged. "It's in their interest to keep quiet, but I understand that some interested parties associated with Father Ignacio will be speaking with those responsible for the default."

Nelson let out a breath. *Cartel justice. It may not be legal, and only partly ethical, but it sure worked. Reynolds was luckier than he knew.*

"Are we done here?" asked Reginald, looking at his son.

Lionel nodded.

"All right, Reynolds," said Miles. "You will resign, and your bonus money will be forfeited and absorbed into Con Union. You will pay one million more to even the books. Is that clear?"

Reynolds looked up at his father. His mouth opened and closed.

"Is that clear, boy?" asked his father, his voice harsh.

"Yes, sir."

"All right." He turned to Lionel. "Thank you, Lionel, for settling this matter so discreetly. It's important to have someone like you who understands the complicated nature of our world and why the law is not always the correct solution to our problems. It's different for us. It's not easy being up here in the stratosphere."

Lionel nodded.

Nelson glanced at Mia, who raised her eyebrows.

"Thank you," said Lionel. "You're know, you're right about the law. It doesn't always apply equally to everyone."

Miles nodded and smiled.

"Justice, however," continued Lionel, speaking softly, "is a different matter."

"What do you mean, son?" said Reginald Bing.

Lionel turned to his father and smiled.

"Justice catches up to everyone, Dad," he said. "Eventually. I believe that. It sure did in this case."

Reginald gave his son a long look, smiled slightly, and nodded.

Miles frowned and glanced at his watch.

"All right," said Miles. "I need to go. Thanks again."

He shook hands with Lionel, Nelson, and Mia, and then left without ceremony, never even looking at his son.

"Well done, Lionel," said Reginald. "Well done."

He turned to Reynolds.

"I would suggest you leave the premises as soon as possible."

Reynolds stood, shrunken and deflated, no longer the bantam cock of a man.

"I'm sorry," he said to Reginald.

"I would think so," said the old man. "Now get out."

They watched as Reynolds left the room, his head down.

Reginald turned to Lionel.

"Well done, son," he said again. "I'm proud of you."

Lionel smiled slightly at his father.

"Tell me," he said. "Was it the cartel that helped Brad launder the money? It wasn't the church, was it?"

Lionel looked down at his hands splayed on the table. They were shaking slightly. "Yes," he said. "It was the cartel."

"The cartel," said the old man, sitting down. "Jesus."

"We spoke to Don Francisco," said Nelson. "He made it clear that his involvement with rebuilding the mine and San Pablo was absolute."

"And Father Ignacio made it clear that Don Francisco is very committed to the Santa Barbara parish in San Pablo," added Mia.

"They are doing the right thing," said Lionel.

"But they're criminals," said Reginald. "Killers, thieves, drug dealers."

Lionel shrugged. "Are they so different from—what did Miles say? Us in the complicated nature of our world? Up in our stratosphere? I mean, Reynolds literally just got away with murder."

"That's different," said Reginald, looking at his son.

"How? Because he steals and kills from inside a boardroom?"

Nelson nodded.

"Dad, you asked me to do this quietly, discreetly, and outside the law, which we did. There was no way to do it without the cartel and without the church, and there was really no way to separate them."

"There is a sort of justice for the people down there," continued Lionel. "They're being made whole again. The people responsible from Alteca and Hermanos Gordos have disappeared." He shrugged. "To me, that looks like justice."

"What about Reynolds?" asked Mia. "Next year, he'll be CEO at a different company. He got away with it."

Nelson smiled.

"What's so funny?" asked Mia.

"Nothing," he said. "Only remember that other people were angry about what happened. They lost family in the accident. Some of them work for Don Francisco."

"Los Gallos," said Mia.

"Could Reynolds be in danger?" asked Reginald.

"It's possible," said Lionel, glancing at Nelson.

"I'd put a watch on him," said Nelson. "Maybe hire some security." *Not that it'll do much good*, he thought.

Lionel stood up, gathered his papers, and smiled.

"I guess that wraps things up," he said.

His father looked at him and smiled.

"Okay. Thanks, son. I appreciate it."

"Anytime, Dad."

They shook hands, and he and Lionel left together. Mia and Nelson followed.

Chapter 23

NELSON UNWRAPPED ONE OF THE new button-down shirts he had purchased that morning. Seven shirts, four slacks, two suits, three pairs of jeans, two new pairs of shoes, and some ties—he wasn't sure how many. Mia had offered to help him shop, but he had declined. It wasn't that he didn't appreciate the offer—he just knew what he wanted.

He had also started hunting for a new apartment—something closer to River North, where Lionel lived.

Steady work does have its perks. Now he'd be able to keep up with his bills, including his alimony. *It'll be nice getting the ex off my back,* he thought.

He got dressed and looked at himself in the mirror. A black shirt and jeans, comfortable and casual. It should be appropriate for Lionel's study hall. Casual but put together. He glanced at his watch and left, walking down to the train station. He could have called an Uber, but part of him still wanted to keep that workingman vibe in his life. He got off at the LaSalle Station. Lionel's place was only a couple of blocks away. It was a cool night, and fall was on the way. The crisp air was nice and refreshing, although part of him missed the Mexican sun.

I'll have to get back there, he thought. *I'll talk to Lionel and figure out a vacation time.* He got to the building and nodded to the doorman, who let him onto the elevator. When he stepped off at the penthouse, he could hear the party already going. He knocked, and Mia answered the door. She was wearing a black turtleneck and jeans.

"Hello, Nelson. How are you?"

"Good. I see you've got the beatnik thing going on."

"Funny. You look good. For once. Come on in."

She went back in and he followed, closing the door behind him. He glanced around the living room. It was nearly full. There were quite a few more people here than last time. He recognized Derrick Nickleby, Preston Angelis, and John Sellers. Mia's astronomer friend Violet Birdsong was standing in the kitchen, but that Professor Enderby was not there. Lionel came out of the kitchen, carrying a bottle in each hand.

"Ah, Nelson, you made it. I was beginning to think you weren't coming."

"No chance, boss. I've got a lot to learn."

"Very true," said Lionel. "Excuse me a minute." He sauntered over to pour a glass for Sellers and his date, a neatly put-together Asian woman with a pixie haircut. He walked around a little, just checking things out.

"So," said a voice at Nelson's elbow, "have you met with Lionel's dad yet?"

Mia. They were standing in the doorway to the dining room, out of earshot from the party guests.

"Not yet, but I've been expecting to be pulled into a limousine any day now."

"I think he'll make an appointment this time," she said.

"Have *you* met with him?"

"Yesterday."

She looked out over the guests.

"Well?"

"I told him the truth—that things got a little dicey at times."

Nelson shrugged. "It wasn't that bad."

"Really? Are you talking about when you got beaten up, or was it that time we were kidnapped by a cartel chief?"

"He had a nice house."

"Or when Lionel lost it and tried to kill that guy?"

Yeah, he thought. *That one was scary.*

"It's a rough business, Mia. Besides, isn't the point of all this to help him deal with his past? His inner demons?"

"It's supposed to happen in a controlled environment."

Nelson shrugged. *That's not even worth commenting on. Nothing is controlled.*

Mia frowned.

"Has Lionel said anything?" he asked.

"Not to me," she said. "He's already looking forward to the next case."

"What case?"

"You'll see," she said. "Shh."

Lionel was coming. He was holding a bottle in one hand and a wine glass in the other.

"You have to try this, Nelson," he said, handing him the glass. "It's a 2013 Joseph Drouhin Premier Cru—a beautiful wine."

"Sounds good."

"You, too, Mia," said Lionel. "We deserve to toast ourselves for a job well done." He filled her glass and raised his own. They toasted and sipped. The wine had a red and black fruit taste with a tinge of vanilla in the back. *Shit*, thought Nelson, *I'm starting to sound like a wine commercial.*

"I got an email from Bradley Baker today," said Lionel.

"Oh, how is he?" asked Mia.

"Well, he just started his divorce proceedings. He's hoping for a clean break, but he thinks it'll get messy."

"How's the work on the mine going?"

Lionel nodded.

"He says they've finally cleared out all the casualties and given them proper Christian burials. They're starting to rebuild. The work on the school is going very well. Father Ignacio is quite pleased."

"How about Don Francisco?" asked Nelson.

Lionel shrugged and smiled. "He didn't say, but I imagine the Don is doing quite well. I gather he moves around quite a bit."

"Did you fill Baker in on our meeting?"

"Yes, of course," said Lionel. "He understands it would be in his best interest to stay in Mexico and do the Farragut public relations thing."

"Well," said Nelson, raising his glass again. "To happy endings."

"As happy as they can be," said Lionel.

"I do think this turned out pretty well," said Mia.

Ever the optimist, thought Nelson.

"Nothing ever turns out completely right," said Lionel. "By all rights, Reynolds, Baker, and Don Francisco should be in jail, and Father Ignacio should be defrocked."

"Not in your complicated world," said Nelson. "Realistically, I think we got the best possible outcome. The stolen money is being put to good use, those responsible for blowing up the mine are gone, presumed dead, and Reynolds has reimbursed the bank."

"Lionel is right," said Mia. "Reynolds should be in jail."

"Sure," said Nelson, "and I should be a movie star."

"I understand he's left town," continued Nelson, sipping his wine.

"What? When?" asked Lionel.

"Day before yesterday. I keep in touch with his security team. It seems as if there's been some interest in Mr. Hanson from Los Gallos."

"The street gang," said Mia.

"Yep. They have strong affiliations back in Jalisco, their home state. I think they feel Reynolds owes them something."

They sipped their wine.

"Well," said Lionel. "I suppose that, realistically, in the real world, that might be called a satisfactory outcome. At least as satisfactory as it can be. And, I think with Don Francisco's help, I might be able to find some justice of my own. For my mother and me. I got a message from Armando, his valet, today."

Nelson looked at him. Lionel wasn't usually so glib about his mother.

Lionel smiled slightly and turned away, heading toward the kitchen.

Nelson frowned. He'd been around long enough to know that very few people paid for their crimes completely—at least not through the legal system. Happy endings were rare, especially when it came to dealing with crimes of the rich and famous.

He'd given up on happy endings for himself a long time ago. Reginald Bing was right. The world was a complicated place. Good things happen only occasionally, and usually by accident. Was this outcome perfect? Hell, no. Was it—as Lionel said—satisfactory? Yeah. Not everyone had been brought to justice before the law—in fact, no one had, but it had all worked out.

He sipped his wine and watched Mia and Lionel in deep conversation. Would Lionel find his closure, his satisfaction, his justice? His peace? Maybe. With their help.

Will I? thought Nelson. *Will I ever be satisfied with the Hightower case? Not likely. My world has different complications than Lionel's.*

He smiled to himself.

"What's so funny?" asked Mia. Lionel looked over and smiled. Nelson smiled back.

He sipped his wine. *Maybe,* he thought, *we can get Lionel to a point where he's okay with what happened to his mother, where he thinks he's done enough to forgive himself. And maybe, just maybe, I can work past Hightower and forgive myself, too. Maybe.*

Acknowledgements

I would like to thank Kira Henschel, my publisher, for her unwavering support. I'd also like to thank Lesley DeMartini for her outstanding skills as an editor. I need to recognize Michael DiMilo for his phenomenal artwork, Tom Linn for his advice about the world of finance, Nick Chiarkas for his expertise on financial crime, Les Huisman and Ben Christiansen for their encyclopedic knowledge of fine wines, Robert Carter for his photographic skills, and Leslie Martin Geddes for her outstanding support. I also want to thank Nick Chiarkas, Dennis Curley, Mark Mamerow, and David Riemer for their invaluable input as beta readers and to thank the rest of my family, particularly Maryann Carter, Paul and Susanne Carter, Sue Kletzke Carter, Rae Williams DiMilo, Barbara Gillespie, my wife Kris, and my daughter Frankie for their unconditional love and support.

About the Author

Geoff Carter grew up attending public schools in the Milwaukee area, eventually graduating from the University of Wisconsin at Madison with a degree in Communication Arts. He has been teaching English in Milwaukee Public Schools for twenty-eight years in both traditional and non-traditional settings, working almost exclusively with at-risk students. Mr. Carter is a proud and active member of the MTEA, the local teachers' union.

He holds a PhD in English and has also taught at the University of Wisconsin-Milwaukee.

Mr. Carter lives in Milwaukee. He is married and is the proud father of a remarkable daughter. In his spare time, he enjoys fine wine, sailing, fly-fishing, organic gardening, and reading.

Please visit his website for more information and blog:
https://geoffreymalcolmcarter.com/

www.ingramcontent.com/pod-product-compliance
Lightning Source LLC
Chambersburg PA
CBHW052004020726
47501CB00004B/997